The Crescent Stone

Book 1 of The Crescent Stone Series

Coming: Book 2
The Fallen Child

E. G. McNally

The Crescent Stone

By
E. G. McNally

The Crescent Stone
©2010 by E. G McNally
Cover Illustration by Tiffany Toland

Dedicated to my wonderful daughter Kali.
I hope that one day you love reading as much as I do.

Contents

The Crescent Stone

Chapter I: Lake Crescent

Taylor woke up early on what she thought would be just another typical morning, hoping to avoid confrontation with her new caretakers. When she appeared in the kitchen, the doorbell rang, completely catching her off guard. She wasn't expecting anyone for another ten minutes and he should have known to knock. She'd explained to her best friend before, that he couldn't wake everyone up or they'd both get into trouble, but apparently her lecture hadn't stuck.

Afraid that everyone in the house had awoken from the sound, she rushed to the door and caught Jake's hand before he pushed the button again. She scowled at her tall, athletic, pain-in-the-butt best friend, standing outside the door.

"I thought I told you to knock." She said with irritation pouring through her whisper. "If you wake everyone up, I'll never be able to hang out with you in the morning."

"Good morning to you too," he pertly responded and brushed past Taylor.

"I'm just saying if you want to hang out and watch cartoons before school starts, you can't wake everyone up." Taylor reminded him. She wasn't really sure he understood how much she needed his company. If it weren't for him, she'd probably be drugging up with most of the dropouts that hang around the pier late at night. They were all headed nowhere fast, and she was thankful to be apart from them.

"Yeah, yeah, I just forgot to knock, okay. Don't get your panties in a knot." Jake replied, sauntering over to the sofa, plopping down in front of the television.

Taylor glared at him for a moment, before retreating into the kitchen for some breakfast.

"So tell me, how is this new foster home treating you?" He hollered into the kitchen.

"Shush Jake, keep your freaking voice down, you're gonna get us both in trouble." She scolded him again.

"Sorry," he replied, this time in a whisper.

"Oh, and in response to your question, the place isn't bad. But I couldn't tell you for sure, because I've only been here a couple of days, and you know how appearances can be deceiving. Anyhow, you've already made me miss the first part of the show because you keep pestering me, so just shut your trap, okay." She eyeballed him, watching as he returned his attention to the television, ignoring the edgy tone in her voice. "I know you don't eat breakfast, but are you sure you don't want anything?"

"Maybe, what's on the menu?" Jake responded, distractedly watching the television.

While glancing back at the television, Taylor shuffled through a couple of different shelves in the pantry.

"Well, there's reduce your cholesterol a little," she said, pulling out the box of Cheerios. "Reduce your cholesterol a little more," she said, this time pulling out a box of oatmeal, "and... Ooh, this looks good, how about some high energy now, you'll be hungry in an hour, and have a wicked bad sugar low later?" The sarcasm pooled in her voice.

"What's that?" Jake mumbled, still fixated on the morning cartoons.

"Lucky Charms," she replied, pouring herself a large bowl, before joining Jake on the couch.

"So, is everything ready for today?" Taylor asked, munching through the cereal.

"Uh," he had to pause to think about her question. "Oh, you mean the lake – yeah. We just have to pick up Joe, before we head out there. His parents let him sign his own excuse notes, for the school, so naturally he's off the hook." Jake replied, as he glanced away from the TV, fumbled in his pocket for a second, and then handed Taylor a note. She read it.

> Please excuse Jacob Stevens from school for the day; he will be attending a family divorce counseling session. The sessions are always difficult, and we don't expect our son to return to school for the day. If there are any questions, please don't hesitate to call our home number.
> Sincerely,
> Loretta and Frank Stevens

"Nice! Is it real?" Taylor asked, handing back the note.

"Yeah unfortunately, my parents really know how to embarrass the crap out of me. Doesn't matter though, it's not like I'm gonna

● ● ●

show. Stupid divorce crap," he said, shoving the note back into his pocket.

"Speaking of which, how's that going?" Taylor asked, and then realizing her mistake, gave Jake an apologetic look.

"Don't ask," he huffed, then reached around the couch for the remote and turned off the television. "We should probably get Joe now, or he'll start to think we forgot about him." Jake mumbled, then halfheartedly rose from the sofa and fumbled for the keys in his pocket. As he wandered to the door, he ignored Taylor's silent apology for bringing up his parents' divorce, groaning the entire way to the door.

Taylor tossed the empty cereal bowl into the kitchen sink, and then grabbed her trusty backpack from the coat closet, before following Jake outside. She slid comfortably into the passenger seat beside Jake. As they sat in silence, she admired the tight little curls of his light brown hair and the way his temple pulsed when he was frustrated, until her thoughts came to an end when they arrived outside Joe's house.

Joe was readily waiting as always, decked out in his designer shirt and matching stylish trousers, outside the steel gates, practically guarding his parent's super expensive house.

"What took you guys so long?" He asked, tossing a rather suspicious brown bag of what was probably beer into the back seat, and then scooted beside it.

"Don't be such a pansy; we're not going to leave you behind." Taylor rolled her eyes at Joe, awaiting one of those boring, be where you say you're going to be, when you say you're going to be there lectures that parents always give, but Jake intercepted before Joe could begin.

"Plus, if we left you behind, who would provide the beer and endless entertainment, right?" Jake said, cutting Joe off before he could retaliate.

"Rough couple of days?" Joe commented while glancing at Taylor, uncharacteristically picking up on her body language.

"I don't want to talk about it." Taylor sucked in a deep breath, pausing, allowing the boys a chance to change the subject, before unloading all of her frustrations on them. But neither spoke, knowing that Taylor would have more to say, because she always did.

○ ○ ○

"I just can't believe this crap," she paused to regroup her thoughts and then continued. "You know, I've moved six times this year and it's not even December yet. I'm not sure how many foster homes are left. But no . . . the state keeps finding more, and they expect me to just keep taking it, as if nothing bad ever happens. Who the hell are they to keep bossing me around? I mean why can't I just get emancipated and come live with one of you or something? I bet your parents have room." Taylor glanced back at Joe, "It's not like I wouldn't be just fine without their ridiculous attempts at help." Taylor clenched her fists and gave out an angry groan. "And everyone at school looks at me like I'm a dang freak show, I hate it." She sighed, nearing the brink of tears.

In order to hide her tears, Taylor's expression was replaced by a scowl. Her pitch-black eyes practically burned a hole through the car window while she glared outside. Her attitude had clearly changed and both Jake and Joe had clearly decided that silence was the only remedy, or at least the only one they were willing to risk. Both boys slumped against their seats, defeated and ill-equipped to deal with a Taylor sob-fest.

Oblivious to the tension, Taylor eased out of her foul mood, daydreaming about flying through the green canopy of evergreens, lucidly envisioning herself as a castle gargoyle, come to life, twisting and winding freely from the tensions of the hurtful world she lived in.

Taylor dropped back into reality when Jake turned the car, onto a side road, hugging the northern side of the lake. The tall evergreen trees nestled within a thick blanket of fog gave the lake a serene and almost eerily vacant appearance. The tops of the mountains were hidden, and the grey lifelessness of the fog reflected in the sheen top of the lake. It was empty, as it often was, and that was good.

The lake was perfect. Everyone was in school, and the lake was barren. She would have plenty of time to reflect on her new situation. With the help of her two best friends and the silent seclusion that the lake brought, she would be able to overcome the depressing feelings of self-degradation that she often struggled with.

Her life felt like a snake pit of loss, full of poisonous obstacles. Every time she moved, she had to accept that she would lose half of her clothes, most of her jewelry, and basically all of her valuables. It was always very difficult and upsetting, with each move becoming consecutively rougher. A little time alone often helped her feel better and it was comforting to be around the boys, especially Jake, with his good humor and sensible views on everyday life.

As Jake pulled onto the trailhead, Joe loaded up Taylor's backpack with junk food and the beer.

"Let's get hammered," Taylor said, winking at Jake. "Not," she mumbled.

Jake chuckled in response, and then both he and Taylor took off after Joe, down the trail, until they arrived at the small, cleverly crafted, wooden bridge that joined one side of the cliff to the other. Contained within the alcove was a small swimming hole known as The Devil's Punch Bowl.

Rumor had it, that it got its name from the trapped souls wadding around in the water. It was said that the devil had collected them, over the years, from the kids who jumped off the cliff and crashed into the jagged rocks below, instead of cheating the devil and landing in the water.

"Go get the wood," Joe pointed to Taylor, and then to Jake, "You figure out how to light this thing," he signaled toward the extinguished fire pit they'd used in the past, "And I'll start on the beer." He shuffled through the backpack and pulled out a bottle.

Simultaneously, Taylor and Jake rolled their eyes, releasing complementing chuckles.

"No surprise there," Taylor mumbled, and then browsed through some of the surrounding ferns and bushes until she had found enough wood to start a fire.

"The lake is pretty dead this morning," Jake commented, surveying the surface for any unwanted guests. "There's someone in a boat far off, but I can't tell if it's a ranger or not. We'll just have to try our luck." He said pulling a lighter from his pocket. He squatted down and rearranged the small pile of wood Taylor had placed in the fire pit.

"What? Is the wood pile not good enough for Mr. Ex-Boy Scout?" Taylor jeered, hovering over Jake, as he placed the wood in a cone shape. "You know, the wood is going to burn, regardless of how pretty you stack it."

"That's true," he responded. "But I'm never going to get the fire started, arranged the way you had it," Jake smartly pointed out. "So, chill out dude – go jump off the cliff or something." He said, waving her away, returning his attention to the fire until he had it hotly burning.

"Fine whatever," Taylor mumbled, walking out to the bridge. She pulled her worn out shirt quickly over her head and shook loose her hair. The long black strands fell limply against her shoulders. She tossed the rest of her stuff over the side of the bridge and onto the ground, where she could easily reach them after plunging into the icy glacier water.

Jake watched as Taylor climbed up the jagged cliff-side and stood at the top staring down at the crystal-clear, eerily, blue-hued water of Lake Crescent.

"She's so nuts." Joe commented, cracking open a second beer. He pulled out two more and cracked them open, before handing one to Jake and placing the second one beside the fire. "Taylor's," he guiltily responded, as if Jake had him on trial.

"Sure," Jake said, looking at him accusingly.

"What, you know I never drink alone," Joe quickly added.

"Right, because we all believe that" Jake rolled his eyes. After sipping some of the beer, he leaned back against a tree and waited for the soaking wet, freezing cold, completely chilled-out version of Taylor to emerge from the lake after jumping.

Taylor stood at the top of the cliff and looked down, picking out the perfect spot, mapping out the jagged rocks, and hoping to avoid hitting them on her way down. She backed up five paces, took a deep breath, holding it briefly, and then released it, whispering into the wind, "Please get me out of this stupid town."

As if in response to her silent plea, the wind rippled up around her, swirling her hair across her face and causing goose bumps to form on her arms. She smiled at the playful response the wind had given her, knowing it was probably just coincidence, and felt comfort in the silly idea that maybe something out there really did care about her.

Three long strides and she went over the cliff-side, quickly adjusting her body, angling it in just the right way to break the water without breaking a bone. She felt as though the air was sucked right out of her chest and her arms waved wildly. She pulled her legs together, preparing them first for the break. Hardly seconds before she crashed through the water, her arms made it to her side, and she looked like a professional who'd done it thousands of times.

Taylor shuddered, as she felt all the living cells in her body scream in response to the chill of the glacier water. She had to think, before panic instinctually took over her body. Which way was up? She wondered, waiting in the cold dim water, until her body finally began rising in the direction of the surface.

She began frantically swimming for the surface, peering through the dimly lit water for signs of the shore, always in the back of her mind praying that she didn't run out of air before reaching it.

And there it was. Lodged between a rock and some murky lake plants. A diamond looking stone, or at least what she thought might be a diamond, faintly glowing. Taylor reached out and grasped it from between a rock and some plant muck. After several thoughts of leaving town flashed through her head, using cash from pawning the diamond, she refocused on reaching the surface, and finally broke through the water gasping desperately for air.

And then a negative thought crossed her mind as she quickly pulled herself up, out of the water, and onto the shore, brushing off the cold water dripping down her skin. What if someone thinks it's stolen, and what if they come after her for stealing it? Not only would she end up in jail, but also, she'd never get out of her stupid town.

"Hmm, better not tell anyone about it," she mumbled, shaking the cold water from her hair, before finding her way to the warm fire Jake started.

"Tell anyone about what?" An authoritative voice startled Taylor.

She glanced up at the fire, where both boys were standing erect, stern frowns pulled tightly across their faces, and then whipped her head toward the voice. A uniformed man, a forest ranger, was standing beside her, his boat pulled up alongside the bridge. Her lighthearted feeling, brought on by the freedom and grace of the jump, dissolved, leaving only a feeling of disappointment.

"Guys . . ." She groaned, frustrated that they didn't say anything.

"Up there, with the others," the ranger instructed.

"It's not what you think," Taylor began to explain, her usual sarcastic tone missing, replaced by a pleading whine. Then she paused, looked at Jake with an empty beer bottle in hand, then at Joe with his and several empty ones beside him, and sighed. "Oh, never mind," she added.

"So, what do you have in your hand?" The ranger said, pointing to Taylor. "I came over here thinking I was just going to bust the group of kids who've been starting fires, but instead I find you guys. Not only with a fire, but cutting class, and drinking? Wow, talk about racking up the points. You kids don't know what's good for you. Anyhow, open up your hand – let's see what you've got." He tapped his flashlight on her hand.

She was nervous, agitated, and a little frightened. She began to think about getting caught with it. Wondered if it was lost or stolen and thought about how much trouble she'd get into if she were caught with it. Her imagination began to run away with her. What if the diamond actually belonged to some majorly wealthy businessman? What if he would stop at nothing less than sending some unknown, mob connected, source to deal with her, in order to get it back, and then no one would ever hear from her again? The thoughts flitted through her mind before settling on something more realistic. Then her eyes widened with fear as she realized they could put her in jail; stealing such a huge diamond was sure to be a felony.

She weighed her options hastily, and then almost instinctively, popped the diamond into her mouth and swallowed, forcing the rough chiseled edges down her throat, nearly choking.

"NO! Don't do that," the ranger belatedly pleaded. "Now, I'm going to have to," he stopped, distracted by the green color rapidly flushing across Taylor's face.

Immediately after she felt the diamond enter her stomach, it felt like a wave of electricity jolted through her body. An undulating series of nauseous waves surged from her stomach to her mouth, and then a buzz rang in her ears, fluttering around in her head, blocking out all her sensations. Suddenly, in one long surge, a thick blanket of electricity rushed from her chest out into her fingertips and toes and rippled through the land around her, like an aftershock ripping across the lake and past the mountainside.

Once the wave of electricity vanished beyond view, Taylor, with much effort, glanced around, embarrassed and confused, but no one appeared to notice what just happened. She started to say something, but instead was overcome by a severe wave of nausea, and then leaned over and vomited.

Chapter II: Monitoring Station

While Taylor and her friends were getting busted, Richter scale readings were pouring in from all over the country. Seismology labs had picked up a large spike in electromagnetic energy, flooding the Pacific Northwest National Laboratory with information that indicated a massive multi-continental earthquake had just ripped through the globe.

The men at the lab were frantically recording information as they jumped from phone call to phone call, finally coming to the realization that something needed to be done.

"Go get Major Bradshaw!" The director in the monitoring room said, sending a messenger for him.

"Yes Sir," the messenger replied, racing down the hallway until he had stopped just outside a conference room, waiting for a break in the speech in order to interrupt.

"The PS injection 20-03 proved generally ineffective, inducing Tachycardia in some patients and in others, the complete breakdown of the cell walls causing the patient to exsanguinate. On the other hand, the PS injection 20-03 has had some very promising results. Some patients responded to the tests with a 75% increase in brain matter usage and their telepathic abilities have proven to be unparalleled," informed one of the six men, at Major Bradshaw's monthly meeting.

"Are there any improvements with the side effects?" Major Bradshaw asked. "I can't take results with a 10% success rate back to the president. It's too difficult to procure enough candidates."

"Well, we've only lost six in this batch so far, the rest are showing various degrees of disassociation and autism, or hyperactivity shortly followed by psychosis." The man explained, rather excitably. "As you can see, it's very promising."

"Yes, well..." the lights in the office flickered, interrupting, his thought process.

"Excuse me, Sir. You're needed in the monitoring station." The messenger quickly chimed, as he interrupted Major Bradshaw in his morning meeting.

"What's this?" He asked, as the young man handed him a handful of files filled with data from the seismology labs. "There are calls coming in from all of the major Seismograph stations. Edmonton, Cerro Bola, Monterey Bay Ocean Bottom, you name it, they've all made calls, and more are coming in as we speak. The data is overwhelming." The young man continued to explain, informing Major Bradshaw of all the details.

Major Bradshaw, head of the Research and Development Sector of the Pacific Northwest National Laboratory, quickly reviewed the updated information of the massive energy disruption centered somewhere in his region.

"And this just happened?" he asked.

"Yes, not five minutes ago," the messenger finished, as they entered the monitoring station.

Major Bradshaw browsed over the large screen plastered on the far wall. He was surprised by the thousands of little red dots popping up all over the screen, on the advanced national seismic system, implying that each location, a national earthquake monitoring station, was greatly affected by the energy surge.

"Figure out where the epicenter was, and I mean now. Find out the damage done, and what the reading was," Major Bradshaw ordered. "Don't spill anything to the press, and get the President on the line," he shouted. "I can't believe this happened in my region, and we didn't see it coming. Someone is going to pay for this."

"I've got the President, Sir," someone hollered in the background. Major Bradshaw quickly hurried over.

"I'm so sorry, Mr. President, there were no indications," he began to explain.

"It was a 9.2 on the Richter scale," someone else shouted in the background.

"What in the devil are you talking about, Major?" the President asked.

"There's been a major quake, we're still assessing the damage, and data is flowing in as Far East as the Atlantic Ocean." He continued.

"Dear lord, what kind of damage is there?" the President asked.

"Sir, you might want to hear this." One of the men in the station interrupted the Major's phone call.

"One moment Mr. President," the major said, and then turned his attention to the young man.

"Sir, I'm not sure what to make of it, we're getting calls in with reports of no damage, nothing. Some stations are admitting to the possibility of equipment malfunction, only most of the stations don't know about the other stations. Our equipment shows all the activity cleared. What do you make of it?" the young man asked.

"First off, there's no way all the equipment from here to the Atlantic malfunctioned at the same time. That's not coincidence, possibly an extremely well-coordinated terrorist attack, but not coincidence. It's possible were looking at some sort of EMP technology." he said.

"I would agree, Sir, except that an EMP always kills power, that, and we know of no one with the capability to strike out most of the western hemisphere," the young man explained.

"True, true..." Major Bradshaw said, rubbing his chin in thought. "Did you hear that, Mr. President?" he asked, over the phone.

"Yes. Major, are you thinking what I'm thinking?" the President asked.

There was a brief silence over the phone while both the Major and the President pondered over the same question.

"Maybe," responded Major Bradshaw. "You know, when Dr. Ambler worked for us back in the sixties, he did hypothesize that the stone fragment, found in the forties, was part of a greater whole. The freak energy wave could be some form of activation on the other half."

"This could be it; this could be my answer. After decades of Presidents before me, who've failed to accomplish anything, I could be the one to unite the stone and harness all of its power. Imagine the serums I could create with the entire stone. Imagine the armies I could build and the support I could give to our allies. It could be endless," said the President. "Find it, and I mean now. I want this kept quiet and done swiftly, report back to me as soon as you've got something – this conversation never happened." The line went dead.

"What do I tell the stations, Sir?" One of the young men asked, as Major Bradshaw put down the receiver.

"Tell them to run system checks, find the fault if there is one. Let all the labs think they've experienced some major equipment failure. Keep the other labs busy enough so that they don't communicate with each other. We'll locate the epicenter from this lab. Also, don't allow this to slip to the press. If you have any pestering news reporters, tell them we performed a nationwide seismological

● ● ●

equipment test, and no other comments." He explained, leaving the room with the monitors.

Someone shouted from the monitor room, "Sir, I think we've found the location."

Major Bradshaw hurried back through the doors, looked up at the large monitor, and pointed to the small undulating red circle, marking the epicenter. "I want to be there by this evening," he said, pointing to the small town of Port Angeles.

"We can have a caravan ready in an hour, Sir," one of the men said.

"Good, I'll be waiting in my office," he said, and walked off. He sat down in his desk chair, picked up the phone, and called his secretary. "Can you get the Director of the F.B.I. on the phone?" he asked.

"Just one moment, Sir," her mousy little voice responded, followed by silence. Within seconds, she returned to the line. "I have Director Paul Realer on the phone, Sir."

"Thank you, Lola," said Major Bradshaw. There was a click, and he knew he had been connected. "Hello director, I need a nationwide APB put out for Dr. Jacque Ambler. It's about time we locate him. I'll fax you all the old files, see if you can come up with a picture of what he'll look like."

"Sure thing, John, anything else I can do for you?" he asked.

"No, that's all for now . . . Actually, let me know if you get wind of anything, odd," he replied.

"I never know what you mean by that until I stumble upon it, but I'll let you know . . . Hey, have you heard from your little girl? It's been a long time since we've talked?" the director asked.

Major Bradshaw fell silent for a moment, picking up a small picture of a little girl on his desk. A smile pulled across his face and his eyes became misty as he remembered the day his wife captured the photo.

He was carrying Shyla on his shoulders at the Zoo. She was twelve and loved seeing the animals, especially the tiger. He held her over the rail near the fence, as close to the tiger as possible, and his wife snapped the photo, just as the tiger was passing the fencing. The smile on Shyla's face, to this day, was so bright and amazing, that it made him feel like she was standing right next to him.

He turned away from the photo, cleared his throat, and replied, "No, nothing, but I haven't lost hope. I need to go, let me know if you find anything."

"Sorry, John – look, I know we had a falling apart, but if you ever need to talk to someone . . ." he was interrupted.

"That's fine; I need to go – Bye Paul," Major Bradshaw said, and hung up the phone.

Major Bradshaw put together a stack of papers on his desk and closed out of his computer for the day.

Lola handed him his jacket on his way out of the office and asked, "Will there be anything else for the day, Sir?"

"No, thank you Lola, but I'm going to be doing some traveling for the next couple of days, so please keep your pager on, in case something comes up. Take care," he said, grabbing the jacket and joining the caravan outside, several hours away from arriving in Port Angeles.

Chapter III: Goodbyes

"When are my foster parents coming to pick me up?" Taylor asked, watching as Jake's parents escorted him through the front doors of the police station, a solemn expression stretched across his face. I hope he doesn't get into too much trouble, she thought.

"They're not," a gruff voice responded.

Taylor whipped her head around and noticed a tall, disheveled man with a sheriff's badge pinned to his jacket.

"Well then, what are you guys going to do with me?" she asked. "It's not like you can keep me here overnight. I wasn't drinking, I didn't start the fire, and you can't prove that I had anything illegal. Not that I did," she said, confident that a little smirk attitude would buy her some answers. "So, what are you going to do with me?" she finished, glancing at the clock, noticing the small hand nearing the eleven and the large hand nearing the six.

"One of the officers will be taking you over to the children's correctional center when their shift ends at eleven. It's my understanding that you will be staying there for a while. At least, until they schedule you a hearing," he said.

"Hearing for what?" Taylor asked.

"New placement, I believe. You've basically used up all of your options out here, and now the state needs to figure out what to do with you," he said.

"Well, that sucks," she mumbled. "What's wrong with the home I just moved into?" She fiddled with a pencil, trying desperately to act like she didn't care.

"They decided that teenagers are too much work," he said, trying to keep the conversation impersonal.

"Oh, I see," Taylor responded, sinking back into her chair. "No one wants a teenage foster kid, especially not one that might have issues. What teenager doesn't have issues?" She paused for a moment, silently venting the anger inside - "So CCC huh?"

"Yup, afraid so kid – try and take it easy, alright. I'm sure something good will come of all this," he said, and exited the conference room leaving Taylor alone for the remainder of the shift.

Wow, this suck, she thought. No one ever wants me, and the ones that do, usually beat me. Maybe the judge will throw me in jail and then I won't have to worry about all this. "What now?" Taylor asked, as a young police officer interrupted her thoughts.

"Just here to take you out to the children's corrective center," he responded.

"Oh, sorry," she said, apologizing for the harshness in her voice. After the long day she'd had, she didn't have the energy to sass anyone else. "I'm tired, can we just go now?"

"Yeah, if you'll just come with me out to the car, then we can get going," he said, escorting Taylor out to his traditional black and white police car.

He held the back door while Taylor slid into the seat and strapped in. Feeling awkward being escorted by a stranger to a place she didn't want to go, Taylor said nothing to the man during the drive, and instead, she found her thoughts spiraling around the sharp pain in her stomach and the strange pinching in her chest.

Oh, that was a bad call, she thought, considering the effects the stone was having on her stomach. If this pain gets any worse, I'm going to have to see a doctor and then they'll cut me open to remove the stone, and that would just make this week even better, she added to her thoughts, sarcastically.

"We're there – just follow me and I'll get you set up for the night, okay," the officer said, turning off the ignition. He helped Taylor out of the car, after getting out himself, and escorted her into a large set of double doors followed by another set of double doors, locked. He punched a code into the small, numbered pad on the door-lock, waiting for it to open, and then nudged Taylor inside, quickly following her and replacing the door.

"Can I help you?" An older woman asked, from behind a large desk, monitoring the activity on several screens that indicated different locations in the correction center.

"Sure thing, Ma'am," the officer responded to her and then turned his attention to Taylor and said, "wait here – this might take a moment," motioning for her to stay on one of the benches attached to the wall.

Taylor sat for what seemed like an hour, until exhaustion finally took over and then she dozed off, using her hands as a pillow on the hard bench surface. Taylor awoke to the older woman nudging her.

"Come on, let's get you set up. Sounds like you'll be here for about a week," the woman said, helping Taylor up.

"Mom, I had a really bad dream ... Oh," Taylor flushed with embarrassment, no sooner than the words escaped her mouth did she realize that she wasn't a kid, nor was her mother around, and that in fact it wasn't a dream, and her bad day really did happen.

The officer gave the old woman a sympathetic look and then commented, "See you in a week kid," and left the center, punching in the locking code on his way out.

"Sorry about that, sometimes I... um forget. Let's just leave it at that," Taylor said, trying to hide any signs of weakness she might have shown, in her sudden desire to seek out her mother's reassurance.

The old woman quickly shared a few words of encouragement, "there, there. You know dear, everything eventually gets better, it does." And then paused, before escorting Taylor back into the barracks section of the facility where she would sleep for the week.

The woman briefly disappeared into a closet and returned with a pile of linens and a stack of several old gray institutional uniforms. "I'll collect your things in the morning. Everyone wears these while they're here. Breakfast will be brought to you in the mornings as well as lunch and dinner, later on. If you've any questions, someone will be around at all hours; otherwise, your room is that one." She pointed Taylor toward one of six doors in the hexagonal shaped room. "I'm sure you're very exhausted, so I'll let you get to bed now. Goodnight," the old woman said, and then left Taylor, locked in the darkened room.

She dragged herself over to the bedroom and draped the linens over the old mattress that was carelessly placed on the top of a cement slab propping out of the ground. She kicked off her shoes and dropped her shorts beside the bed, before crawling under the scratchy wool blanket from the pile of linens, and quickly fell asleep.

"KNOCK, KNOCK, KNOCK!" An attendant was knocking on the door.

"Breakfast is here," she said, placing a small tray beside Taylor.

"Thanks," she responded.

"I've brought you some clean clothes so that you can look refreshed for the hearing today," she said, and then set a pile of folded clothes beside the tray.

"Wow, the hearing's today, already?" Taylor asked.

"Yeah, it's been a good week since you came here. It's about time they had your hearing if you ask me," she said.

"With nothing to do, I guess I lost track of time in here," Taylor responded.

"Well, that's understandable, it can be boring. Anyhow, an officer is going to be here soon to escort you, so get ready." And with that final note, she left the room, leaving Taylor some privacy.

Taylor quickly undressed, leaving the old prison uniform clothes in a pile on the floor and replaced them with the cleaned clothes on the bed. Juggling a muffin and apple in one hand and a milk carton in the other, she scarfed down the food, cramming as much into her stomach as she could before the officer arrived.

"Taylor, Officer McGraidy is here," the attendant hollered, from down the hall. "Come up to the front and I will let you out."

"Coming," Taylor responded back, taking one last bite of her apple before tossing it back onto the tray and leaving the room. She waited inside the door, at the far end of the hall, until the attendant buzzed her through.

"Oh hey," Taylor said, surprised to see the officer that had dropped her off at the center a week ago. "So, what did you do to end up as a taxi driver for delinquents?" she said, the sarcastic tough-kid facade that Taylor perfected returning to her as naturally as riding a bike.

"Nothing, I just thought you might like to see a familiar face, that's all," he said, winking at the attendant.

"Whatever," she sighed, rolling her eyes, secretly glad to see Officer McGraidy. Any familiarity was better than none when faced with the unknown.

He finished signing a couple of release papers and then motioned for Taylor to follow. "Come on kid," he said.

"Take care, Taylor. Who knows, maybe you'll like the next home," the attending lady said, offering a few kind words of encouragement as Taylor followed the officer out to his police car.

"Hey, have you ever been in the front of a police car?" the officer asked Taylor.

"No way, really – I can sit up front," she asked, relieved that she wouldn't have to be toted through town in broad daylight, in the back of the police car. "You're not going to get into trouble for that, or anything?"

"Nah, hop in, it's nothing special," he replied, strapping himself in and starting the car.

"Where are we going anyway? I thought the hearings were held in the building up the street," said Taylor.

"They are, but it's my understanding that you are going to have a very long day so I thought we'd get some coffee, unless that is you don't like coffee?" he said.

"Cool, I think," she said, wondering what the officer was buttering her up for. "Does that mean you know where they're going to send me?" she asked, raising her eyebrow to the officer questioningly.

"Unofficially, but I'm not allowed to say anything, so don't bother badgering me," he said.

"Fine," she said, as they pulled into a little drive-through coffee hut. "I'll take a caramel macchiato, of the large sort – as long as you're buying," she said, clearly feeling smug.

Unconcerned with Taylor's obvious self-righteousness, he ordered for the two of them. "I'll take a large caramel macchiato, and a medium black coffee."

"Four-fifty please," the lady said, waiting for the change that Officer McGraidy pulled out of his uniform pocket and handed to her. Once he received both the drinks, he handed Taylor hers and they began the drive back to the correctional facility where the hearing would be held.

"Thank you," Taylor mumbled, realizing the rudeness in her attitude towards the officer, and then went back to silently sipping her coffee.

Once they pulled back into the parking lot of the correctional center, Taylor broke the layer of silence that had fallen in the car and asked, "Can you at least hint at where they are going to send me?"

"Sorry kid, you'll just have to wait," he responded, locking the doors behind him as he escorted Taylor into the judicial side of the correctional center.

"Bummer," Taylor groaned, flopping into a seat in the lobby and fidgeting with her coffee.

"Can I help you, Sir?" an attendant asked the officer, in an all too familiar way that reminded Taylor of last week, when Officer

McGraidy dropped her off for her initial stay at the correctional facility.

"Yes," he said, automatically responding to her question. "I'm here escorting Taylor Saskia for an eight-thirty hearing with Judge Rynfield."

"Okay, will you please fill out an informational packet on her behalf?" she asked, handing him a clipboard with some papers.

While Taylor sat silently browsing through some magazines, the officer quickly filled out the paperwork, returned it to the attendant, and then rejoined Taylor in the lobby.

"Any last words, before they call you in?" he asked, watching as Taylor actively fidgeted with her nearly empty coffee cup.

"This is really nerve racking," she responded honestly. "I've never actually been to one of these hearings; usually they just cram me into a room for a day and then drop me off at a new home. I'm not usually involved in these placement hearings."

"Don't worry. It's nothing serious, and I think you'll be pleasantly surprised by the end of this one," he calmly reassured her.

"No offense, but aside from the Judge saying, congratulations you've just won a million dollars and emancipation, I don't think I'll be very thrilled," she said ironically.

"Will Taylor Saskia please report to hearing room three," a loud scratchy voice called over the intercom.

"That'd be us kiddo," Officer McGraidy stood up and motioned for Taylor to follow, briefly stopping near a trash can, allowing Taylor a moment to swig the last drop of coffee and toss the cup into the can. "After you," he said, waving his hand at Taylor.

Her heart began to pound, and she could feel the perspiration build up on her brow as she entered what felt like a courtroom. The Judge was waiting, fixated on her every movement, or least that's what it felt like. And once she sat down beside her caseworker, she noticed that the officer had disappeared, leaving all the staring eyes stuck on her.

"Good morning Taylor," the annoying caseworker whispered to her. "Today is going to be a great day for everyone," she exclaimed in such a bubbly manner that Taylor wanted to slap the smile right off of her face.

A succession of thoughts rapidly flashed through Taylor's mind, as the caseworker pulled out a file with her name plastered onto it. How does she know that today is going to be a good day? What does a happily married woman, with no kids, and both her parents still alive, have to say to me about a freaking bad day? And who in their right mind starts a good day by being escorted by a cop, from a correctional center to a hearing.

"What a nut," she said aloud, finishing her thought just as the Judge interrupted, plunging right into the business of relocating Taylor.

"What? Did you have something to say, Taylor?" the judge asked quizzically.

"Nope, sorry, that was nothing," she blushed, sinking into the back of her chair.

"Okay then, to continue . . ." the judge began after clearing his throat. "Due to the exhaustion of resources in Clallam County, the State of Washington would rather place Taylor Saskia with a living relative rather than move her into another county. Although the state prefers a ward to maintain residency within the state for legal purposes, we are willing to draw up an interstate compact on behalf of the child."

"Seriously! He says that like I'm not here," Taylor mumbled. Irritated by the Judge, Taylor pretended that she wasn't listening to him and glanced around the room. Sitting on the opposite side of her caseworker, Taylor noticed three officials that must have represented the State, two policemen, and two men that didn't look like they belonged at all. Both were dressed in military uniforms, and the taller, older looking one had a file that he was browsing through, periodically looking up from it to evaluate Taylor. That's odd, she thought.

"Furthermore, we have contacted the Grandparents and they are more than happy to claim guardianship," the Judge continued, catching Taylor off guard.

"What . . ." Taylor gasped, dropping her jaw.

The caseworker gave her a pleased smile. "Don't you think that's great," she whispered.

"I don't know what to think," Taylor mumbled. I didn't realize I had Grandparents, alive even, she thought.

The Judge continued. "The caseworker has suggested permanent transfer of the guardianship to both of the Grandparents with immediate relocation. On behalf of the child, both the State and the Department of Social and Health Services agree with the recommendation and have decided to get the ball moving, so to speak," he chuckled. "Anyhow, your caseworker is in charge. There have been arrangements made for you to leave later this afternoon. I trust you won't make this difficult for anyone. It is a lucky child, whose Grandparents can step in and take on the parenting job. Good luck Taylor." He said the last part directly to Taylor and then concluded the hearing and left the room.

"Oh, what a great day, don't you think Taylor?" Her caseworker chirped, ushering her out into the lobby.

"Maybe . . ." Taylor groaned, hiding the nervous edge in her voice.

"I've only ever heard bad stories about my grandparents, from my mom," she explained.

"Nonsense, we've spoken to them, and they seem like very gentle and realistic people," the caseworker responded. "Now, if you please. You've got packing to do and little time to do it." She turned her attention to Officer McGraidy, "If you'll be as kind as to escort Taylor back to her foster home to pick up her stuff and then off to the airport, we can all be on our way." She handed him a folder, which contained a flight plan and some meal vouchers, along with a copy of Taylor's file.

"Thanks," he said, grabbing the folder and escorting Taylor out to the car. "I'll make you a deal, okay kid," he said, holding the passenger door open, while Taylor plopped into the seat.

"Yeah, I guess. It's not like I'm in any sort of position to argue with you anyway," she responded despondently, preoccupied from the proceedings of the hearing. Taylor was both confused and anxious, as things that her father had said flashed through her mind.

"Your mom's parents are the most horrible people in the world," he'd say. "They once threatened to blow my brains out if I didn't leave their house right then and there. They were hateful people - didn't even want us in their lives." Taylor remembered how he'd say all sorts of terrible things about them when he was drunk, but that was the problem. He was always so drunk and angry that who knows how much of what he said was exaggerated or even made up.

Taylor shook her head, knocking away the images of her angry father that remained while she sat in the car. Trying to hide the obvious tortured look that commonly overtook Taylor's face when she was reminiscing, she cleared her throat a few times and refocused her attention.

"Are you alright there? You kind of spaced out on me for a while." Officer McGraidy gave Taylor a concerned look.

"Yeah, sorry . . . Now what about a deal?" she asked.

Officer McGraidy pulled up alongside a cute little ranch style house at the corner of the street, parked the car, and leaned over to Taylor to speak. "Well, I figured . . . If you promise to behave and not give me any trouble, not that I think you will, I'll let you meet up with those troublemaker friends of yours to say goodbye, after you finish packing here."

"Cool . . . I mean, yeah, that sounds like a good deal." Taylor responded. This guy is pretty cool, she thought. I'm glad I got stuck with him, instead of my lame caseworker, for the day.

They both got out of the car and walked up to the house. Taylor rapped on the door, until her foster mom answered.

"Come on inside," she said. "Taylor, you know where your things are. I left some bags in the room you were staying in."

"Thanks," she replied, and headed back to her old room where she quickly called Joe, setting up a rendezvous point. When she finished up her phone call with Joe, she rummaged through the few things that were hers and tossed them into her backpack, then proceeded to call Jake.

"Can you meet me at the coffee shop downtown?" she asked, once he'd answered the phone.

"The one near subway," he responded.

"Yup, that's the one." She scanned the room for any last items.

"Sure, is Jake coming?" he asked.

"Yeah, apparently I'm leaving town today, so this is my only chance to say bye," Taylor explained.

"Okay, well I'll be there shortly, wait for me." He finished and hung up the phone.

Taylor zipped up her backpack and glanced around the room one last time. The room looked about the same as it did before. Taylor shrugged a little, accepting that she didn't really have much to change a room in the first place, but maybe that would change someday. She gave the room that she had stayed in fewer than three days a final farewell, and then rejoined Officer McGraidy in the living room where he was chitchatting with her old foster mom.

"Officer McGraidy and I were talking, and he told me about taking you to say goodbye to your troublesome friends. I think that's awful nice of him, don't you?" the foster mom asked, exaggerating her face as she asked the question.

Taylor gave her a scrutinizing look. What was she trying to get at, she thought? And then like a light bulb flicked on, Taylor realized that this woman, like so many foster parents before her, was trying to act like she was her mother, and it was her duty to enforce good manners. Keeping in mind the deal she had made with Officer McGraidy earlier, Taylor kept her sarcastic thoughts to herself, and instead said to Officer McGraidy, "Thank you, that's very awesome of you to let me meet up with my friends." Taylor flashed a small glare to the foster mom, and then exaggerated a smile.

"Better," the foster mom said.

Taylor let out a disgusted noise. She was annoyed that a woman who had only watched her all of three days felt so in control of her behavior. What nerve, she thought.

"Can we go now?" Taylor pleaded, scooting over toward the door.

"Sure thing . . . Is that all you have?" he asked, pointing to the backpack she had slung over her shoulder.

"Yeah, it's not like I have much these days." Taylor gave the backpack a quick shake and then opened the door, walking out onto the front porch, before replacing it over her shoulder.

"Well, it was nice to meet you again, Mrs. Chialto," the officer waved her goodbye.

"You too," she responded, and then added in a scrutinizing tone to Taylor, "Mind your manners young lady, and take care."

Taylor pretended she didn't hear her, sitting inside the car, quietly waiting for Officer McGraidy.

He sat down beside Taylor, strapped in, and started the car before asked Taylor, "So where to?"

"I asked Joe and Jake if they could meet us downtown at the coffee shop near Subway, if that's okay," she said.

"Yeah, that's fine. Quit stressing already. I'm not Mrs. Chialto." He winked at Taylor, and then pulled the car away from the sidewalk.

"Oh, so you caught that too," Taylor sighed in relief.

"By that, you mean that holier than thy attitude?" he asked.

Taylor nodded in agreement.

○ ○ ○

"What was that all about?"

"Honestly", Taylor answered, "I have no idea. I only lived there for like three days before I was moved into the CCC place. The funny thing is that that is normal. If a foster home isn't bad one way, then usually there's some other catch, like an abnormal addiction to etiquette."

"Well hopefully your grandparents will be pretty cool," he said, nearing the downtown coffee shop that Taylor loved.

"Yeah, let us hope," She murmured.

Joe and Jake were both patiently waiting outside the coffee shop, Jake carrying a little something shaped like a card. Taylor jumped out of the police car, eager to catch up with the boys, before running over to them and affectionately in turn punching each in the shoulder. "Hi guys," she said, disappearing inside the coffee shop before either one could hit her back.

"Ouch, not gonna miss that," Joe flinched.

"I will," Jake muttered, and then followed after Taylor. He walked up to the counter where Taylor was browsing through the display of drinks and ordered for all of them. "I'll take two large caramel macchiatos and let me guess," he paused to glance at Joe. "The Oreo madness blended coffee as well, oh and make that a large," he said, testing Joe's approval.

"Hey, you don't have to order for me, Jake," Taylor said, pulling out a handful of change from her pocket.

"Nah, my treat, we'll call it a little farewell gift." He quickly paid the cashier and waited to pick up the drinks while Taylor and Joe went to sit beside a window.

"Nice escort," Joe commented. "Is he not coming inside?" He nodded in the direction of the car outside.

"Nope, guess not. But don't worry he'll drag me out of here when it's time to go," she said.

Jake ambled over balancing the three drinks, before distributing them, and joining Taylor on the loveseat in the shop. "Speaking of dragging you off, where are you going anyway? You haven't even told us what happened at the hearing yet."

"Well, there's good news, and there's bad news. I'll start with the good. Apparently, I have Grandparents that want to take care of me, so I don't have to be moved around anymore," she said.

"Wow, that's really cool. I know you've missed having a real family and all," Jake responded, sounding as cheerful as he could manage to fake.

"Yeah, only the bad news is that I'm moving away – to another state, I think. Also, I really don't know my grandparents. I mean what if they totally suck, and are really mean and strict?" She sighed. "I won't be able to hang out anymore, and I'll have to make new friends and all that jazz."

"Yeah, I could see how that might suck," Joe responded, slurping up some of his Oreo blender.

"Hey, just look at it this way, it's a new school so you could totally join cheer squad or something hot like that, and we could still come visit anyway . . . maybe," Jake teased.

"Yeah right, cheerleading, there's something I'll look into. You'd love it if I was bouncing around in one of those skimpy little skirts wouldn't you, ya pervert." Taylor playfully smacked Jake's arm. "Okay, but in all seriousness, I'm not even sure where I'm going. They didn't divulge that information to me." She straightened up her face and let out another long-disappointed sigh.

Joe stiffened and both Jake and Taylor turned to follow his gaze. The officer had left the car and was coming inside.

"Looks like it's your time to go," Joe regrettably pointed out.

Officer McGraidy popped his head into the door, catching Taylor's attention, bringing a dampened end to her little get-together. "Taylor we've got a plane to catch, let's go."

"Sorry guys guess I've got to get going," she said, while staring Jake in the eyes, and then mouthed the word sorry again.

Both the boys casually walked with Taylor out to the car, chitchatting about the latest Seahawks game. Taylor tried to ignore the banter assuming that both boys felt just as uncomfortable about the goodbye as she did, fidgeting with the car door, until the officer stressed the importance of leaving again.

"Well, I guess I'll call you guys once I get settled in, assuming they allow me to make phone calls." She crossed her fingers in an exaggerated attempt to lighten the uneasy feeling settling in her stomach.

"Sounds good," Joe replied, and gave Taylor a goofy handshake bump fist custom. "Stay cool girly," he added and then nonchalantly strolled back into the coffee shop.

Taylor's heart began to race, as Jake's stunning blue eyes peered down into the barren black sea of hers, in one final attempt to say goodbye. Almost like an electrical shock, a tingly surge sprung into Taylor and flushed the cool ivory skin of her cheeks, causing her to look away in embarrassment and breaking the silent trance shared between the two of them.

"Yeah . . . I've got to go now – guess I'll see ya later," he said, brushing Taylor off and then walking back toward the door. He paused for a moment and then Taylor heard him whisper, "Never mind," before disappearing into the coffee shop. Her eyes fell to the ground, focusing on the little uneven cracks of the cement, in a futile attempt to distract herself from her bleak thoughts.

"Now, that we've got that out of the way, let's get going," Officer McGraidy interrupted her pity party, once again stressing the importance of leaving.

Taylor slumped into the car, strapped herself in, and browsed out the side window for the remainder of the drive out to the airport.

Chapter IV: Strange Dream

"So, what'd he give you?" Officer McGraidy asked, as he helped Taylor with her backpack, locking the car doors behind them before entering the small airport.

"Nothing, what do you mean?" She asked. "Oh, right – I forgot he was holding something that looked like a card. He must have forgotten as well," she said, making a sad pouty face.

"Ah, don't worry. I'm sure it was something silly anyway. It was probably just an easier way to say goodbye or something like that. Guys are never very good at those sorts of things. Cheer up, maybe he'll mail it to you," Officer McGraidy commented.

Taylor followed him up to the check-in counter and waited patiently beside him as he spoke with the attendant.

A thought crossed her mind. "Where am I going anyway?" She interrupted Officer McGraidy.

He responded while handing his I.D. to the associate at the desk. "They didn't tell you? That's odd."

"And whom do we have flying with us today, Sir." The attendant interrupted, before he could respond to Taylor.

"Taylor Saskia," he replied. "She'll be flying alone, so she'll need to be monitored during the layovers at the airports. There have been arrangements made for Mia and Pat Donalow to pick her up at her final destination," Officer McGraidy explained.

The attendant nodded her head in understanding and typed some information into the computer. Once she was done, she printed out a boarding pass and some other information. She handed the pass and packet to Taylor and said, "Make sure to give this paperwork to the associate once you get off the plane and they will take care of you." Taylor nodded her head in agreement.

"Any check-in luggage?" The lady asked.

"No, I just have this backpack, and I'll take it with me," Taylor responded, clinging to her only possessions.

"The plane is already boarding. Officer McGraidy is more than welcome to escort you out to the staircase. Have a nice flight," she cheerfully added, then turned back to her computer, motioning for the next person in line to come forward.

○ ○ ○

Officer McGraidy walked with Taylor outside until they reached the small staircase outside of the airbus. They paused for a moment.

"Well, I guess thanks are in order." Taylor smiled at him. "I couldn't have been stuck with a cooler guy for the day."

"Yeah, it was no problem; just try not to get into any trouble out there, okay." He paused, then handed her a wad of cash. "It's just a couple bucks for some snacks or something, nothing big."

Taylor smiled at him once more. "Thanks again."

"Don't mention it, kid," the officer said to Taylor, waving her off.

Taylor swung her backpack up and over her shoulder, ascended the stairway and disappeared into the plane. There were only a few people on the plane, and most of the seats in the back part were vacant.

"Sit wherever you'd like. This is a pretty empty flight," the flight attendant told Taylor, pulling the file out of her hands. "I'll keep a hold of this. When we land in Seattle, I'll give it to the escort there, just to ensure you catch all the right flights."

She picked out an empty pair in the back row beside the lavatories, propped her bag on one and sat in the other, leaning her head against the window. Taylor tried to clear her mind and fall asleep while the plane was taking off, but before she knew it; her thoughts were racing with anticipation. By the time she had settled her nerves, they had already arrived at the Seattle-Tacoma airport, and it was time to get off of the plane.

"Good afternoon, ladies and gentlemen. This is your captain speaking. We have arrived at the Sea-Tac airport. The local time is three-thirty in the afternoon, and it is fifty-five degrees outside, on this overcast day. Thank you for flying Kenmore Air, we hope you enjoyed your flight and have a good day." The captain's monotonous voice droned over the intercom.

Taylor watched as all of the passengers left the plane and then waited for the flight attendant.

"Please follow me," she said.

Taylor picked up her bag and walked quietly behind the lady until they reached the inside of the terminal, where she was turned over to an airport escort.

"Marko will bring you to your next terminal. Have a good day," the flight attendant said, disappearing back outside.

"Hello, my name is Marko, and I am in charge of making sure that you make it to your next flight, so don't run off. Now please come on," he said, after browsing through the flight schedule that the stewardess had handed to him. "Portland, Maine, is it?" He asked Taylor.

"Why, is that where it says I'm headed?" She asked.

"Yup that's what the instructions are. You've got this last flight that will take you there and then we hand custody of you over to a Pat and Mia Donalow," he said.

"Portland, Maine? That's a long way away," she replied.

"Oh yeah, this next flight is a five-and-a-half-hour flight. That'll suck for you. I suggest sleeping or reading, something that will help pass the time, if you know what I mean," he explained.

"Yeah, I think I've got it under control," she commented, and then silently followed him. Ugh, this is like being babysat by the most boring person in the world, Taylor thought. I'm almost seventeen. Can't I just travel alone? I'm not even going to be able to use the cash that Officer McGraidy gave me because this guy isn't going to let me stop anywhere. The annoyed babble rambled through Taylor's mind until they arrived at the next terminal.

"Yay, we're just in time for boarding," the escort dryly said. He ushered her out the doors, down the long corridor, and into the plane, where he handed her file over to another flight attendant. "Bye," he said to Taylor and exited the plane.

"Bye," Taylor mumbled, and then turned to the next stewardess. "Hey, I guess you're in charge of me now."

"Let's get you situated. This will be a long flight. If there is anything you need, please let me know." The flight attendant walked Taylor down to a middle row of seats and waited while she strapped in and pushed her backpack under the seat in front of her. "There are some headphones in that pocket," she said, pointing to the back pocket of the chair in front of Taylor. "You can plug them in here and listen to music or watch the movie. Just adjust the channels with the buttons there." She pointed to the little headphone jack on the armrest and explained the buttons. "I need to go prepare for takeoff, but please, once again, let me know if you need anything."

○ ○ ○

"Thanks," she mumbled, slumping back into the chair. She pulled out the headphones from the chair pocket, placed them over her ears, blocking out the loud roar of the engine, and then closed her eyes and focused on the music until she drifted off into a deep dreamy sleep.

As Taylor drifted away, her thoughts embarked on a strange journey through her mind.

Where am I? She thought, opening her eyes up inside a cozy living room. She looked around, noticing a fireplace with a new stack of wood freshly burning away, and a comfy sofa set placed around a couple of bookshelves arranged on both sides of a large window. She stepped up to the window and peered outside into the dark evening night. A large black car pulled up into the driveway and out stepped a familiar looking face, along with three others.

What is he doing here? She thought, recognizing the military man from her hearing.

"Search the perimeter first, and then you two take the back and you, follow me into the front. Get the girl quickly and quietly." The military man ordered the others, pulling out a handgun.

"Huh," Taylor gasped.

"In the window," one of the men yelled. All four men snapped their attention towards the window that Taylor was peering through, just catching a glimpse of movement.

She quickly covered her mouth and slipped out of view from the outside and then glanced around the room looking for some sort of escape route. She noticed stairs on the other side of the room. Instantly dropping to her knees to avoid being seen through the window, Taylor scuttled over to the stairway and then scurried up, stumbling over a couple of stairs in her frantic hurry.

"On three, one . . ." Taylor could hear one of the men outside begin to count, before knocking in the door.

"Oh my God, oh my God, what the heck is happening," Taylor gasped, tears pouring down her face as she rushed into the room upstairs in a panic, locking the door behind her, and browsing the room for an exit.

"Upstairs," she heard another voice yell, quickly followed by the pounding of boots marching up the steps.

Her heart pounding harder with every second and her chest heaving with every hastening breath, her focus narrowed in on a window across the room. She flew to the other side of the room and fumbled with the lock, until she was able to push the window up and open, reaching outside for a grasp of something to hang onto. She reached out, completely oblivious to the black claw that replaced her own hand, and grabbed tightly onto the wood siding, pulling herself out of the window and climbing onto the roof.

"There, tail out the window," another man yelled, just as they smashed into the room and caught the final glimpse of a long black leather tail, sliding hastily out the window and vanishing into the night.

Taylor sucked up her breath and crawled quietly over the shingles until she was hidden behind the chimney and watched silently. A head bobbed over the ledge of the roof and browsed around, pausing to gaze at the chimney, and then giving up, returning back into the room.

"She can't be far," she could hear one of the men saying. "Get outside now, cover the area, and find her," a different, stronger voice ordered. It must have been the leader, the one she had recognized from earlier, but what was he doing here, and why was he after her.

Still out of view from the armed men outside, Taylor waited patiently against the shingles on the roof, until she had heard them drive off. Struggling to calm her breathing, she stood up, and peered around the neighborhood. Silhouettes of treetops against the moonlit sky and smoke plumes funneling out of chimney tops filled her with tranquility, and she closed her eyes, enjoying the light caresses the wind left against her skin. Remembering how the wind had responded the last time she jumped off of the Devil's Punch Bowl, Taylor thought that maybe it was playing with her, with all of its innocence, and urging her to play back.

Instantly, in response to the wind's gentle plea, Taylor lunged right off of the rooftop and into the air, joining the wind in its innocent swirling dance. To Taylor's sheer delight, she found herself soaring through the air, rising with the thermals and falling with the playful dives of the wind. All the anxiety from earlier had drifted away and she was soaring off into the distance without any concern, or at least until it began to get cold.

The night began to fill with a white wall of blindness and the playful tease of the wind turned into a battering of harsh kisses, stinging against her cheeks, drawing tears from her eyes, and burning the tips of her fingers. She had flown so far and so long that she no longer knew where she was, or when it was, but rather that it was extremely cold, and she couldn't see more than a couple of yards in front of her.

As the bitter cold chipped away at her light-hearted free feeling, she began to panic. She peered desperately through the white night, searching for something recognizable or at least a hut or cabin in order to escape the relentless storm. A small glow caught her eye. As she drew in closer, the glow became brighter. Once she was close enough, a large mansion began to outline in the storm, and the bright glow was visibly coming from a large fire roaring inside one of the rooms.

Taylor swooped down onto a ledge, just outside the large window, and peered inside, looking for a way in.

Oh, that fire looks so welcoming, she thought.

Just then, two men walked into the room and Taylor quickly pulled to the side of the window so as not to be seen and listened silently to their conversation.

"It seems that the second half of the stone has been activated. The only way to save her is to remove the stone, young man," one voice said. Taylor peeked around through the window, trying to make out the figures that she saw.

"I'll do anything to save her, just name it," the second voice, a familiar voice, proclaimed.

"Good, I'll need you to . . ." The voices became too hard to make out as the men stood closer to the fire, but now Taylor was distracted by the conversation and wanted to get in closer to hear better. She clung to the outside wall, and almost like a gecko, climbed sideways on the stones until she reached a second window, in a separate room, that opened. Pushing open the window, Taylor crept into the room, shaking off the cold, and then froze as a majestic figure stared back at her from a large mirror in the room.

"Wow," she gasped. "Is that me?" The words escaped her mouth.

Standing in front of her was a slender and mysterious gargoyle. Her skin was the color of night; the same color of her hair, except that

● ○ ●

a shiny black crown of ridges had replaced her hair. Ridges she'd expect to see on a dragon, riding all the way down her back and disappearing at the end of her long muscular tail. Her ears were tall and pointed, and her face jutted out much like the muzzle of a lioness of tigress. Her body was slender and graceful, yet still muscular. She looked down at her arms and legs.

"No wonder I was climbing on the walls," she whispered, admiring the deadly claws that replaced the dainty shape of her hands and feet. She playfully slashed the air with her claws and smiled, as exhilaration pooled in her nerves. And then, last but not least, as she returned her gaze to the mirror where she was admiring the new shape she had taken, she gasped, "How cool."

Taylor gazed upon two of the most incredible wings she could ever have possibly imagined. One on either side of her shoulders, leathery and sleek, each one a good ten feet long, the size impeded only by the walls of the room. Transfixed on the beautiful and yet horrifying angelic shape, she was startled when suddenly they collapsed, folding down like drapery and wrapping around her neck, locking together like a cape. The movement happened so instinctually that Taylor didn't even realize the wings were attached until after they enrobed her.

"Hey, you!" Someone startled her.

"Who's there?" She said, frantically glancing around the room.

"Wake up . . . Wake up." She could feel an arm pushing on her shoulder, and then unexpectedly the dream vanished, replaced by a dim glow of lighting and a strange boy standing over her, as she opened her eyes.

"What," she said, waking from the dream, realizing she was still on the plane.

"Everyone is getting off," a boy who must have been sitting somewhere behind her said, then grabbed his bag and followed the other passengers.

Taylor's heart sunk into her chest as she realized it was only a dream.

"Oh, thanks," she muttered, watching the boy disappear. She tiredly pulled out her backpack and joined the remaining passengers as they exited the plane. As she neared the door, the stewardess stopped her.

"You must have been pretty tired. You were out like a light the entire flight," she said.

Taylor moaned in acknowledgement.

"I'm sure it made the flight go by faster though . . ." She spoke. "Well, I guess I'll walk you out and turn you over to your grandparents, if you don't mind," she politely added.

Taylor hesitated, "Okay, I guess." It's not like I have a choice, she thought. Her nerves began to jump. And although she was rattled from her strange dream, the idea of living with her grandparents, people she didn't know at all, began to settle in, and suddenly she found herself nearing the brink of a panic attack.

Hardly keeping a cool façade plastered to her face, Taylor followed the stewardess down the corridor that connected the plane to the terminal, and out to where her grandparents were, with exception to airport protocol, waiting.

"Taylor!" chirped a small, elderly woman. "My dear sweet child!" she exclaimed, running up to Taylor, embracing her tightly like a long-lost friend.

"Well, you look just like your mother," A tall, old man commented, overshadowing the smaller woman.

Uncomfortably wedged between the new stranger's arms, she pulled away from the old woman, and brushed herself out. Pushing back the long strands of hair, tossed in her face, and straightening out her shirt, Taylor, uneasily watched the two of them as the stewardess interjected.

"I'm assuming you must be Pat and Mia Donalow." She said.

Pat responded, "Yes Ma'am, I believe you've got some paperwork for us."

The stewardess signed something in the file, and then handed it over to him. "You won't mind if I see some identification, just for security purposes please?"

"No problem. I can appreciate that. It's not like you'd want to hand her off to the wrong people." Pat said, nodding in agreement before pulling out his driver's license and showing the stewardess.

"Thank you, I believe that's everything then. You folks have a nice evening," she paused, directing her attention to Taylor, "good luck with your new home Taylor." She said, and then gave a brief wave, before turning around and walking back towards the terminal.

Taylor silently stood, watching her grandparents for a moment. What kind of people are you, she thought, creating character profiles from their stature? Tall, confident and handsome in an old man way - not what I expected, she thought, looking up and down her grandpa. And you, petite, amiable, nonthreatening, with quaint old lady curls – not what I expected either, she thought, glancing over her grandma. Where are the guns, and attitudes, and hatefulness that my parents used to talk about? Reflecting back on the old stories, she realized neither of them lived up to the horrifying monsters that Taylor had depicted from her parent's stories over the years, and now maybe she did have a chance to start over.

"Oh honey, I know this is all new to you. And I know we must seem like total strangers, but you don't have to figure us out tonight. You've got lots of time to get to know us and we've got lots of time to get to know you." Mia lovingly explained, slipping over to Taylor and pulling her back into a big hug. "And the important thing is that we'll love you no matter what."

Taylor became tense and very uncomfortable again, the words echoing in her mind. We'll love you no matter what . . . Yeah right, she thought, brushing away the warm feeling that threatened to tear down her wall of safety, built up behind her tough-girl façade. "Okay, okay . . . can we just get going already? I'm really tired and I'm sure you've got thousands of questions you want to pelt me with." She said, readjusting her backpack over her shoulders.

"Oh yes, sorry dear . . . let's just be on our way then." Mia commented, leading the way out to the car.

"We've got a good hour and a half until we're home, please let us know if you want anything to eat or if you'd just like to sleep. We understand how exhausted you must be." Mia exchanged a look of agreement with Pat.

"Anything at all," he said, holding the door for Taylor as she jumped into the back seat, before jumping into the driver's side himself and starting up the car.

"I am kind of hungry. I haven't really eaten for a while." She commented. "A burger or anything like that would be fine, if you don't mind."

"Of course, dear, there's a stop up the road a little way, we'll grab a bite there. We won't bother you for anything else tonight. We know you must be exhausted." Mia said, before zoning off while they drove up to a burger joint.

"A cheeseburger is fine," Taylor relayed to Pat, as he ordered it through the window, paid for it, and drove off. She chomped down on the sandwich, enjoying every last ketchup smothered bite, "Thanks," she muttered, keeping a fresh and polite tone with her grandparents.

This time it was Pat that responded. "Not a problem, like we said anything you need."

Taylor began to feel uncomfortable with all the nice gestures and the sympathetic attitude. "Okay, just so that we're clear here - you guys don't have to keep pretending like you care about me. I know how to take care of myself, and I've been doing it a long time. I'm not trying to be rude or anything. I just know how this works, and the sooner you stop pretending to care, the less likely I'll get hurt, okay." She came out and said it, what she'd always meant to say to other foster parents. It was important to her that they are honest and upfront, she was tired of being moved from one home to another and tired of all the emotional games they play. The worst thing that could happen now is that they would decide they didn't want her and send her back but being sent back now would be better than being sent back later, when she might actually like them.

"Darling, darling, darling . . ." Mia sighed, and then turned to Pat. "How I wish they'd notified us about her years ago." She leaned over the side of the chair, gazing at Taylor, and empathetically whispered to her. "My, how the system has messed with you, you can't trust anyone, can you?"

A lump formed in Taylor's throat, she wanted to cry. She wanted to tell Grandma about all the awful things that had happened to her in foster care. She wanted to tell her how lonely she felt and how nobody cared to listen. And mostly she wanted to share with her how horrible it'd felt the day she'd lost her mother. She wanted to tell her all those things, but her mind wouldn't let her unleash the flood of emotion that would inevitably leave her feeling vulnerable and lost. So instead, she huffed at her grandma, turned away, facing the window, and muttered, "What would you know," while gazing out the window.

The remainder of the ride was quiet, both Grandparents listened to music on the radio up front, and Taylor glared out the back window, recalling fragments of her strange dream, trying to lighten her mood, and distract her mind.

● ● ●

That was such a strange dream. It felt like I was really there, and that man in the uniform, he seemed familiar, like maybe I've seen him somewhere else, she thought. Maybe I'm so stressed out from everything that's happened the last week that my normal life is spilling into my sleep. It's not like I normally remember my dreams.

I wonder if I could dream about being a gargoyle again, she thought, while staring into the shadowy trees. A dark figure soared quickly through the treetops vanishing as suddenly as it appeared. Yikes, Taylor thought, peering into the darkness, finding nothing. It must be time for me to get some sleep. Now I'm seeing things.

No sooner did Taylor close her eyes to relax, did she find the car pulling into the driveway, and her grandpa making the announcement that they were home. Taylor peered out the window, barely making out the two-story shape of the house and the glinting surface of the moonlit river behind. It was dark and cold, as she stepped out into the driveway, and yet a warm feeling emanated deep inside as the words "we're home" sank in.

Chapter V: At the Tracks

The next morning Taylor awoke to the irresistible smell of bacon wafting into her room from the downstairs. She couldn't remember the last time she'd woken up to such a great smell, and so she pulled on some pajama pants and hurried downstairs into the kitchen.

"Good morning darling, how was your night?" Her grandma pleasantly greeted her with a plateful of scrambled eggs, strips of bacon, and fresh from the oven biscuits.

"Oh, everything smells so good," Taylor said, smiling, and then she quickly corrected herself, before snatching a plate and disappearing into the dining room. "I mean . . . eggs are good."

Grandma brought in a few glasses of orange juice and a pitcher situating herself across the table from Taylor.

"So, how was your flight, yesterday?"

"Long and . . ."

"Did you sleep well?" Grandpa chimed in, joining them at the table.

"I guess, but . . ."

"Do you like your room? I painted it myself." Grandma interrupted before Taylor added anything.

"How're the eggs?" Grandpa asked.

"Oh my God, I don't know, you're asking me too many questions. I can't even breathe." Taylor tersely replied.

"Oh, sorry honey, we must have gotten a little excited." Grandma said. "You just tell us whatever's on your mind." She added.

Taylor gobbled down the eggs and began on the bacon before she said anything, leaving both her grandparents waiting in anticipation for something to come out of her mouth. "The flight wasn't too bad, but that was probably because I slept the whole time. I did have a really strange dream though, actually I sort of had the same dream again last night, and it was really weird." Taylor didn't continue realizing that she would have to describe it now; maybe if she changed the subject then she wouldn't have to say anything. "The room is nice, but do you mind if I add some personal touches to it, you know, make it my own?"

"Oh, sure thing honey, just don't do anything outrageous, like taking out a wall or adding a greenhouse." Grandma smirked.

"Funny, but I was just thinking about drawing some pictures on the walls and putting up some posters, nothing to permanent." She smiled, successfully changing the subject.

"So how about that strange dream you've been having, wanna tell us about it?" Grandpa asked.

Taylor frowned.

"Yeah, you know Pat here used to be a psychologist back in the day, maybe he can help you figure out the deeper hidden message within the dream. They say that dreams are just the subconscious speaking out in abstract ways." Grandma said.

Oh great, now I get to play someone's guinea pig, she thought. "It's actually really stupid now that I think about it anyway?" She said, doubting they seriously wanted to her a dream about gargoyles and men dressed in military uniforms. They probably thought she was just having dreams about boys and school.

"Come on, give your old grandpa something to think about." He spoke.

"Okay, but I'm telling you it's out there."

"That's fine, I like a good challenge." He replied.

"Well, it began with me in a house. Much like this one come to think of it." Taylor said looking around at the room and finding it strange that it was really similar to the dream, if not the same.

"Then some men dressed up in military uniforms came to the house. They were looking for something, but I don't know what. They scared me so I snuck onto the roof, hiding so that they couldn't find me." She continued.

"After they left the house, I began flying, and then I flew into a snowstorm in the mountains and found a mansion. I heard some men talking about something. It sounded like something about a stone, and saving a girl, and activating it, but then I –um, just woke up." She cut the story short, too embarrassed to say anything about the bit where she was a gargoyle, or about the fact that she had found a large diamond recently and it was probably still inside her stomach.

"Interesting," said Grandpa, keeping a straight considerate look.

"Wow that really does sound strange." Grandma smirked, throwing a wink at Grandpa.

Grandpa sat for a while eating the remainder of his breakfast while Taylor sat wondering about the harsh thoughts crossing Grandpa's mind. Maybe he thinks I'm crazy. Or maybe he's not even thinking about it, maybe it was so stupid that he doesn't even care and regrets that he asked about it in the first place.

"Right, well that's pretty cut and dry." Grandpa finally interrupted the silence.

"I'm not crazy, I swear." Taylor quickly defended herself.

"No darling, you're not crazy. I just mean that all the things in your dream symbolize fairly obvious rolls in your life that could easily be bothering your subconscious." He replied with a chuckle.

"So, what do you think?" She cautiously asked.

"Well first, I think the men in the military uniforms symbolize authority, and because you recently had some problems with the police, I could only ascertain that your subconscious is still bothered by the incident. When you hid on the roof in your dream it could just mean that you're hiding from yourself, and not confronting the way you feel about the whole debacle.

"Secondly, imagining oneself flying is a rather common occurrence in dreams, especially in adolescent females, but in your case, it could just represent the trip that you took to fly out here on the airplane. That seems a fairly simple inference.

"And lastly, along the same lines, the mansion in the cold mountains that you found, could easily be a subconscious view of how you see our house and the trip it took to get here. The cold could symbolize an emotionally distant association you have with us, and the long trip into the mountains to find the mansion could represent the emotional toil you must have traveled through to arrive here at your new home." Grandpa finished, with a smug look on his, satisfied that he'd gotten it all right.

"Wow, I never really thought about it that way, but I guess it makes sense. Thank you." She said, dissatisfied with the analysis. She felt like there was more to it than that. A chill ran down her back as her entire body acknowledged the genuineness of her dream, the bitter cold nipping at her face and hands and the amazing feeling of flexing those beautiful black wings. Something about it seemed real, but she couldn't tell anyone that, not even Grandpa.

As she sat at the table thinking about the analysis that Grandpa had given her, she heard the disturbing headline of a local news channel drifting in from the living room, where Grandpa had retreated.

"Four more children vanished from an elementary school early yesterday morning, this time in Concord, New Hampshire, bringing the national total to forty-seven in the last three weeks. The FBI is investigating each case, but further information has not been released to the press. So please keep a close eye on your children and make sure all arrangements to and from school are explicit. Next, we'll be speaking with John Yodel, who is on the scene in Hong Kong, where a new terrorist group is claiming responsibility for the attack on the Shanghai World Financial Center . . ."

"There you are honey." Grandma said, causing Taylor to jump.

"Yikes Grandma, did you hear the news? It sounds like the world is having a total meltdown. I missed a lot the last few weeks." Taylor replied.

"Now, don't go minding the news, there's always something terrible going on now-a-days. You just worry about, Taylor, and everything will be just fine." She reassured her, sending a cross look at Grandpa in the living room. "Now come on, I'll show you around the house and then afterwards, the yard. I'm sure you didn't get to see anything when we drove in last night." Grandma said.

"Oh cool, I'd like to see what's around here. I couldn't tell for sure, but it looked like there was a river out back." She replied, pushing the newscast into the back of her mind.

"Yes, there is one; it runs out to the sea you know. The tides change the direction of flow in the river, so you have to keep a close eye on it, especially if you're going to boat or anything daring like that." Grandma said.

She followed her grandmother around the house discovering the different rooms, an office, two bathrooms, three guest rooms, one of which had been converted into her room and the main living room where Grandpa was finishing up the news. Then Grandma stepped out into the back yard with Taylor right behind.

"It's beautiful," she gasped, gazing at the magnificent oak cascading shade over a vast portion of the back yard. And like a post card picture, an old rope swing hung below one of the larger branches, with the picturesque winding river looming behind.

"That's not all," Grandma walked down a rickety staircase and stopped at the little dock floating on the river's edge. "I used to fish with my dad on this dock when I was just a little girl, of course back then the river was so polluted you couldn't eat any of the fish that came from it, but it was still fun."

"You've lived here that long?" Taylor asked.

Grandma chuckled at the comment and raised her eyebrow at Taylor.

"I didn't mean that you're really old or anything. I just meant that I've never known anyone to live in one place for so long. I mean look at me; I've never lived in one home for more than a year. That's all I mean." Taylor quickly defended her comment.

"Oh, don't worry, it just doesn't seem like that long ago to me, I suppose." She said, and then an idea struck her. "You know, I've got all my old fishing gear in the shed if you'd like me to show you how. And I'm sure grandpa would love to join us, the old guru. What he wouldn't do for an excuse to fish." She chuckled some more, cautiously leaning over the edge of the dock, and then tossed some water into Taylor's face.

"Hey, cut it out, that's cold!" Taylor snapped, secretly enjoying the sense of familiarity and closeness she was sharing with Grandma.

Taylor peered across the river, soaking in the beauty of the old town. She could make out a boat park, a large bridge, some classic Victorian houses, and a curious old railroad track.

"Enjoy it, while you can, this river will be solid ice in a few weeks, and the days will be so cold you won't want to leave the house." Her grandma said.

That gave Taylor an idea.

"Can I go explore in town later today, maybe?" She sounded pleading, hoping that she wasn't pushing her boundaries.

"Of course, actually we should all go together. Considering you'll need to be starting school no later than next week, and all you seem to own is a backpack with a few measly items, we should probably get you some school clothes and supplies." Grandma replied.

"Okay cool," she said, taken aback by the idea that someone other than herself was thinking about her needs, and genuinely seemed to care. She hadn't even begun to think about school, and with only a couple of items in her backpack, it was probably a good idea that she purchases some new things. She was still hesitant to fully open up to Grandma and Grandpa, but she felt less and less like she needed to be on her guard around them and decided to soften her tone. Hoping that they won't hurt her like everyone else has.

"We better get going, Grandpa will wonder if we've drowned." Grandma said, clambering back up the old staircase, waiting for Taylor at the top, before entering the house.

Taylor caught another snippet of the news as she wandered over to Grandpa in the living room.

"Forecasts suggest an early winter this year, with expected snowfall accumulation to rise above last year's thirty-two feet. Experts claim global warming is the cause; others claim it is a test. Join us with local weatherman Jim Boneo while he discovers just what kind of test the locals believe this is. Jim . . ."

"Thanks, Tom." The local weatherman replied as the camera switched to him. He was standing beside a frumpy looking old man outside a Hannaford grocery market, holding a microphone. "Sir, can you tell us a little about global warming, do you think the ice caps are melting?"

"Oh, global warming, that's just some well thought up scam to get people to buy all these new 'energy efficient' vehicles and crap."

Jim pulled the microphone back to himself. "So can you explain why the weather has become increasingly severe and dangerous?"

The frumpy old man shook his head vigorously in agreement. "Oh yes I can, indeed, Sir. You see it's the end of days coming, it is." He proclaimed it like it was matter-o-fact. "You see the problem is all this racism and terrorism, and the government using all those chemicals that people don't even know about, and killing people, and all those underground porn rings and stuff, you know. I'm telling you it's the wrath of God coming down on us. If you ain't a Christian than you better be saying your prayers, cause bad stuff is coming." He waved his hands at the sky as if proclaiming the truth.

The reporter stood speechless for just a second before responding. "Well, there you have it; bad weather is the Wrath of God, ladies and gentlemen. Tom, back to you," the camera switched back to the news reporter sitting in his cozy desk. Taylor decided it was a good time to interrupt Grandpa.

"Wow, you believe that crap Grandpa?" She asked, confused why the news was broadcasting such an extremist view on the weather changes.

"Well darling, I'm not sure what to believe anymore, especially with all these kids disappearing out of school. It's like no one is safe anymore."

His comment reminded her of why she came into the house in the first place. "Oh, speaking of which, Grandpa. Grandma was going to take me into town to get some school supplies; did you want to come with us?"

"Oh, that sounds fine, I've been meaning to pick up some medicine from the pharmacy." He replied, easily forgetting what they had just watched. He noticed Taylor's gaze, fixated on the front door. "Feeling a little cooped up, are we?" He asked, regaining her attention.

"Oh sorry, are you guys ready to go?" She spoke. As far as she was concerned, the sooner they left, the sooner they might get the shopping done, and then the sooner she might get a chance to explore before dark. Not that she was afraid of the dark, but she doubted they would let her stay out after dusk, with it only being her first day in town.

Grandma grabbed her purse and followed Grandpa as he went out to the car to start it. Taylor ran upstairs and fumbled through her backpack until she'd found her trusty old pocketknife, placing it in her back pocket and then ran quickly outside, joining both her grandparents in the car.

"Taylor, did you know that even as close as these two towns are together, with only the bridge separating them, they are still two separate towns, because the river is a boundary line . . ." Taylor peered out the window as her grandmother rambled on about the history of the town and the neighboring towns. Not particularly fascinating information to Taylor, however, the rustic appearance of the buildings and the over a hundred-year-old dates engraved into the more senile looking ones, caught her attention and she wondered about what life would have been like before cars existed.

"I guess that makes sense why they're so close together." Taylor mumbled, as Grandpa pulled alongside one of the older buildings and parked the car.

"What makes sense?" Grandma asked.

"Sorry, I was thinking out loud. I just figured that back before cars, people would have had to walk, or take horses to get into town, and so having each little area be its own town just made sense. No one wanted to walk very far to get where they needed to go unless they had to. Well at least that would be my guess." Taylor explained, shrugging her shoulders. She didn't really care if her guess was right or not, but she thought it was a pretty good assumption.

Walking into the building together, an old musty smell welcomed the three of them, causing them to crinkle their noses in response to the aging smell of the store. Grandpa disappeared down the opposite end of the building and Grandma escorted Taylor over to the clothing section, handing her random articles of clothing for her to try on in a dressing room.

"Do all the buildings smell like this?" Taylor asked, finding a place in the two-stall dressing room to try on the clothes Grandma had handed her.

"Just the older ones, but you get used to the smell." She replied. "Almost all the buildings on this side of the river have experienced some level of water damage or another. Anytime the river fills over twenty-five feet, it floods into this part of town." Grandma casually explained, as if a river rising twenty-five feet was a normal occurrence.

Of course, maybe around here, the river rising twenty-five feet was a normal occurrence, she thought. The idea sent a shiver down her spine.

"Well, these all fit just fine," Taylor said, stepping out of the changing room with a pile of clothes. Two longer sleeved sweaters caught her eye, hanging on one of the racks. As she hurried over to pick them both out, she flashed a puppy dog look to Grandma, waiting for her approval of the two Dot Rosette Crew Cardigans, one in black, and the other in a silvery grey color.

"Well, those certainly look nice, although I'm not sure how warm they'll keep you." Grandma commented.

"Yeah, well I got to have something my style for school." She replied, a satisfied smile stretched across her face.

After they finished picking out all the new clothes Taylor needed for school, she followed Grandma into the school supply section of the store and rummaged through some basics, like notebooks and pens, until they found everything she needed.

"Now, where do you think Grandpa went off to," Grandma said, looking around the aisles.

"I thought he went to the pharmacy?" Taylor replied.

"Oh, I'm sure he did, honey. But it's been over two hours, I'm sure he's done with that by now."

"Wow, two hours, already? It didn't feel like that long." Taylor replied, amazed with how fast the day was passing. Still enjoying the time, she was spending with Grandma, Taylor diligently followed her, aisle by aisle, until they finally found Grandpa in the fish and wildlife section.

"There you guys are," he sounded all innocent, like he'd been searching for them the whole time.

"I should have figured you'd be in the fishing area. Silly me, for thinking you'd be anywhere else." Grandma chuckled.

"Well, I figured if I'm going to teach Taylor how to fish, then I'd better get her, her own fishing pole." He said, winking at Taylor.

"Grandpa, you don't have to do that." Taylor said, frowning.

"Just think of it as a welcoming present, that's all." He replied.

"So, you're really going to teach me how to fish?" She asked, half afraid that he'd say no, he was just messing with her, but he didn't. He just shook his head yes with a big smile and led the way out to one of the cash registers to pay for everything.

Taylor held back a huge smile that was forming across her face. She didn't want to give away the excitement that she felt. Parents never wanted to spend time with her, especially doing something like fishing together. Hopefully she wouldn't do anything that might mess this up because so far, she really liked Grandma and Grandpa.

Taylor followed behind in thought as Grandpa pulled out his credit card to pay.

"Can you believe it about that attack in Hong Kong?" The cashier said, making quick conversation with Grandpa. "They say it's going to hurt the global economy worse than the World Trade Towers."

Grandpa's face hardened, as if the mentioning of the towers brought up some bad memories. "It's too bad, that's for sure. I don't know how much more the economy can take these days, although I'm not sure if I believe it was an uprising from China that caused the accident."

The cashier nodded in agreement, bagging up the merchandise and handing the receipt to Grandpa. "You folks have a nice day now, and don't let any of this bad news ruin a nice day like this."

"We'll try not to," Grandpa responded as they were walking away.

"Shall we grab a bite to eat and head down to the boat park? I'm thinking there's a certain railroad track that leads along the river and that a certain someone might want to explore around before dark." Grandma smiled, directing the question to Taylor.

Taylor beamed with excitement, "How'd you know I wanted to explore the old tracks?"

"Just a hunch I guess, plus it's not hard to imagine with you staring over at the tracks every chance you get." Grandma smiled a warm understanding smile. "I was a kid once."

They dropped the shopping bags off in the car and then walked over to the dinner next door and picked up some pizza slices, before strolling down to the boat park. Grandma and Grandpa picked out a bench overlooking the river with an open view of the railroad tracks and sat down to eat. Something about the way they sat silently together enjoying the peace from the river, made Taylor realize just how much in love the two of them must have been. She liked to imagine that they needed only the comfort of each other's presence to feel completely happy. And then she remembered that she felt like that sometimes, with Jake.

She didn't live in Port Angeles anymore, and that was unsettling to say the least. Would she ever see him again? The thought crossed her mind; she never did get a chance to date him, a chance she might take now.

In order to keep from becoming depressed, Taylor decided that she wouldn't think about it anymore. There was nothing she could do about it and therefore she should just move on.

"Are you going to eat that?" Grandpa interrupted Taylor's otherwise complete thought, pointing at the pizza.

"Oh no, you can have it. I'm just too excited to go explore, I think. Do you mind if I take off?" She replied. She was hiding the fact that her little bought of depression actually caused the loss of appetite.

"Sure thing, just be back here in a couple of hours. We can wait around a little while. Plus, I can give the fishing pole of yours a test to make sure it works." Grandpa explained, giving Taylor the okay to take off.

"Oh, I forgot something earlier." Taylor whirled around toward Grandma and Grandpa, realizing she hadn't thanked them for anything they'd done.

"And what's that?" Grandma asked curiously.

"Thank you, guys, for everything so far, the clothes, the school stuff, the fishing pole, and even for giving me a home." She struggled with the words. "Sorry, I'm not used to being taken care of," she admitted, nervously picking at her fingernails.

"Well, you're welcome darling, now you just go have some fun." Grandma dismissed her, and both she and Grandpa watched as Taylor held back a skip in her step and quickly disappeared behind some bushes, hiding the old railroad tracks.

Taylor thought about the news clip she'd caught on the television earlier. It was strange how the world seemed so chaotic at a time like now, especially when she was becoming so comfortable in her new home. Leaping over a fallen tree branch and onto the next track, she noticed a bridge just barely visible among the river's edge further down the tracks, and that caught her attention.

Collecting some stones and thinking back on the boring week she spent in juvenile hall, Taylor slowly but surely made her way down to the bridge, hidden within a small alcove of the river, and sat, legs dangling, on the edge of a large wooden tar covered track. She fidgeted with the stones until she found just the right shaped one to skim the surface of the river as she sat. The flat, smooth rock, nothing like the stone she'd swallowed, reminded her of the day at Lake Crescent, the one that would forever change her life.

Wondering why the rangers never pushed the issue of what was in her hand, she realized that they didn't even notice the strange surge. She could have sworn it felt like an earthquake. Of course, she did throw up after she swallowed it, so maybe something was wrong with her vision. And she did see a strange shape in the trees last night, maybe she's just too stressed out from all the changes in her life, and she really is seeing things. But just then, another shape distracted her, hidden in the bushes across the river.

"What," Taylor gasped, peering desperately into the thick shrubs. Closing her eyes as if to rub the shadow out of sight, Taylor looked back at the same spot in the trees, but the shape had disappeared.

Looking frantically around, hoping that she wasn't going insane, she noticed the sun was setting and it was casting a heavy stream of shadows across the riverbanks. Maybe it was just the shadows, hopefully, but still, seeing shadows twice in the last twenty-four hours was bad.

"Oh my God, oh my God, this is soooo not good. I need to get back to the house, I'm going nuts." She said to herself, as a sort of command to force herself up from the ledge, easily hanging over a small part of the river.

She hopped over the rail and back onto one of the wooden tracks, but a rustling noise in the bushes caught her off guard. She slipped. Crack. Her leg twisted unnaturally between the tracks, as the rest of her body thudded on the hard tar covered planks catching her from crashing into the water and rocks below.

"Ah," she screamed out in pain, looking around at the absence of humanity in the fading light. If no one could hear her, then she'd better try and get up or else who knows what could happen.

She pressed both her hands firmly against the wooden beam and tried to lodge her other leg against the opposing beam for leverage, but as she lifted to bring her leg out of the gap, the weight of it dangling forced her to scream out in pain again and drop her body back against the beams.

She shifted around to get a look at her leg, hanging lifeless in the air, and as the rusty scent of iron hit her nostrils, and seeing the gushing wound where the bone snapped through her thigh, caused a wave of nausea that sent her head spinning.

"Help," she yelled, "somebody help."

But nobody could hear her. She'd been so lost in thought during her trek it never occurred to her that she traveled close to three miles down the track which led her quite a distance from the town.

She cried for help nearly ten minutes before the loss of blood and mind-numbing pain began to beat away at her consciousness. As the last few pleads, barely escaped her mouth, the dark engulfed her, and she surrendered to the calm of the deadly sleep threatening to take over.

Her eyes were closed as she sniffed the air outside, forgetting about the sharp pain in her leg.

"Yum, that smells good," she said, blinking open, her eyes.

There was a strange old man standing beside her, and a thick smoky bacon aroma filled the air, enhancing the familiar seawater smell on the beach, which she recognized as Salt Creek.

"What's roasting in the fire?" She inquired, startling the old man.

"Oh my, you surprised me." He steadied himself, bracing her shoulders.

"Let me help you, Sir." Taylor offered a hand, as he looked up at her face and paused in pure disbelief.

"Oh no . . . you shouldn't be here." He pushed away from her.

"Oh yeah, and where should I be?" Taylor became defensive; realizing that the last thing she did remember was passing out on the bridge with her injured leg. Was she in some sort of afterlife, she began wondering?

The old man grumbled as he reached into the bonfire and pulled out a long walking stick, burning at the end with a strange blue flame.

"Do you know what today is?" He cocked his brow, leaning his weight on the stick.

"Of course, I do . . . it's Tuesday," she proudly replied.

"Of course, you wouldn't know. That's why you don't belong here.

"But aren't I dead? Isn't this like my afterlife or something?"

"No, it's not, and you wouldn't be here if you were dead. So please try to understand and go back home."

"But I don't even know where I am. How can I leave when I don't know where to go?"

"You must leave the same way you came here and do it soon before you change anything." He waved the glowing end of the stick in her direction.

"What, what do you mean?" She glared at him, because he was only confusing her more. "I don't know how I got here. I hurt my leg and passed out. I most certainly didn't do anything crazy to get here. Will you just tell me something useful, old man?" She barked, but before she had a chance to yell at the old man again, a distraction in the sky caught her off guard. Four brilliantly colored gargoyles crossed the sky, like the blue angels at a super-bowl game, until they disappeared beyond the mountains. "What on earth was that?" Her jaw dropped.

"I can't tell you more about this place, only that you are not allowed here. You have a purpose sometime else." He said ignoring her question, "and you must leave."

"Sometime, don't you mean someplace else?" She was becoming extremely frustrated with the man's ramblings.

"If you are here, then you cannot be there, and without you there, then here cannot be, so return to there, where you belong, and make it possible for here to be." The man was ever so patient, even as Taylor was boiling.

"I don't understand your riddles old man; just tell me where I am already, so I can go home, okay." Taylor glared at him.

"Just wake up," he swung the blazing stick from the bonfire and smacked Taylor upside the head.

"Ouch, what'd you do that for," Taylor rubbed her head as the throbbing ache surged through more than just her forehead, and the realization that she was still dangling with a broken leg over the railroad tracks settled in.

"Sorry, I'm just trying to get you out of here. You could die if you lose too much blood." A husky voice informed her.

As she tried to open her heavy eyelids and see clearly who had come to her rescue, she was only able to make out a hazy shape. One that looked strangely like the shape she kept spying in the bush, but that was about all she could see in the dark, with her consciousness drifting in and out.

"This is going to hurt and I'm sorry but soon you'll be at the hospital, okay." He spoke.

Taylor attempted to nod but all she managed was a grunt. He scooped her up like a baby, holding her as still as possible, and then lunged out into the sky.

Taylor felt like she was still dreaming, maybe she was. This strange guy came out of nowhere and rescued her. She didn't know what to believe. She could feel the wind rushing against her face as they soared through the night air. The chill in the air suggested that winter was coming soon, and the aching pain in her leg began to subside as shock began to settle in.

She tried to tell the man about her grandparents and how much they must be worrying about her, but the words only came out of her mouth in fragments and pieces of gibberish.

"Shh, we'll be there soon. Save your strength Taylor." The man said.

Normally she would have worried that some stranger knew her name but right now she was just so exhausted from the pain and blood loss that she felt right at home in his arms and allowed his comforting words to sink into the depth of her soul. She tried again to make out his face but finally gave up and nestled into his collarbone after recognizing the shape of a gargoyle face from a statue and decided that she must be too far gone to make any realistic observations.

Finally, with a thud, they landed in what must have been some garden outside of the hospital. They didn't move for a long moment, something felt strange to Taylor. Like maybe his arms had gotten fleshier, or smaller. And the cold leather that she was leaning against on his chest became warmer and fuzzier, but regardless of what changed Taylor couldn't focus on any one thing for very long as the pain in her leg began to pound even harder than before, until finally he began to move.

He walked her up to the entrance of the emergency room and waited for a nurse to run out with a stretcher to place her on. As he shifted her over to the stretcher, she was able to make out his face just a little. He was a boy, maybe her age or a little older, and rugged, but that was all she could tell before he nodded to her and took off. The nurse didn't even get a chance to talk to him before he disappeared.

"Hey, hey, come back here," the nurse hollered at him as he vanished down the street, "We've got questions for you. Dang kids, hope he didn't do this to you." She mumbled.

Another nurse came out and helped the first one push the stretcher into the emergency room, where the on-call doctor popped out, checked Taylor's pulse, looked at her leg, and then sent her into an operating room.

Chapter VI: Miraculous Recovery

"Try and relax we'll take good care of you." One of the nurses said to her.

"Check her pockets see if you can get any identification." The same nurse said to the others then looked to Taylor and tried to ask some questions. "Can you tell me who to call, dear?"

Taylor could see nurses around her hooking up fluids and injecting shots into her. She choked out, "Pat and Mia Donalow," and then she faded out as the pain medication began to take effect.

Taylor woke up the next morning thirsty and tired and sore. She looked down and saw that her leg was in a cast and Grandma was sleeping in a chair beside her. The curtain separating Taylor from other guests in the room waivered and Grandpa walked in holding three coffees.

"Oh, I'm glad to see you're up. You had us worried all night. Do you remember what happened?" He asked.

"Um," Taylor rubbed her head trying to piece together the events of the strange night. "No, mostly I just remember what happened before I fell."

"Oh well, that's alright I'm sure you'll remember over time, so how did this happen?" He pointed at her leg.

"I was sitting on one of the tracks hanging over the water at the bridge, until I noticed it was getting late out. Then I got up to head back but something in the bushes distracted me and I slipped on the track, and I guess I twisted it just right, or just wrong I guess." She touched the hard plaster over the leg.

"Well, I guess it's a good thing some random boy found you out there or who knows how long you would have waited before someone came along." Grandpa replied.

Grandma began to fidget just as a doctor pushed open the curtain and stepped into the room.

"I'm glad to see you awake and talking." He commented browsing through her chart. "How are you feeling this morning?"

"I'm sore and my leg is throbbing but otherwise okay, can I go home?" Taylor asked him.

"Well, I don't see why not. Your grandparents have the medication that you can take for the pain, and we'll need to see you back here in a few days to make sure the bones have set properly, but otherwise you're good to go today. Any questions?"

"Um, how long do I have to wear the cast?"

"I'd say at least six weeks in this one; if all looks good from there then we can probably put you into a smaller removable cast. Just take it easy." He spoke.

"Okay," she mumbled, disgruntled that she'd have to begin at her new school with a broken leg.

"Anything else?" The doctor asked, handing the chart to Grandpa, waiting for his signature.

"No, that's all I can think of, thanks, I guess."

"Well then you're free to leave, just make sure to check back in, in a few days." He reminded them and then left the room pulling the curtain closed again so that Taylor could get dressed.

"Well let's go home then, shall we?" Grandpa asked.

"Sure, but do you mind leaving for a minute so Grandma can help me get dressed." Taylor flushed, embarrassed to think about changing her clothes with Grandpa in the room.

"Oh, yes of course, I'll just be waiting in the hall." He said and slid behind the curtain and out into the hall.

Grandma helped Taylor out of the hospital gown and into a clean new shirt from home and then with difficulty into a pair of pants.

"We're gonna have to get you some bigger pants for school if you are going to fit that cast into them." Grandma commented.

"Oh, please no, I'll find a way to make them fit. I don't want to look like a complete idiot at my new school. Its bad enough that I have to wear a cast, just let me figure out something." Taylor pleaded, disgusted by the idea of wearing sweats into school. At least she had some fashion sense.

"I guess, but if I think you need something different, you'll have to surrender okay." Grandma said.

"Sure, but I promise I'll figure something out. Now can we go, please?" Taylor hopped out of the bed and reached for the crutches leaning against the wall. "This isn't so bad," she said, hobbling out into the hallway where Grandpa was waiting.

"You look like a champ," he commented following behind Taylor as she headed out to the parking lot. By the time they made it to the car her arms were exhausted, and she collapsed into the back seat with her leg propped up on the other side of the seat. They drove home, careful to avoid potholes and any unnecessary bumps that might cause Taylor some pain.

Once home, they set up a nice reclinable chair for Taylor with end tables on both sides so that she could have whatever she might want and just relax and watch the television.

A few days went by, as Taylor stayed at home, mostly switching from the chair in the living room, to her bed, and then back again. She practically went through Grandpa's entire movie collection and read her favorite book twice through. She found the news to be rather disturbing and avoided watching it as much as she could. It was nearly every day that another two or three elementary and middle school kids went missing all over the country. It was really strange, but they all appeared to be the brightest of their classes or they excelled in something like art or music. It might have just been Taylor, but she really thought the kids were getting targeted by a specific group and not just randomly abducted.

Shutting off the television once again, after Grandpa had finished watching his disturbing morning news; Taylor decided to call Jake for the first time since she'd moved out to Maine.

She dialed his phone number area code and all and waited for him to answer.

"Hello," his familiar calming voice echoed through the phone.

"Hey Jake, long time no talk, right?" She asked.

"Hey, I was starting to think you forgot about me. So how are you doing, what's it like out there?" He asked, excited to hear from Taylor.

"I'm doing okay. I kind of had an accident, but all and all it's not too bad out here, and my grandparents are really cool. Like surprise, right?" She relaxed enjoying the sound of Jake's voice.

"Well, that's good, except that you're going to have to tell me about this accident."

"Don't freak out, but I broke my leg, like really broke my leg. Like bone poking through skin broke my leg, but I'm in a cast now and I'm fine."

"Holy crap that sounds terrible. Sorry I wasn't there to stop you from being a klutz."

"Nah, its okay, I turned out just fine. I don't even feel any pain from it anymore, but I do have to wear this crazy huge cast to school for a while, which I haven't started yet. So, I can't tell you what its like yet."

"Oh, speaking of pains, there's been this pain in the butt guy going around asking all sorts of questions about you here in town. He's dressed in a military uniform and goes by the name Major Bradshaw. He's already questioned Joe like four times about you and some stone. He's talked to me a few times too, but I have no clue what he's talking about. So anyway, heads up there's some strange dude asking around about you." Jake informed her.

"That's good to know, I wonder if it's the same guy that was at my placement hearing. Hmm oh well. I guess if he finds me, he finds me." She replied, wondering if Jake or Joe had noticed the diamond, she had found at Lake Crescent.

"Well, it was nice catching up with you, but I can hear my dad yelling in the background. He wants me to go do some lame daddy son dinner thing. He's not taking this divorce very well. And yes, it's been finalized, they just keep exchanging me every other week, but I'll tell you about it some other time. Stay safe and don't do too much crazy stuff without me." He waited for Taylor's reply and then hung up the phone.

"Bye Jake," the words drifted off into the back of Taylor's mind and her eyes moistened, getting home sick for Jake for the first time. She hasn't had a boyfriend yet. She knew he'd dated a couple of girls but never for very long, and never anything serious.

But if she had to date someone, she would have liked to have dated him. Oh well, she thought drifting off into a little nap. Dreams of the night she broke her leg replaced the sad thoughts of missing Jake, and she focused on the figure she saw across the riverbank. She couldn't make out any details, but it was shaped curiously like one of the gargoyles she had seen soaring through the sky in the strange future dream she had. She snapped out of her dream and woke up after reliving the part of that night where she broke her leg.

Grandma noticed the painful grimace across Taylor's face. "Is everything alright, Taylor?" She asked. "Do you need a pain pill?"

"No, I'm fine. I just had a bad dream. Sorry to worry you." She responded. "My leg hasn't actually been hurting since we left the hospital, come to think of it."

"Is that why you don't want any of the pain meds? I figured you were just trying to pull the tough girl stunt and deal with the pain.

Well maybe that's a good sign. You can always ask the doctor today when they x-ray your leg to make sure the bones set."

"That's today? I completely forgot." Taylor was surprised.

"We should probably leave in about an hour." Grandma informed her.

"Okay, I'll be ready."

Taylor drifted off into thought again, wondering about the boy that had rescued her. Because she was so out of it that night, and could vaguely remember making it to the hospital, she wondered how the random boy must have even transported her to the hospital in the first place. It must have been a car, or something like that, there's no way he flew her there, like she imagined. Then she wondered what he was doing out there, maybe fishing? Or who knows, sketching the sunset, and then he must have heard the pathetic screaming from some strange girl, and came to the rescue. There had to be an explanation. She started school in a few days; maybe someone there would know something. There was bound to be rumors going around the school in such a small town.

Just then Grandma interrupted her. "Time to go, Taylor. We don't want to make the doctors wait; they have other patients to see."

"Alrighty, alrighty, just give me a second." Taylor brushed off the crumbs that had collected on her shirt while she'd been sitting in her recliner chair munching on random snacks throughout the day then fumbled for her crutches. Hobbling slowly out to the car where both of her grandparents waited, she tossed the crutches in and then clambered into the back seat propping her leg up on the seat again.

Once at the hospital, Taylor went to a special room where a trained x-ray technician shot several images of her leg from different angles and then joined her grandparents in the waiting room until the doctor was done examining the results. Not twenty minutes had passed since the x-rays were taken when a group of three doctors hustled out of a room and escorted Taylor into a clean and empty room with a bed and a couple of chairs.

"Please have a seat on the bed, Taylor Saskia?" One doctor looked down at the chart, and then up at Taylor as she nodded in response to her name.

"We must have mixed up the charts, or maybe the x-rays." One of the doctors said to the one with the chart.

"No, I'm telling you I saw her just a few days ago, this is the same girl. Those x-rays match her."

"Then why do they look like the x-rays of a person whose injury is in week five or six?" The three doctors just kept bickering.

"There's just one way to settle this, the cast has got to come off.

Grandpa and Grandma were standing back watching, as the three doctors discussed the possibilities of what, they did not know, until finally Grandpa had had enough.

"Before anyone does anything I'd like to know what's going on here." He demanded.

"We're not really sure what is going on. That's what we're going to find out." The doctor with the chart set it down, rummaged through a drawer, and pulled out a mini saw. The other two doctors helped Taylor situate her leg on the bed and Grandpa and Grandma sat back in the chairs, out of the way, unsure of what to do.

They started up the saw and carefully began to cut through the large cast that covered most of Taylor's leg, from her upper thigh all the way down to below her knee. White powder filled the air as the saw ripped through the plaster until finally, they reached the end of the cast and began again on the other side. Once they finished cutting a straight line along opposite sides of the plaster, they were able to lift off the top half and reveal the bruised, ripped, and stitched skin below. Only the skin wasn't stitched, there was no scar from the bone that had protruded through the skin, and there were no signs of bruises anywhere along her leg.

The doctors were stunned in awe as were her grandparents.

"Hey, you know this doesn't really hurt anymore and I bet I can move it, look." She explained lifting her leg from the bottom half of the cast and tilting it side to side.

"Stop that! You're gonna make it worse." Her grandma yelled, worried that she'd damage the healing bones.

"No, wait, it's fine." The doctor set down the plaster piece and motioned for Grandma to sit back down and relax.

All three of the doctors took turns pushing and bending different parts of Taylor's leg, inspecting every inch. "That's really astonishing." One commented.

"And this doesn't hurt at all?" Another asked.

"No not at all, is that good?" Taylor smiled, pleased that she was healing so well. Maybe it was all the healthy food Grandma fed her or maybe because she did so well staying off of the leg, but realistically she didn't have any better an answer than the doctors did.

"Good, this is amazing. You really appear to have healed completely in what would take a normal person six weeks at least, in only four days. This is a medical anomaly. We're going to want to take some more tests. Check your blood, and bone marrow, there has to be an explanation." One of them said overly excited.

"So, if you don't mind, we'd love to have you stay for a while and we can begin some basic tests and see where to go from there."

"Actually, we do mind. I'm not subjecting my granddaughter to all sorts of science experiments and tests. She's not a lab rat and she's got to be starting school, and if what you say is correct and her leg is all better than she can start on Monday. And we don't want to be hanging around here." Taylor's grandma responded. Realistically Taylor assumed that Grandma didn't want any of them to deal with all the press and drama that goes along with these weird science anomalies.

"But you don't understand what kind of possibilities this could mean. And just think about all the . . ."

"Let me stop you right there, I do understand. And what I also understand is that a couple of doctors want to play science experiment on my granddaughter for some journal entry or science award but guess what. I'm looking out for my granddaughter, and she is number one. I have final say on her behalf and she is not going to be participating in any experiments. Now if you'll kindly prep us to leave so we can go home, we'd greatly appreciate it." Grandma interrupted the three doctors and put them in their places leaving them astounded and disgruntled.

"Yes Ma'am, we'll see what we can do to get you guys out of here." One of the doctors spoke up, grabbed the chart and followed the other two out of the room.

Taylor and both her grandparents watched as a nurse pulled one of the doctors over nodding and saying something they couldn't make out from inside the room. The nurse pointed at the room Taylor was in and then the phone. The doctor walked over to the phone, looked again at the room Taylor was in, spoke for a while, and then hung up the phone, saying something to the nurse. After he was finished, he returned to the room to release them.

"You're free to go, but are you sure you won't let us do some tests?" He tried one last time.

"We'll think about it, but for now, we're absolutely positive we won't do any tests." Grandpa confirmed, leaving the doctor with a disheartened look.

"Okay, you guys may head home then. Have a nice day." He surrendered, allowing them to leave.

"Well congratulations Taylor, are you ready to go home without a cast or crutches or anything." Grandpa reached over and patted her on the back. He picked up the remaining cast pieces before handing one to Taylor. "Would you like to keep them for a keepsake item?"

"No thanks, they'd just smell bad and take up space in my room, but it was a nice thought." She responded, tossing the plaster onto the bed.

Grandpa set the other piece beside the first and helped Taylor stand up. She took a second to balance herself, no longer wearing a cast or using crutches for support, and then placed all her weight onto the healed leg and gave it a couple of steps to test it out.

"Wow, this really does feel cool. My leg feels just like new, and nothing hurts. And most importantly, I don't have to wear a cast to school, Yay." She bounced once and then settled down. No need to press her luck or get careless. She followed Grandma and Grandpa back out to the car and plopped into the back seat poking and prodding at her own leg. Wondering how on earth it could have healed so quickly. She thought about the stone and how long it's been since she swallowed it. There was definitely a strange aftershock that happened when she swallowed it and she'd been having all these strange dreams ever since. She began worrying about whether something really bad was beginning to happen to her like John Travolta in Phenomenon. Nobody likes to get all sorts of cool abilities and then find out they are dying from a brain tumor.

"I bet she gets that from my side of the family. You know my sister once had cancer and after all the chemotherapy treatments, you know what happened?" Grandma distracted Taylor.

"She got better and lived a long happy life, with no . . ." Grandpa began to explain.

"Yeah, she got better and lived a long happy life, with no reoccurrences of the cancer, ever. So I bet there are just strong genes in the family." Grandma beamed.

"There sure are strong genes in your family but you have to admit her leg healed awfully fast. Maybe it's all the garlic you use in your cooking." Grandpa teased.

"Well, my my my. . . There is nothing wrong with a little garlic." Grandma responded defensively.

Grandma and Grandpa continued bickering for several hours and halfway through dinner. They finally gave up when Taylor was so fed up with the bickering that she just excused herself from the dinner table, leaving a plateful of mashed potatoes and half a chicken breast, and stormed off to her room for the night. After that they both calmed down and finished the evening watching their favorite sitcom together.

Chapter VII: Bad Press

Taylor could hear the theme song to jeopardy echoing downstairs and assumed that Grandma and Grandpa must have made up, but she was too exhausted to join them. She kicked off her shoes, pulled on her pajamas and snuggled into bed drifting off into a dreamless sleep.

She woke up abruptly, she felt a bit of unease and her stomach felt tense. It was very early, so early that it was still very dark outside, and there were no cars on the streets. Her ears hurt a little and her back felt very sore. She propped herself up on her bed and wiped the sleep out of her eyes. She was still tired but couldn't sleep.

Her window was open, and a cool breeze was tossing her curtains about. She walked over to the window and put her hands up on the top of the open window thinking she might close it. Then she stopped and gazed outside.

She could see far down the river, and with amazing clarity. As she looked up and down the riverbank, at the dark houses she became fixated on a spider, building its pristine web. It was sitting on a green stem of a weed, growing at the far side of the riverbank, under the bridge. The wind was tossing the grass back and forth and still the spider meticulously spun its web. Each strand was connected to another strand and each strand had its own perfect place.

"Look at that, there's some movement in her room . . ."

Taylor's trance broke. Strangely, she could hear someone talking, but she wasn't sure if it was about her. If it was, she had to be hearing things, because there was no way she could hear some random conversation from inside her room. She gazed around anyway, thinking there might be someone right outside, but the only life outside was a dim light in the house across the river and there was no way she could hear anyone in there. And now that she was alert, she realized that there wasn't any way she could see the spider either, all the way across the lake, in such detail.

Something wasn't right. She stepped back from the window and looked down thinking she might clear her head and stop dreaming. Taylor gasped as she noticed that the creature, she continuously dreamt about was her. Disbelieving her own senses,

Taylor jumped over to the mirror above her desk and examined her face.

"Oh my . . ." She gasped. This had to be one of the coolest dreams she had ever had. Staring directly back at her was one of the most beautiful gargoyles she could have ever imagined.

Her black eyes were larger and more pronounced, but still a cold dark black. Her ears weren't hurting anymore but they had become long and narrow and extended like a cat's, above her head. Her eyebrows were now just pronounced ridges of black shinny skin, and her hair was gone, replaced by ridges, forming a crown, on top of her head.

She stepped back away from the mirror and gazed at her side. She was staring in disbelief, fixated on the large leather black wings in the mirror. Feeling some new muscles she had never used before, she stretched out, and her wings opened up as far as they could inside the bedroom. She bumped a nightlight off the table, but her tail, with monkey like reflexes, swung over and curled the lamp into itself before it could hit the floor.

Content on the idea that she was dreaming, she decided there couldn't be any harm in trying the new body out. She had wings, maybe she could fly. It was still dark out so no one would probably see her anyway, especially since she was as dark as night itself.

She stepped back to the window and reached her arm outside to grab a ledge. Once she had a hold of something she pulled herself out of the window and up on to the roof.

"Well, let's see how these wings work." She chuckled, then stretched the wings far open and sprung from the roof. The wings caught the wind with ease and Taylor felt instantly relaxed. She caught a light updraft that lifted her high up into the sky, far above the houses.

"Wow, this is amazing," she couldn't help but yelp with excitement.

Her eyes could see far, far away and with such amazing detail. She wondered if she was seeing how an osprey would see, or an owl. The dark didn't seem to have any interference with the level of detail that her eyes could see. She could hear finite sound as well. If she saw something moving, she could tunnel her hearing toward it and listen with amazing detail to the little changes in the movement or tone.

Taylor wanted to fly down to the river and glide along the surface, and then thought that it might seem a little cliché, but then again who wouldn't want to give it a try anyway. She arched her wings back and plunged downward toward the river and then spread her wings out, end to end, and glided just at the surface along the river until she had reached the next river town.

Taylor pulled away from the river and flew above the town. She saw a large building with a gold statue at the top, and a church further away that looked like an old cathedral. The cathedral looked like a perfect place to stop and admire the city. As soon as she was close enough, she spread her wings out to slow her speed and launched her legs forward to grasp the outer edge of the bell tower.

She pulled herself into the bell tower and stood up, amazed that her wings naturally folded around her chest clasping together at the nape of her neck, as if they already knew what to do. She gazed out over the city, watching as individual cars passed through the streets quietly. The sun was just barely breaking dawn when she could see lights popping on in random houses hear and there signaling life beginning for the morning.

"Oh no," she gasped; realizing that with dawn came light and with light came the ability to be seen. She didn't have time to head home, and hopefully she didn't have to. Hopefully she would just wake up from this amazing dream and already be in bed, but until then she decided to retreat into the cathedral.

It was dark inside, she didn't hear anyone moving, and so she found a stairwell and made her way down inside the tower of the church. The tower opened onto the back of a large balcony in the far end of the church. There were pews all around, and the walls were covered with stain glass windows and images of angels, doves, women, and men. It was beautiful. It reminded her of her childhood, when her mother would take her to the early morning mass and the sunlight bursting through the stain glass windows would dance with color on the walls all around the church.

She walked up to the balcony and leaned over the edge.

"I wonder if God really exists. If he does, I need to thank him." She mumbled. "If I'm dreaming, I don't ever want to wake up. I've never felt so free." She chuckled some more with a large grin plastered to her face. "What if this is real? Can I really heal myself at an amazingly fast rate? How cool would that be?" But then her smile was replaced by a nervous strain. "How am I going to hide this? If people find out about this, I'm going to become some sort of science experiment, dissected and mutilated. I don't want that to happen, and I don't want to run away."

Taylor hushed her thoughts before someone stepped out of the corner and startled her.

"What are you doing here?" The young man said, unrecognizable in the dim light of the stain glass windows.

"Who are you?" She hissed, defensively.

"What the heck are you doing here? You shouldn't be out . . . if they find you . . . who knows what they might do." He grumbled, quickly scanning the room.

"What do you mean?" Taylor replied. She was more confused that the sight of her didn't surprise the guy.

"Did anyone see you come here?" He quickly replied.

"No, I don't think so. I mean this is just a dream anyway, right?" Taylor was freaking out. The strange boy was scaring her.

"I followed you here, and if I did, then someone else could have." He added, finishing up his paranoid sweep of the balcony, before settling near the back wall.

"No one knows anything about this, I don't even know about this, at least not until now. Wait, who are you anyway?" She asked again.

"Who I am, is of no importance to you, but you need to stay out of trouble and lay low. Keep out of the press or anything like that, Major Bradshaw has an eye out for you, and you better bet he's going to find you." The boy explained, still hidden in the poor light, nervously glancing around the room.

"Are you looking for something?" She asked, wondering why he was so apprehensive.

"No!" He snapped. "Just making sure no one followed you."

"You know what, I don't know who you are or what you want, but I can take care of myself just fine, and you're giving me the creeps. I don't need some crazy little hobo boy, sulking around in a church, to tell me what to do, not to mention that you obviously haven't looked at me. Do I look easy to catch?" Taylor proclaimed, but actually felt frightened. The boy knew much more about what was going on than he led on to believe, and she needed to know more about it.

"Sure, you can take care of yourself. I bet that's why someone already had to keep you from bleeding to death." He snapped at her.

"Hey, that was an accident. Not to mention, he was probably the reason I got hurt in the first place . . . He startled me." She mumbled under her breath.

"That doesn't matter. What does matter is the stone." He said to her, looking her up and down. "I can see you've made good use of it." He raised his voice in agitation.

"The stone, is that what this is all about?" She asked.

"Where is it?" He remarked, moving closer to her.

"What are you talking about?" She said trying to sound oblivious. "I can't give it to you, if that's what you want."

"Oh, don't play stupid. Give it to me. You didn't just randomly get all those powers. Give it to someone who knows how to harness them. I can keep it safe." He barked at her, and then quieted down as he got close enough to touch her skin.

"You're telling me that there's more power than this?" She waved her hands over her chest.

"Yeah, but it's dangerous in the wrong hands," he tilted his head as he responded.

"Well, I've got bad news for you. I can't give it to you." She cocked her eyes to the side, so as to avoid eye contact with him when she answered.

"Why not," he said more calmly now.

"It's kind of, sort of, well, inside me. . ."

"WHAT!" He screamed at her.

"I swallowed it, maybe a couple weeks ago, I'm sorry I didn't know it wasn't going to, you know, come out in my," She hesitated to say the next word, blushing, "poop."

"Crap, are you serious?" He replied, very agitated now.

"That would explain your appearance." He said letting out a huge sigh.

"Well, you're no use now." He commented rather disappointed and turned around to leave.

"Wait." Taylor exclaimed.

"So, what am I supposed to do, hmm. You seem to know a lot about this stone. Why am I useless?" Taylor spit questions at him, hoping he'd help her.

"Can't you see no one else can have it now? Once it's a part of you it's always a part of you. If it's removed, you die." He added, disappearing down the staircase.

"Wait, but what else do you know . . ."

Just then, the front doors to the church burst open underneath her, and some voices cut in.

By the time she had looked back at the stairwell, where the boy was, he was gone, and she needed to make a quick exit, as well.

"Get her . . . on the balcony!" One voice yelled.

"Don't let her get away!" Another one shouted.

And just as she moved to jump over the edge of the balcony, something sharp hit her in the neck, and she fell. Her mind blanked out as she fell over the side and crashed onto some pews below. The voices around her faded out as she tried to listen to the conversation. She could tell they were moving her, but that was as much as she could tell before she blanked out completely.

Taylor woke up in bed with a headache and a sore shoulder. She felt groggy and poorly rested.

"Boy that was a strange dream." She said, rubbing her sore head. Just to make sure, Taylor stepped over to her desk and checked the hanging mirror.

"Normal ears, normal face, check, check, and check. . . What a strange dream." She said with a grunt, rubbing her neck in the spot where she dreamed of getting shot by the dart.

"This is really strange, weird stuff has been happening to me ever since I left Port Angeles. First that really strong pulsing feeling that no one else seemed to notice, then the strange dreams that keep haunting my sleep, then my leg, and now last night's really strange dream. What the heck is going on? Oh, and that guy Jake said is looking for me, hmm maybe he would know." Taylor grumbled, pulling on some tattered jeans and a shirt before heading downstairs to join Grandpa and Grandma for breakfast.

As Taylor was slowly walking down the stairs, the doorbell rang, and caught her off guard.

"I'll get it. I'm right next to the front door anyway." She hollered into the living room. She jumped down the last few stairs and answered the door. She was very surprised when she opened the door and sudden flashes of light burst into her face.

"Snap, Snap, Click!" T.V. reporters and journalists were standing at the door and in the yard taking pictures of the "Demon child." That's the name people were yelling out in the yard.

"That's her, that's the girl." Reporters pointed to her. "She's the one. She sold her soul to the devil." Someone shouted. Someone else threw something at Taylor, it splattered on her chest, rolling off of one of her new shirts for school, leaving a long trail of brown grossness.

"How does it feel to be on the side of the devil?" An old woman with brown hair and a nasty scowl asked her, shoving a microphone into her face.

"Grandma, something happened?" Taylor stuttered, trying to get retreat back into the house. But she was cut off while a couple of people jumped in behind her. "Grandma. . ." She hollered again.

Someone ran up to Taylor while she was distracted by all the cameras flashing and with an extremely sharp knife, sliced a large chunk of her skin off of her arm.

"Ahh, GRANDPA!" She screamed and started crying while grasping her injured arm. All the reporters and journalists had questions for her. Tears were running down her eyes and blood was dripping onto the porch as she tried to move through the people blocking her door. But no one would move, they were intent on making a spectacle out of her, and the crowd was getting larger in the streets. People were rushing to see about all the commotion.

Grandpa ran out of the door with a baseball bat and started swinging at people who wouldn't move out of his way. Grandma rushed over to Taylor and held her tight, pushing through the people to get Taylor back inside.

"You 'all ought to be ashamed of yourselves, harassing a little girl like this. Go find some real stories somewhere else. How about figuring out where all those missing children are going, instead of hurting my little girl. Get out of here." Grandpa swung his bat around a few more times and then retreated into the house, locking the door behind, and pulling all the curtains closed.

Grandma snatched a small quilt from the side of the sofa and placed it over Taylor, to comfort her. Grandpa rushed to the bathroom and brought back with him an emergency kit with some gauze and Neosporin. Taylor's arm was bleeding very badly, the cut was about an inch long and deep enough to need stitches, which means that they would need to return to the hospital.

● ● ●

"What was that all about?" Taylor said through breaks in sobs.

"I bet one of those doctors at the hospital decided to get some credit from the press." Grandpa muttered. He grabbed the phone and dialed the hospital.

Taylor listened as Grandpa had some harsh words with the staff member on the other line, and then he set up an appointment and hung up the phone dialing the police station next.

Grandma sat on the sofa comforting Taylor and dressing her wound, while Grandpa talked to the Police Chief. When he was done, he hung up the phone and peered out of the curtains hoping the crowd had died down, but no one had left.

"They're sending someone over to clear out the crowd, and then they'll set up a regular drive by to keep the reporters at bay, but until then they said to sit tight and wait until someone arrives, which could be a while because they're really tied up with a new missing child case, here in town." He explained.

While they waited, Taylor turned on the television and placed it on the news channel. She could see the front door to her house on three different stations. There were several people in the yard and they kept replaying the shots of her opening the door and getting her arm cut, before her grandparents rushed her back into the house.

"Are you serious?" She mumbled. "These people are freaking psychos." She said, tossing the controller over to Grandma. She realized that if the guy that Jake said was looking for her didn't know where she was, he soon would. The thought made her feel sick to her stomach. Her arm was already throbbing, but now a bad feeling sent a chill down her spine, and the nausea became overwhelming.

"It's going to be okay, Taylor. We'll get to the hospital in no time and they'll fix that right up." Grandpa commented. He must have noticed the sickening look draw upon Taylor's face.

A couple of hours passed as they waited. Taylor dazed off, pushing the pain to the back of her mind.

"Honey," Grandma got her attention. "The police are here, so let's get you to the hospital, for some stitches."

"Do we have to go back there? I don't want to go back there again. What if they want to do some more tests? I'm sick of tests." Taylor whined. She was more afraid that they might not let her leave this time.

"Sorry dear, but you need some stitches." She replied.

The car was outside, and so they needed to wait until the cop had cleared all the people away. Once they retreated back a safe distance, the three of them walked through the kitchen and out into the driveway, avoiding the commotion on the lawn, and waiting for the cop to give them the okay.

Once they arrived at the hospital, a doctor came right out and directed Taylor and her grandparents into a room.

"Here, just lie down on the bed and rest your arm on the side." He told her. "Your leg is doing great, I see." He commented, pulling out a container of gauze from the cabinet and a bottle of iodine, placing them on the small tray already arranged beside the bed with some sutures and a couple of operating tools that looked like pliers.

"Yeah, it healed up pretty good, I guess." Taylor responded.

"This might hurt a little, but usually it doesn't, I do have to clean the cut before I stitch it up though." He grabbed a cotton ball and poured some iodine on it, before pulling off the gauze and preparing to rub down the large bloody area. As he removed the gauze both he and Taylor stared in awe. Grandpa stood up and walked over to the bedside, peering at the unusual scene in front of him, and Grandma braced herself against Grandpa, shocked.

They all stared frozen with confusion and possibly fear as the last small splice of skin merged together on Taylor's arm, sealing itself closed like a Venus Fly Trap, leaving only the outline of a scar, and then that too, disappeared into the normal color and shape of her arm.

Everyone was still staring when Taylor noticed a strange look form upon the doctor's face. He reached over to tray, swiped a scalpel, and more quickly than Taylor could pull her arm away, he sliced another strip of her arm.

Taylor squealed and pulled her arm back.

"What on earth do you think you're doing?" Grandpa yelled at the man.

"Just watch, don't tell me you aren't curious. You're a man of science. You would do the same." The doctor replied to Grandpa.

"I'd like to think I would get someone's permission before I just start hacking away at them." Grandpa claimed, glaring at the doctor.

"Well, I'm sorry I didn't ask, but just watch." He commented again, pulling Taylor's arm out and bracing it on the bed.

Grandpa and the doctor leaned in, both fixated on the newly exposed flesh trickling blood down her arm. The doctor glanced back and forth between his watch and her arm. After a minute the blood stopped running, and so he wiped it away, but nothing else happened for close to ten minutes.

"Enough is enough, why don't you two just stop acting like kids and stitch that thing up, so we can get home. She's been through a lot." Grandma chimed in, tugging on Grandpa's sleeve.

"WAIT! Wait a second, just look at that." The doctor exclaimed. He pointed to the new cut and watched as the skin began to pull together. First the under-layer of dermis and then the upper layer tightly zipped together, leaving another scar, imprinted on her arm, until that too melted into her perfect ivory skin, and vanished.

"Well, I'll be frozen in hell." The doctor exclaimed. He rubbed his chin, staring at the arm, puzzled, until a nurse came in, pulling him outside.

"There's a Major Bradshaw on the line. He's asked that you detain Taylor Saskia for questioning." Taylor could hear the nurse say.

"This isn't a police station. You'll have to let him know, there's nothing I can do. I can't keep them here, especially with her grandparents breathing down my neck. If he wants to talk to her, he can come out here, himself, and deal with them. I'm a doctor and I have patients to deal with, especially if this is a matter of national security, then I don't want anything to do with it. You tell him that." Taylor and both her grandparents heard the doctor firmly explain to the nurse, before returning to the room.

"You guys are free to go. You have an amazing gift there, Taylor, just be careful." He gave her a firm look, and then left the room, leaving Taylor and her grandparents confused.

"What'd he mean? Be careful!" Taylor asked.

"I don't know, you heard as much as I did out there. Something about national security, let's just go home. This day can't get any stranger.

Chapter VIII: Leaving Port Angeles

Meanwhile, that morning, Major Bradshaw was back in Port Angeles harassing the police station for more information on her whereabouts. He'd had no luck at Taylor's relocation hearing because the child protective services wouldn't release her new location.

"So, who do we have in there now? Jacob Stevens, is it?" Major Bradshaw asked, browsing through a police file. "Haven't we already talked to him a couple of times?"

"Yes, Sir, but he isn't giving us the information we need. He and that Joseph Smith boy must be collaborating stories." Dan, his right-hand man, commented.

"Any luck at the Lake?" Major Bradshaw inquired.

"Nothing there, and quite frankly, I don't think we are going to find anything. The monitors show no levels of activity at all, as a matter of fact, the only real activity we've seen has been some minor quacks on the fault lines in Seattle, California, Colorado, and something strange on the East Coast, other than that, this entire area has been dead as a doorknob." Dan explained, leaning back against the one-way mirror of the conference room Jake was sitting in.

"No way, that's crazy." A voice bellowed down the hallway of the police station.

"Chief, you should see this!" Another man yelled out from the lounge.

Major Bradshaw followed the Police Chief as he wandered down the hallway and into the conference room, where all the commotion was coming from.

"You're not going to believe what some crazy news reporter just did."

"Yeah, Chief, they'll show it again. Check it out." A couple of the cops in the room chimed. There was a small television centered on a table with a bunch of guys chilling around it, sipping coffee and eating doughnuts.

Major Bradshaw and the Police Chief both watched the replay of the news clip several times. He was rather surprised to see a news crew with several people standing in a yard harassing a young girl.

"Hey that's the girl you're looking for, Major." The Chief commented. "She came in here after the little incident at the lake, but

I guess she was a foster kid, so the state had to make different arrangements for her and those files are almost always ironclad."

"Hey maybe that news crew can tell you where she is. As far as I know she was shipped off to Maine to live with her grandparents." Officer McGraidy offered.

"How'd you know that McGraidy?" Chief asked.

"I dropped her off at the airport. Remember?" He asked.

"Oh right, you volunteered because you felt bad for the little girl. Softy," Chief teased. "Shh, let's catch the whole thing." He turned up the volume on the television.

"We would like to interrupt you with the brief glimpse of what the fountain of youth might look like, or as this town puts it the 'Devil Child.' This young girl, of Randolph, Maine, no less than one week ago was in the hospital with a broken leg." The news reporter pointed to a picture in the upper corner of the screen. A photo from the hospital popped up. There was a large creamy bone, jaggedly protruding from an even larger fleshy wound on the left thigh.

"Now imagine that leg, on this girl, less than a week ago. You can clearly see that she is walking, and now standing here, as if nothing had ever happened." The little picture changed back to the girl at her house, live, with a large group of people swarming into her yard.

"Just one second, and one of our guys will show you the leg." The news reporter commented and then watched as a young reporter leaned down at her leg and pulled her pant up to show everyone the leg. Dozens of flashes went off from several cameras.

"They're calling her the Healing Girl. Her blood quite possibly holds the secret to health and longevity. Healing Girl, or Devil Child you decide for yourself, just stay tuned as we keep you updated on her status. Oh," The reporter cringed as someone sliced a large chunk on her arm. "That looks like it hurt. But wait, here come the Grandparents to save the day. Well, that looks like all for now folks, but stay tuned and we'll keep you updated. This is KNBTY always giving you the best news." The reporter finished, and then the station reran the clip several times, before continuing on with other news.

"Randolph, Maine, did they say?" Major Bradshaw commented to the Chief, and he nodded his head in reply. "Well, that's where we're headed then. Thank you for your help. I think we've gotten all the information we came to get." He said to him.

● ● ●

"What do you want me to do with that Jake boy in the holding room?" Chief asked.

"Just let him go, whether or not he knows something won't matter now. I know where she is. Have a nice day Chief." Major Bradshaw shook his hand and left the police station with Dan following behind speaking rapidly on a cell phone.

"Airport will be ready in twenty minutes, if you want to head out there now?" Dan informed the Major.

"Good, it's time we find that stone before she has any idea what it is capable of." Major Bradshaw reached into his pocket, pulling out a small clear tube, and stared at it in his hand. He clenched his teeth together, shaking the shard of stone back and forth inside the tube examining it, and then placed it back inside his pocket.

The flight wasn't too long on their nice jet. Dan stayed very busy on the phone scheduling meetings and negotiating with the reporters in order to put a hold on all the broadcasts with Taylor. The words national security and threat were thrown around quiet a bit, but eventually his phone calls died down and he joined Major Bradshaw skimming through files.

"I contacted the Police Chief. He said that they will be taking Taylor to the hospital for some stitches or something. Assuming that we land soon then this might be our only chance to get in there and search the house." Dan explained, and then contacted the pilot up front.

"Okay sounds good," Dan commented from inside the cabin, and then rejoined the Major. "He says another ten minutes and we should be at the airport. There's a cab there waiting for us as soon as we land."

"Good, we'll have just enough time to get in there and do some readings, see if we can't find where she might have put it." Major Bradshaw said.

The plane landed and the two men rushed off and into the large Black sedan, waiting with a driver and all.

"104 River Road, Randolph, and step on it." Dan ordered, knowing the address from talking with the Chief.

"Get the hospital on the phone, will you Dan?" The Major ordered. Dan punched in a few numbers and before long handed the phone to Major Bradshaw.

"Nurse Amanda, she's talking on behalf of the doctor currently treating Taylor."

"Hello, Amanda, lovely name." He said.

"Oh, thank you," she replied.

"You have a girl in your care under the name of Taylor Saskia. She is a major threat to homeland security. I want you to keep her checked into the hospital as long as you can. Don't act like anything is wrong, she may be very dangerous." The Major lied to Amanda. His main purpose was to keep her there so that he might have more time to search the house.

"Dangerous, Oh dear. What should I do?" She began to panic.

"Don't do anything unnatural, act like everything is fine. I don't want her to know that anything is going on. Understand?" He stressed.

"Sure, I'll tell the doctor. Is there anything else we can do for you?" She replied, calming herself down.

"Not really, thank you." He replied.

"Just a second, I'll go speak with the doctor." She placed the phone on hold, and he waited, watching as the driver pulled across the street from a large white two-story house on a large lot above the river.

"We're at the house," the driver informed Major Bradshaw while he was on hold.

"Hello! Major?" Nurse Amanda returned to the phone. "I've spoken with the doctor, and he's made it clear that you already understand his position and there is nothing more he can do to keep them here. I'm sorry we couldn't help more. Have a nice day." She hung up the phone.

Major Bradshaw tossed the cell phone back to Dan and led him over to the side entrance of the house. Dan pulled out a little gadget and messed with the door lock before it clicked, and they rushed into the house.

"We've got a good twenty minutes and then we've got to get out of here." Major Bradshaw said, pulling a tool from Dan's hand and pointing for him to cover the second floor. They both scurried around the house, pointing what looked like radar guns, at different places in the house. Dressers, drawers, boxes, closets, anyplace they thought a stone might fit, but no luck. Nothing was registering on the guns. Seventeen minutes had passed, and they had covered most of the entire house, finally Major Bradshaw called for Dan, but was surprised to find him sitting at the table in the kitchen.

"I didn't find the stone anywhere but check this out." He said handing the old hospital forms to the Major. They were Taylor's checkout forms from the leg injury and solid proof that she had in fact injured her leg and then healed four days later.

"Well, the stone's not here. So, either she has it or someone else does, but I'll bet she has it." Major Bradshaw said, grinding his teeth together again, frustrated that he'd have to track around a teenage girl. This was starting to become a delicate situation, one he did not like the look of.

"Let's get going. We don't want anyone knowing we were here. I think it's best if we keep a tail on her for the next few days. I want to know if she knows about the power of the stone, and I don't want to bring her in just yet. If the stone has become part of her than we may have some bigger issues." Handing the papers back to Dan, so he could put them back where he found them, the Major stood up, and walked out the door, waiting for Dan in the car.

"I've got some work to do, so I'll be returning to the Cyndac Facility, but I'll have two guys join you. I want you to put a tail on her. You guys keep an eye out for any unusual behavior and keep me posted.

Chapter IX: One Bad Game

Taylor stretched her arms out, slowly waking up for the day. Today would be very exciting; she gets to start her first day at her new school. Setting up and gazing out her window thinking about the finite detail she dreamt of the other night about the spider building its web, she listened for the sound of any life stirring.

However, she wasn't very surprised to hear her grandparents moving around in the kitchen downstairs. No doubt, they were preparing something for breakfast. They probably wanted Taylor to start her first day of school on a fully satisfied belly.

Taylor had a quick shower and then dressed herself in some of the new clothes she had set out the night before. She hurried downstairs and joined her grandparents in the kitchen for breakfast.

"I called ahead while you were getting ready. The principal will have someone waiting in the office to escort you around the school. They should have all your books and your class schedule ready. Hope you don't mind." Grandma smiled, handing Taylor a plate of scrambled eggs and Mickey Mouse shaped pancakes.

Taylor wolfed down the pancakes and shoveled the eggs into her mouth. Satisfied with the tasty breakfast Taylor found her old backpack and hurried out to the car waiting patiently for Grandma to catch up.

The drive was short, only about five minutes. She made sure to watch the road names so that later on she could walk to school alone. The school was tucked back, among some houses and a hill, on the far side of the river. Many students were gathered out front waiting for the first bell to ring.

Taylor clung to her backpack and waved by to Grandma.

"Wish me luck," she called back to the car.

"Don't sass your teachers and good luck." She responded with the window rolled down.

Taylor collected her thoughts, held her head high and walked up to the main doors, strolling left, once inside the hallway until she entered into the office. An older lady at the front desk looked to her and asked, "May I help you?"

Taylor leaned over the desk and responded, "I'm the new girl, Taylor Saskia. I'm supposed to meet a student here to show me to my classes."

"Oh yes, just one moment." She said and backed out of the desk chair she was sitting in. She disappeared into a back room to file some paperwork and then returned to the desk. When she sat back down, she seemed to have forgotten what she was doing and began working on some files in front of her. She glanced up at Taylor, scrunched her forehead, and then nodded her head as if she had suddenly remembered.

"Oh, um," she fumbled with her words then signaled to a boy sitting on a bench in the office. "Derek, this is Taylor Saskia, you'll be escorting her to all of her classes and showing her around." Then she turned to Taylor and said "Taylor, this is Derek Willem, he's new as of last week, so I'm sure you'll have a lot to talk about. He just took an editor position on the school newspaper and will be joining the football team this spring, so if you have any questions about what's going on around here, I'm sure he'll know." She handed Taylor her class schedule and dismissed her, returning to the work on her desktop.

Derek held open the door and allowed Taylor to walk out before he released it and then joined her in the hallway. Taylor handed him her class schedule and he browsed through it then handed it back to her.

"I've got first, second, and sixth period with you, but I know people in those other classes so you shouldn't be alone. I'll meet you outside of class if you'd like, in case you need to figure out where to go next." He winked at her, and then led Taylor on to the first class.

When they walked into the room several of the kids stopped what they were doing and glared at Taylor.

"Hey, you're that girl on the T.V." One kid pointed out, gathering the rest of the class's attention.

"That's right, you are. What'd you do, sell your soul to the devil?" Another kid sneered at her and then several of them chimed in.

Most of the kids stayed in their seats but a couple of kids grouped up and formed a half circle around Taylor.

Completely acting innocent, as if he didn't know what the kids were getting at, Derek turned to Taylor and said "So you're the girl all this fuss is about. I'd herd rumors around school and parents talking about it, but I didn't realize it was you."

"Nice, now you're part of this stupid crap also?" Taylor asked, glaring at him.

"Is it true? Can you really heal with amazing speed?" He asked.

"No, people are just stupid and will believe anything they see on T.V." Taylor said a bit scared of what the kids were planning.

"So that was all a fake, on the news?" One of the kids in the group had asked.

"Yeah, you know, they were just trying to get some good reviews. You know how T.V. can be. Throw a little excitement here and there and they get their ratings back." She stumbled over some of her words as she was making up a story. Derek made a sour face at her and then backed off. He didn't really seem to care that much.

"Sure, I don't think I believe that. My dad works at that news station, and he says you're a freak." One kid barely finished saying before another one got up into Taylor's face so closely, that she tripped over the garbage can, and fell against the wall, making a complete fool out of herself. Most of the kids in the classroom laughed at her, before the teacher entered the room and interrupted the debacle. Derek was the only one not laughing, but he was sitting at the far back of the classroom peering at something else, acting as if he didn't care.

"Well, I can see you've already acquainted yourself with the other classmates so please take a seat so I can begin English 200." The teacher wrote the class name and his name on the chalk board in big sloppy letters and began the lecture. "Most of you have finished A Tale of Two Cities I hope." He looked at Taylor, "Just follow along if you haven't."

Her face turned a beet red as she sank down into the already awkward seat in the front row of the classroom, and avoided looking at anyone, knowing that she hadn't a clue about the story. It was actually kind of ironic because she was required to read that book back home for her old English class, but she managed to get out of it with the move, but now she wished she had read it. Everyone was going to know everything that was going on, in this class for the next few days and she hadn't a clue.

"Great," she mumbled.

"You have something to add, Taylor?" The teacher raised an eyebrow at her.

"No," she grumbled and slid down lower into her seat, waiting desperately for the bell.

Finally, it rang, and Derek, true to his word, waited outside the door until Taylor managed to unglue herself from the chair, and mosey on out of the classroom.

"Next is math with Mr. Kriedberg. He's a pretty nice guy and he just lectures us on the math subject for the day, so the class goes by pretty quickly." Derek told her.

"Cool," she replied, feeling confident, walking beside the tall, tanned, gently muscled boy, which was Derek.

"Hey Derek, What's up?" Some kid said passing in the hall.

"Yo," another kid jabbed him in the shoulder. "New chick?" The boy grinned at Taylor.

"New to school, you know it." Derek responded to the boy.

Taylor couldn't help but laugh at the ridiculously cheesy response Derek just made. He turned to her with a teasing glare.

"Hey, I'm just trying to fit in. Lay off." He commented, "You could take some hints from me you know."

"What, I don't think so, Mr. Greasy hair." Taylor teased back, running her hand through his gelled T.V. reporter look.

"Hey, don't touch the hair, it's the Axe effect." He responded, knocking away her hand.

Taylor laughed at him again, rolling her eyes back. "The Axe effect – you've seen way too many commercials."

"Whatever, here's math, just find a seat. I'm sure the teacher will introduce you." Derek huffed and then sauntered into his seat near the back of the classroom again.

Taylor watched as all the other kids found their seats and then a big grin crept across her face when she noticed the only empty seat was directly across from Derek.

"Oops, looks like your Axe effect pulled me in." She laughed again in Derek's face.

"Whatever," he replied and sat ego injured staring at the front of the classroom, ignoring Taylor.

The teacher stood up from his desk when the bell rang and pointed out the name of the class and what section they were studying. Taylor was sure the teachers were doing that so that she could figure out where to pick up from.

"We've got a new student joining us. I'm sure of course this being a little town that I'm the last to know. Taylor Saskia," he pointed back at her as she slightly waved her arm avoiding too much notice. "I'm Mr. Kriedberg, and I'm sure your classmate Derek there, would love to show you where we will be starting in the textbook today."

Derek looked up from his desk, and over to Taylor, then back to Mr. Kriedberg, and finally scooted his desk over until he was just close enough to point out in the textbook where they were and mumble a few things about the lesson.

"Thank you, Derek, and please remember girls don't have cooties." Mr. Kriedberg commented, obviously noticing the hesitation Derek had to speak with Taylor. The whole class snickered at the comment and Derek groaned ever angrier with Taylor.

"You suck," he mumbled, just loud enough so that Taylor could tell what he meant.

"Sorry," she mouthed the words, and then finally turned her attention to the teacher's lecture. She found that she had to pay attention, or she had no clue what was going on.

The rest of the day went pretty smooth. She found that she had to pay attention in most of the classes, otherwise she was completely lost. Art was fun, because she didn't have to do any thinking, just playing around with pencils and paints.

Sixth period was the best. She had P.E. with Derek, and by then he wasn't mad at her anymore. Normally she wouldn't like P.E. but for whatever reason this week they were doing a ton of running activities, and she was really fast.

"Oh look, what a surprise. Little miss devil child can outrun everyone. Let me guess, one of the perks from the man below?" One of the jerks from first period caught up with Taylor on the track and commented. A second, followed shortly behind, sneering little nasty comments between gasps of breath.

"Seriously, why don't you guys get a life?" Taylor brushed against the guy, pushing him aside.

He looked back at the other guy, smirked, and then stuck out his foot tripping Taylor on the tracks.

"How's that feel . . . Satan's child!" He sneered and then fell back on the tracks, acting innocent and curious just like everyone else catching up to Taylor.

She tumbled over herself a couple of times down the track and stopped against the gravel just on the side of the track. Derek rushed over to her side, helped her up, and brushed away the dirt and marks on her back.

"You've got to be kidding me, did you see that?" Taylor pointed at the jerk that tripped her. "He tripped me on purpose." She wiped some blood off of her arms, they were both scratched up and hobbled over to the benches, where she found a spare shirt and rubbed her knee with it because it was bleeding pretty badly.

The P.E. teacher stayed back toward the other end of the track, pretending like he didn't see anything. Derek got his attention, but by the time he arrived, Taylor had already taken care of most of the scrapes.

"Oh sorry, I didn't notice you fell," the teacher commented nonchalantly.

Taylor glared at the teacher. "Can I go and clean up?" She attempted to sound calm.

"Oh, those are just scratches, toughen up and wait until the end of class like everyone else." The teacher harked and then joined the rest of the class leading them in some stretches and stomach crunches.

"What the heck is his problem?" Taylor asked Derek, who stayed behind with her, while the rest of the class finished the exercises.

"Who knows? He's the basketball coach, and very old school, also kind of a jerk to almost everyone. Don't let it get to you." Derek explained.

"I won't, it's just weird, dealing with that attitude, from an adult." Taylor finished wiping off the scratches, realizing that the scrapes had healed up, just like at the hospital, but no one else had noticed yet. Quickly, before drawing any attention, she rubbed some of the blood from the shirt and some dirt from the ground, back onto her arms and knees, hiding the clean uninjured skin.

"Do you need some help with that?" Derek asked Taylor, pointing to her dirty knee, unaware that she had just covered her non-injury up.

"No, I'm fine. I'll just clean it up in the locker room with soap and water. Let it clot for now, you know?" She shrugged.

"Finally," Derek helped Taylor up, while she faked a limp off the field, just after the final bell rang.

"Hey there's a basketball game tomorrow night and I could get you out of a couple of classes if you want to do some school reporting." Derek commented.

"Yeah, how can you get me out of class?"

"Well, we usually leave when the team leaves, that way we can follow the warmup and the rest of the game, and tomorrow the team leaves before lunch. So, if you want out of class for a while you can come to the game and learn the ropes of reporting for the school newspaper." He told her, nudging her shoulder. "It can be pretty fun, plus afterwards we always go out to eat."

"Okay, you've sold me. I'll have to run it through my grandparents, but I bet they won't mind." She replied, pulling the hair tie from her hair, allowing the long black strands to fall against her shoulders. "And at least I won't have to do gym tomorrow."

"Cool, meet me in the newspaper office before lunch and we'll get going." He scribbled the room number down on her hand and took off toward the parking lot. "See ya tomorrow," he shouted back.

Taylor met her grandma out front, tossed her full book bag into the back seat, and joined Grandma in the front seat.

"How was your first day of school?" Her grandma asked.

"Not too bad, some people recognized me from the news, but otherwise, I met a cool guy who showed me around the school and invited me to a basketball game tomorrow night. He edits the school newspaper, and invited me to come along and maybe do some writing for the newspaper, what do you think?" Taylor asked.

"Sounds like fun, I'll run it through your grandpa, but I bet he'll be excited that you're making friends." She reassured her. "Well, help yourself to an after-school snack. I'm sure you've got homework to catch up with. I'll call you when dinner is done."

"Okay, thanks." Taylor responded, reaching back for her backpack, before running into the house and stopping at the fridge for a fruit pie and milk. She gorged out, until she was filled up, and then ran upstairs to her room, rummaging through her backpack until she found A Tale of Two Cities, and began reading, propped up on her bed pillows.

Dinner was no let down as usual. Grandma made some of the best old fashion meals imaginable. A homemade chicken pot pie, followed by an amazing custard for dessert, made the perfect end to a rough day. Taylor hit the sack and eagerly awaited the start of the next day, where she would get to hang out with Derek, away from school, and away from the jerks in her classes.

First period wasn't too bad. Having read halfway through the book last night, Taylor was able to participate in the class discussion and felt less like part of her chair and more like part of the class.

Second period was strange. Derek had been present in the back of the classroom first period, but he was absent second period and she had no idea where he went. She could only assume that he had to get some stuff ready for the game, and she would see him later before they left.

Once the ending bell for fourth period rang, Taylor hurried off to the room number that Derek scribbled on her hand the day before. She peeked into the room, but Derek was nowhere to be found. Thinking that maybe he was just hidden in a corner just out of sight, she walked into the room, and was greeted by and overzealous red head.

She had very long hair, straight and lifeless with green eyes and freckles. She was probably four inches shorter than Taylor, but she was wearing fashionable boots with a two inch heal so the difference in height wasn't much between the two of them. She had on tight fitting jeans and a black overcoat with a hot pink shirt underneath. When she reached out to shake Taylor's hand, she noticed some fancy black netted arm sleeves that attached at her thumb.

"Hi, I'm Kim. Derek said you'd show up. He's supposed to meet us at the game, something came up." She said with a smirk and shook Taylor's hand enthusiastically.

"And I'm Taylor, which obviously you already know." Taylor responded pulling her hand back. She was a little surprised to be greeted by someone other than Derek. She wasn't used to outgoing personalities and was very uncomfortable with the confrontation.

"This is the newsroom if you didn't already guess. Derek got called home for something, so hopefully we'll see him at the game later. I usually do the team write ups but I'm graduating this year so someone else needs to learn how to do it and Derek thinks you'll do okay for now. Basically, we just follow the team out to the game, watch it, take some little notes, and then write a small article about the game. The city likes that we do this and uses our articles for their newspaper as well; it lets the town know how the high school team is doing. We get more support this way. Well, I think that's about it. I'll drive us, just meet me in front of the school in about forty minutes; I think that's around when the team is leaving." She said wrapping up her conversation with Taylor and scooting her out the door.

Taylor stopped, turned back to her and almost started asking a question before she changed her mind and walked off. She needed to stop at her locker and pick up the rest of her schoolwork before leaving.

"She seems cool, a little eccentric maybe, but cool. And at least she didn't ask me anything stupid." She mumbled to herself, stuffing books into her backpack at her locker. Once she was finished gathering her schoolwork, she hurried out to the parking lot and waited for Kim. She wondered what had taken Derek away for the day and then put her thoughts aside hoping that she'd see him later, at the game.

"Honk, Honk!" A horn blared from the little blue Jetta pulling around the drive.

"Come on girly, hop in." Kim hollered out the passenger window from the driver's seat.

Taylor pulled the handle, opened the door, and jumped into the car. She tossed her backpack over her side and into the back seat, then pulled her seatbelt on and relaxed into the seat. Kim pulled out of the school's driveway and waited behind the school bus, which had all the basketball players, and waited until it left following the entire two hours. Taylor felt a little awkward in the car with Kim; she had only just met her, but Kim didn't seem to mind and so Taylor slowly relaxed.

"I have to ask, which I'm sure you get this all the time, was all that stuff on the news real." Kim said, interrupting the silence.

Taylor hated the question, what was she supposed to say? As she found out the day before, people just generally thought of her as some possessed demon child. Would some stranger really care if she told the truth or not, or would she come up with her own hateful conclusion without any concern for who Taylor was?

"What do you want me to tell you? Yes, I can heal myself or no, the news station was just looking for a cheap story?" Taylor mumbled under her breath.

"Well, I'm just saying that if you can heal, or you know . . . Your blood has healing powers in it, that's really kind of a miracle. Don't you think?" Kim responded. She glanced at Taylor briefly and then back to the road then continued talking. "It's just that there are people, you know, that are sick with cancer and treatment doesn't work for them, but what if doctors could cultivate the healing components in your blood and then they could get better." She hesitated for a moment then finished with, "I just think it would be really cool that's all."

Taylor was staring at Kim while she was driving. Tears had formed in her eyes, but she was holding them back. Taylor could tell that someone really close to Kim was sick. If she could do anything to help, she would try, but she had a feeling that there wasn't anything special about her blood.

The car fell silent until they arrived at the competition's school. Neither one of them had the nerve to change the discussion to something else, but neither of them wanted to continue talking about it either.

The school was about two hours northwest of theirs and the sun had already begun to set. It was almost wintertime in Maine and the days didn't last very long. They could tell that school had dismissed for the day because there were only a few kids around the building and almost all the lights inside were off, except for the gym. The bus began to unload in front of them and the boys began shuffling past each other into the gym entrance.

Taylor recognized a couple of the guys that got off the bus and the coach.

"Oh crap," she mumbled.

"What's wrong?" Kim asked.

"Nothing, just those boys," she said, as she sank back into the car seat, hiding from view.

"Oh, don't worry about them, they'll be busy tonight. Coach keeps them on a short leash." Kim reassured Taylor.

"So, where's Derek?" Taylor asked, browsing the parking lot.

"Probably inside, like everyone else. Come on." Kim hopped out of the car and skipped over to Taylor's side, waiting for her.

They walked inside together, found a couple of seats behind their team, and watched as the boys ran layups and suicides across the gym for warm-ups. A couple of the boys stopped, glared at Taylor, and whispered among themselves, but were shortly broken up once the coach noticed.

The game started and not six minutes into it did Taylor notice Derek's lack of presence.

"Man, I hope Derek is okay. I really figured he'd be here by now." Taylor casually remarked.

"You've got a thing for him, don't you?" Kim teased, checking out one of the basketball players intently. "That's Tim Ambler; he's a hotty, if you ask me."

"Yeah, for sure . . . if you like the pale skinned, buzz cut, military looking type." She added. "He's a good basketball player, I'll give him that. It's too bad the team isn't winning." Taylor pointed out the scoreboard with the home team up 42 to 36.

"Yeah, he's so dreamy. . ." Kim trailed off, gazing at Tim running up the court.

The end of the second quarter buzzer rang and the boys all filed into the locker rooms for half time. Kim bounced up out of her chair.

"I'm going to get some comments from the spectators, see what people have to say. You can join me or not. I really don't care. It's up to you."

"I'll wait here, you know, keep an eye out for Derek, in case he shows up."

"Alright, see you in a bit." Kim headed up the bleachers back to some older man sitting at the top. She appeared to be asking some questions and then jotting notes down in her little notepad.

Taylor watched some kids play around on the court while the boys were having heir half time pep talks. Eventually they all began trickling out of the locker rooms. One in general caught her attention. He was standing at the door, talking to the coach. They both glanced at her and then continued talking. It was clear that they were talking about her. No doubt, wondering what she was doing at the game, or planning another mean prank like in P.E. the day before.

Taylor became rather agitated. The coach should have better things to do than join in with the immature harassment of an innocent high school kid. He was acting just as bad as the students and not only that, but they look up to him as a role model and he should be setting a better example.

Finally, the second half of the game began, and Taylor tried to ignore the random glares that she received throughout the remainder of the game. Sadly, their team lost the game. It was a fairly bad loss too. 75 to 58 left the coach irate and ready to punch somebody. After harshly yelling at several of the boys, he disappeared into the locker room and the remainder of the team followed.

"Meet you at the car, okay." Taylor commented to Kim. She decided that it was a good time to duck out of the game and meet her at the car. Better to miss the crowd than get caught up in all of the bitter commotion.

Kim disappeared around a corner looking for more spectator comments, and Taylor left the gym. It was very dark and oddly quiet. The only thing Taylor heard was a couple of low voices chuckling in agreement off where a group of figures stood. As soon as she was away from the school building and out into the dark parking lot the group began to follow behind her. The car was further to the side of the building and a way behind the bus, she wasn't sure if she would make it to the car before the group made it to her. She picked up her pace, heading for the driver's side of the car. As she began fumbling for the keys someone came up beside her and knocked her to the ground.

She gasped to catch her breath as she was trying to sit up and make out the figure, but then another one kicked her in the ribs and knocked her back to the ground.

"Stupid cow, you should have stayed home where you're Momma and Daddy could save you. . . Oh wait you don't have a mom or a dad. Oops, my bad," One of the boys mocked.

"Good one," someone added.

"Where's Derek, isn't he going to stand in and tell us off? Oh, I bet he's just as freaked out by you as the rest of us, or did you eat him, Devil worshiper." Another mocked, before jarring Taylor in the ribs again.

"Stop, please, I never did anything wrong. . ." Taylor stammered, trying to breathe through the sharp pains in her chest.

"Pick her up," a low, angry, and very familiar voice boomed. It was the coach. Two guys grabbed Taylor's arms and dragged her up into a standing position, holding her tightly.

The coach grabbed her belt and started pulling it out.

"Try and screw my guys up. I'll show you. What right do you have coming out to my game and using some sick witch voodoo magic crap on our game?" He continued undoing her pants.

"YOUR'RE SICK!" She screamed and then slammed him in the groin with her knee. He fell back momentarily, the guys still holding her firmly, and then sneered at her and socked her in the stomach, causing her to gasp for air some more.

While she was wrenching in pain, she could feel her blood begin to boil. Not in the sense that she was getting mad, because she was already furious, but in the sense that it was getting hotter. She could feel her veins racing, and her heart pounding at an intense speed. Any doctor listening to her pulse would have said that she was about to seize, but no, it just got faster, and her muscles began to expand.

"What the heck?" One of the guys holding her arms let go and stepped back, as her flesh became black and leathery, and her face began to transform into a gargoyle's.

"Oh my god, she's the Devil." The coach yelled. "Stop her, before she destroys us all." He kicked out her legs, and she fell to the ground.

She was still changing as a barrage of kicks began digging into her chest and back and face. The putrid smell of blood and sweat mixed together and swirled into Taylor's nostrils as she was finishing the transformation. The blood must have been hers, but the nasty sweat and fear that she could smell in the air, was most definitely the coach's and his gang.

"Get the bat," she heard someone yell.

When she looked up, from the pause in the beating, the coach caught the bat midair and swung hard and fast right at her face. But he was not fast enough. Taylor's new agility and powerful hand caught the bat mid swing. She stood up now eye to eye with the coach and challenged him.

"Why don't you pick on someone your own size?" She hissed, crunching the bat like a cornflake, feeling very confident that she was in a position to teach the coach a lesson or two.

"Alright I will," the coach replied. "Tim, you get her." He harked, backing away from Taylor like a coward.

"Na uh, I'm not going to be a part of this." He shook his head and stepped away from the group of guys, backing against a tree.

● ● ●
90

"Fine coward! Jonathan, you deal with this abomination." He yelled at another kid.

"Be glad to, Coach," the kid sneered, giving Tim a look of satisfaction. He pulled out a knife and popped the blade open. "Let's teach you a little lesson, witch."

He came up from behind, thrusting the knife towards her kidney, but before he even had a chance to break the tough skin, Taylor, in one fluid motion, stepped to the side, her tail slicing the air around his feet, knocking the guy to the ground, catching the knife in her hand, and tossing it at the tree.

She turned back around, ready to face the coach again, but to her surprise he held a gun just inches from her face, leaving her stunned, but for just a brief moment.

"Dodge this." The coach grumbled, pulling the trigger.

She twisted just fast enough that the bullet grazed her cheek and passed on, hitting the unsuspecting Tim, leaning against the tree.

"Ah," he screamed out, falling to the ground.

"You shot Tim!" One boy freaked out, screaming at the coach.

"What did he do?" Another cried.

The smell of rusty iron was overwhelming. The injury had to be bad with such a strong pooling smell gushing out from him. The bullet must have hit an artery or something. She snatched the gun from the disoriented coach, crunched the gun between her hands, tossing it at his feet, and rushed over to Tim, kneeling down beside him.

"Get away. Don't hurt him." Jonathan squealed at her.

"Shut up, just give me a minute." She shouted. "I can hear his heart stopping. I think I can do something. . . Just back off and give me some time." She waved the guys back and then ripped open Tim's shirt.

"What are you doing?" A different guy hissed, pulling her hand back.

"Just back off," she yelled at them again, pulling her hand back. She placed both her hands over the gushing wound above his heart, closed her eyes, and began to focus.

Nothing happened at first. She could feel his life pumping away with the remainder of blood gushing from his heart. She felt the pain he was feeling, it was slipping away, almost as if he were falling asleep, only she knew better, he wouldn't wake up if he did. She focused all of her energy into a single ball and directed it into the wound.

Something strange began to happen. Strands of glowing vines crept from her hands, twisting and winding into his chest.

"Stop it! You're going to kill him." Someone screamed at her.

"Shh, he's already dying, can't you see that?" Another shouted at the other.

Taylor ignored the screams coming from the other boys standing around the scene, and focused intently on Tim. It was as if he and she had become one. She had become a gargoyle kneeling over a boy, melded into his chest, and an intense blue glow emanated around them, making it impossible to penetrate the strange shield she had created.

"What's going on?" A boy asked.

"I can't tell. . . It looks like it's healing." One boy gawked. "The bullet, it, it's coming out." He added.

The bullet backed out of the gushing wound in the chest and fell to the ground. The blood slowed to a trickle and then stopped all together, leaving a fleshy wound, and then that too sealed up, leaving a large, rounded scar surrounded by black and blue bruises. Taylor gasped, as the intertwined mess, weaved into his chest, retreated back, and the blue glow died down leaving Taylor slumped over, gasping for breath, beside Tim, who had begun gasping as well.

He sat up, looked at Taylor, and before he could say anything, police sirens blared around the corner, catching everyone off guard.

"Get out of here, before anyone else sees you." Tim said, pushing Taylor up.

She scrambled to her feet still breathless, and hurried off behind the school, after scanning the lot for an escape route. The coach was nowhere to be found. He was probably the one that alerted the police. The boys stayed behind, helping Tim up, with hesitation, unsure of what to think about what just happened.

Once she was hidden from sight, she circled around the school and found an easy climbing route to the roof. She wasn't ready to leave the scene yet. She wanted to know what happened.

She pulled herself onto a dumpster, leaped to the escape ladder beside it, and climbed up the side of the brick school. She shuffled onto the roof and stayed hidden, behind air vents until she was close enough to the front of the building to see what was going on.

The police were taking statements from each of the boys, no doubt spilling their guts about her, but then they amazed her when the coach was placed in handcuffs and tossed into the back of one of the police cars. The local news channel had arrived at the scene, just in time to catch the coach shouting profanities while being pushed into the back of the cab. Taylor recognized the reporter; it was one of the same women that were at her house the other day. After becoming comfortable with the conclusion of the scene, Taylor decided to high tail it out of there and find a way back home.

Staying out of sight, she sprinted toward the back of the building just long enough to get some speed, and then lunged into the air, gliding discreetly in the direction of the highway. She wasn't familiar enough with the area to find her way back freely, so she stayed as close to the highway as possible without being seen.

"This isn't a dream, I guess." She mumbled, speaking to herself as she often did. "Now what am I going to do? There's no way this is going to stay a secret with all those guys knowing."

Scanning the treetops for life and keeping a decent proximity from any houses she continued following the highway until she recognized the river and then branched off, gliding down toward the riverside, hugging the bank as much as possible. It wasn't too long before she arrived at the house, but what would she do when she got there? It wasn't like she could just waltz in the front door, decked out as some badass looking gargoyle. She'd scare the bejesus right out of the both of them, probably causing simultaneous heart attacks, and that would be terrible. She had to be discreet, but she hadn't a clue what to do. With the house in view and no idea of what she would do, Taylor soared over the rooftop and landed, delicately above her room, sitting patiently over her window.

She peered out, over the river, watching the bats nip flies off of the surface of the water. She couldn't go inside now, not while she could still hear her grandparents moving around downstairs. It sounded like they were watching the news. The news that she would have to explain later, once they found out it was about the game she was at. She waited until the movement in the house died down, and she was certain that both Grandma and Grandpa had gone to sleep, then crawled down to her window and slid into her room, quietly resting on her bed.

She wasn't sure what to do at this point, glancing down at her long tail falling over the side of the bed. After staring at the ceiling for a long time, she decided that if she wasn't normal by morning than she would leave. She'd sneak out and leave a note for them to find. Make it say something about how she hated it here, and that she could never be happy with people she didn't know. Something that would keep them from looking for her, which was the best, she could come up with. Content on her plan, Taylor drifted off into a deep sleep, where only a bright light, much like a supernova echoed repeatedly through her thoughts, until one abruptly woke her up.

Alarmed, she jumped out of bed, ran over to her mirror, and sighed, pulling at the sides of her fleshy human cheeks.

"Sweet, I don't have to run away." She groaned, pulling her alarm clock out, gazing at the time. "4:30, yikes," she rubbed her eyes and slumped back down into bed, pulling her sheets over her head and zonked out.

Chapter X: Burning

"Taylor, wake up. You're gonna be late for school." Her grandma said, nudging her shoulder.

Taylor looked up at Grandma, down at her hands, still half dazed from the night, and sighed, plopping her head back under the pillow.

"Sorry, I got back so late from the game last night that I didn't want to wake anyone. I just came up here and passed out on the bed." Taylor mumbled, beating Grandma to the question before it was asked.

Taylor waited while Grandma left, then quickly got dressed. She pulled her hair back, put on some shoes, and hurried downstairs. Both Grandma and Grandpa were watching the news channel again.

"Taylor, did you notice anything strange at the game last night?" Grandma asked. She was watching a follow up about the game.

"Um . . . not really," Taylor hesitated. "Unless you're talking about the coach, he was arrested for something. I'm not sure what though."

"Well, it's a good thing you weren't there then. Apparently, he was so angry about his team losing, that he was threatening the kids and shot a gun off in the woods. A couple of the kids had to wrestle him to the ground and got knocked around a bit, but they're all alright. I don't think that the coach will be coaching anymore though. Could you imagine?" Her grandma exclaimed with amazement.

She released a deep breath and lied. "Oh, that strange thing, that's why I was home so late. Didn't want to worry you, sorry again." Taylor was relieved to find out that nothing had gotten out about her. She wondered why the guys at the game didn't say anything about her, and then noticed the time.

"Grandma, can you take me to school, there's no way I'll make it in time." She asked.

"Sure, go start the car; I'll be out in a second." She replied.

Taylor grabbed the keys off the dining room table and darted out the door. She started the car and moved into the passenger seat. Once Grandma showed up, they headed for the school. It only took a couple of minutes and Taylor was glad. She didn't want to talk about the game, or anything from the last few days, actually. As soon as they pulled up to the curb, Taylor hopped out of the car and hurried over to the doors.

"Watch out for any crazy gun happy coaches, okay," Grandma hollered with a smile, out the passenger window.

"Sure thing," Taylor turned in response and then ran into the school building. She headed straight for her locker. To her surprise, Kim was waiting there, leaning with her back against Taylor's locker holding a newspaper. Taylor walked up to her and brushed her aside in order to gain access to her locker.

Kim looked at Taylor, pointed to the newspaper in her hand, and back to Taylor. "Have you seen this?" She asked.

"Yeah, it was all over the news this morning, the coach got in trouble." Taylor replied.

"You know that's not what happened." Kim whispered, glaring at Taylor.

"What do you mean?" Taylor responded innocently. She didn't remember seeing Kim outside, only the group of boys and the coach.

"I saw you, last night." Kim poked her chest. "I was on my way to the car when I heard some fighting. I ducked behind a tree, and that's where I saw what really happened." She leaned in closer to Taylor and said with a hushed voice. "You're like a gargoyle or something, aren't you? And you can definitely heal people." She added.

Taylor closed her locker door, after she had finished getting out the right books for class. She paused for a moment, crocked her head, and groaned.

"Honestly Kim, I don't know what's going on with me right now, but I've got to get to class and so should you. Please don't say anything?" She begged, before heading to class.

"Sure, but you have to talk to me later, k" she replied, wandering off to her first class.

Taylor shook her head in disbelief, groaned again, and stepped into first period just as the bell rang. No one seemed to care that she wasn't seated. She glanced around the room; Derek was still nowhere to be found, and so, she shuffled back to his seat, and sunk into the chair, keeping to herself for the entire lecture, which concluded with a return of old reports.

Once the bell finally rang, Taylor hurried out the door following the last student. Just outside the classroom, someone snagged her arm, pulling her hard against the wall.

"Tim, what do you want?" Taylor asked, surprised to see him talking to her at all.

"I need to talk to you, but not here. Meet me at the graveyard across from your house, after dark." He whispered, alarming her with his sense of urgency.

"What's with everyone being so secret today, seriously?" Taylor commented.

"Huh?" Tim responded.

"Nothing," she shook her head, "Sure, I'll meet you there." She replied, brushing his hand off of her arm. "Can I go to class now?"

"Sorry, just remember, after dark. . ." Releasing her arm, he nodded at a few people in the hall, and then disappeared around a corner.

The rest of the day was unusually tense; rumors of the coach's episode flooded the halls. Apparently, he'd always been a bit of a hot head and so the story wasn't far from the truth. No one was going to miss the jerk, but the basketball team would be hurting until they found a new replacement.

Taylor ate lunch alone, hiding at the far side of the cafeteria. Derek and Kim were both absent for the remainder of the day. She was a little suspicious, after the little run in with Kim that morning. The cat was out of the bag, and who knows how long it would be, before the whole town formed a lynch mob to hang her. Kim knew what happened, the boys from the game knew, and no one at school was bothering her as usual, Taylor felt the uneasiness of the calm before a storm stroll through the school. Something bad was coming but she couldn't tell what. She just had another one of those chills that made the hair stand up on the back of her neck.

After lunch ended, Taylor sped to her next class avoiding the strange looks people were giving her. A couple in particular even made a point to move across the hall as she passed by, Taylor was very uneasy by now, and couldn't wait until her final class was over. As soon as the bell rang, she lurched from her desk and out of the school, swiftly crossing the parking lot. She wanted to avoid as many people as possible. After the morning rumors of the coach blew over new ones must have started, and Taylor was sure they were about her. But everyone was avoiding her, and with them the afternoon rumors, she was sure were about her.

"Hey Taylor, get in." Kim yelled from her car, pulling up behind Taylor.

"Sure, anything to get out of here, everyone's been acting strange this afternoon, do you know why?" Taylor said, jumping into the car.

"No sorry, I've been at home helping out my dad." She replied.

"Look, I'm not going to tell anybody about anything, but you have to do something for me." Kim commented.

"I guess so, it's not like I have a choice." She replied.

"It's just that . . ." Kim hesitated, "My dad, he's really sick. It'd really mean a lot to me if you could try to heal him. I saw you heal Tim last night, and if you could just try that again. It's just that we've tried all sorts of medications and treatments and he's still getting worse. The doctors don't know how much longer he has, please try." She begged, wiping a few stray tears from her cheeks.

"I guess I can try, but I don't know how I did that the first time." Taylor explained. "But I'll try."

"Good, that's all I want. I really think you can do it." She exclaimed, far more confident in Taylor than she was in herself.

Kim changed direction in the car and drove both Taylor and herself upriver to her house. They pulled up to a large Georgian house. Kim rushed out of the car and up to the front porch. Taylor followed behind a little nervous of what was to come. They walked inside, Kim leading Taylor, through a grand living room and up the staircase. Taylor was alarmed by an old woman staring out of the front window. She seemed distraught, rocking back and forth mumbling to herself.

"Sorry, that's my mom, she's really upset about this whole thing, but she's willing to try anything." Kim explained, redirecting Taylor's attention.

Taylor stayed behind Kim as they entered the room. Kim's dad was tucked into some blankets on the bed. The room was fairly barren, beside a large oxygen breathing machine in the corner. Kim said something to her dad and then looked at Taylor.

"You can try now, he's ready. His cancer is in the final stages and we've little hope for anything else. . . Please make him better." She whimpered.

Not really sure how she did it the first time, Taylor placed both her hands over Kim's father's chest and began focusing. A minute went by, and then another. Kim stayed quiet and watching the scene from the corner. Nothing appeared to be happening. Beads of sweat began to form on her forehead. She stopped, wiping her brow, and then refocused, placing her hands over his chest again, concentrating on healing his body.

"Is it done? Did it work?" Kim scooted toward her father.

"I don't think so Kim. I'm not sure how I did that last night." Taylor apologized, pulling her hands away.

"Change into a gargoyle and then try again." Kim urged. "You have to heal him; I saw you do it last night. Please." She pleaded, tears pouring down her face.

"I'm sorry I don't know how that happened or why. I promise if I can figure it out I'll come back here and fix him, I promise." Taylor replied to Kim nearly crying. She truly was sorry that she couldn't heal him. And furthermore, she was afraid that he might die before she had a chance to figure it out, Kim would resent her forever.

"I'm sorry," Taylor whispered, backing out of the room. She made her way down the stairs and to the front door. Kim's mom looked up at Taylor questioningly. Taylor nodded her head and frowned and then Kim's mother looked away and began sobbing.

Taylor left the house and trudged home. The walk wasn't far. She had to cross the bridge and stopped as she neared the graveyard. She wondered where Tim would meet her later and then continued home.

She wiped off her feet, before entering the kitchen, and then placed her backpack against the wall.

"You're home late," Grandma commented, peeling a potato.

"Sorry, this girl, Kim, invited me over for a little while. Can I help you with anything?" Taylor offered.

"No thanks, everything is almost done. Thanks for the offer though." Grandma replied, finishing up the last potato. "I'm glad you're making friends so fast. New towns can be tough sometimes."

"Yeah, but people have been pretty cool so far," Taylor lied. She didn't really want to involve her grandparents in her extremely bizarre personal issues.

She joined Grandpa on the couch, while he was finishing up the news, sadly picking up on another report of missing children.

"It's such a shame, with all those poor kids going missing." Grandpa commented.

"I wonder why there's been such a spike in abductions lately." Taylor replied, staring off into space.

"I don't know if there's been such a large spike, as much as the news just covering more of them." He added. "But who knows, life's been pretty scary lately."

"Dinner time," Grandma interrupted.

They all sat down for another great meal, made by Grandma, munching away at the steak and mashed potatoes, paired with a hearty salad and French bread. Taylor enjoyed eating with her grandparents; they usually kept up a good conversation and enjoyed a laugh or two, but tonight she was in a rush. Glancing outside, she realized it must have been dark for over a half an hour, and she needed to get to the graveyard. She wolfed down her piece of French bread, jumped up from the table and found a coat at the closet.

"I'm going to go for a walk." She said, pulling the door open.

"I guess so; just don't break a leg or anything." Grandma hollered, with a perplexed look on her face.

"Ha, ha . . . sooo funny." Taylor smiled at them, before closing the door and disappearing down the street.

The night was clear, and a light breeze chilled her bones. She wasn't sure what she might find in the graveyard and didn't want to think about it. She crossed the street, running through the entrance of the graveyard, and looked around, but nobody was in sight. Maybe he was waiting somewhere in back. She wasn't sure where he'd be waiting, and so she hurried toward the back, figuring that a walk around the graveyard couldn't hurt.

"Psst, hey, over here," a voice whispered.

She looked around and saw a hand, behind a large tomb with a statue on top, motioning her to come closer. She crept in closer, until Tim reached out and yanked her coat, forcing her to slam against the side of the tomb.

"Look, I needed to tell you this before anything else happens. They rest of the guys are planning something serious. They have no intentions of saying anything about you. Instead, they just want to get rid of you and make it look like an accident. They're keeping me out of the loop because they think I'm a softy. But I got wind that they are planning some sort of attack on you, and you need to get away before they do.

● ● ●

"My uncle deals with this sort of thing that you've got mixed up in. I can send you to him, but you're on your own from there. Here's some cash, just take it and go." He said, pushing a clip of money into her hand.

"But . . . what . . ." she was interrupted, as the sound of breaking glass echoed through the neighborhood. Someone down the street screamed, and suddenly the air began filling with the thick smell of kerosene and smoke.

"Oh my god, the house is on fire." Someone down the street shouted. "Call the fire department."

Taylor and Tim both ran to the edge of the graveyard peering down the street.

"No, that's my grandparent's house!" Taylor screamed, lunging into the street, but Tim grabbed her, pulling her back to the curb.

"They're inside! I have to save them." Tears streamed down her face as she was screaming and prying at Tim's grip.

"Do you want them to see you and kill you to," he yelled back at her. "You can't go back there. Please, just take the money and go find my uncle."

"Let me go, let me go! Please let me go!" She whined, as they both watched the fire eat away at the house.

The fire department finally arrived, pulling out the hoses and blasting the roof with heavy streams of water. Two men ran into the house and moments later carried out a body. Once the ambulance finally arrived, Grandma and Grandpa were placed in gurneys and wheeled into an ambulance, but the scene didn't look good.

Taylor's cries where now sobs, and she was grasping consciousness of the situation. What was she going to do? Her grandparents were the only family she had left. She tried to figure out a solution when Tim interrupted.

"Take my car." He shoved the keys into her shaking hand. "It's the only car up the road. Take it and drive north, until you hit Canada, and then look for a town called La Baie. Once there, find an inn called The Thirteen Moons. My uncle owns the place. His name is Jacque. No one will look for you up there. Just get out of here and lay low. I know what you are, we talked in the church. Now get out of here and find my uncle, he can help." He shoved her toward the car, sprinting off down toward the fire.

○ ○ ○

She clenched the keys tightly, looking back at the smoldering house, and wiped the snot and tears away from her face.

"I'm so sorry I brought this on you guys," she whispered, running up the street until she found a black Lexus, the only car on the curb.

She didn't want to leave, but at this point she had no better ideas. She looked around for Tim but found no sight of him. Strapping into the car, she glanced down the street once more, and then left the curb heading north for the intersection.

Chapter XI: Long Drive North

It was late and Taylor was tired. She had just experienced one of the most excruciating days of her life. She watched as her grandparent's house burned to the ground and the paramedics carried their bodies out from the house. She had no idea if they were dead or whether the boys that started the fire thought that she might be dead as well. She had to leave. She needed to find someplace safe, and she needed time to figure out what was going on with her body. Time, which she had plenty of, as she began her long journey north towards Canada.

"Tim Ambler. . . Who would have guessed? The so-called basketball hotty was the guy I met at the church. And apparently I wasn't dreaming." She mumbled.

The interstate was about thirty minutes away from town and she was already sick of driving. Normally a good drive was relaxing now and then, but with all the crap that just happened, she didn't want to be left alone with herself.

Signs started to blur, not recognizing one town from the next, and so she pulled off in Orano, to fill up the gas tank. She wiped her eyes, pulled off on the exit, and drove down the circular road to the gas station. She filled up the car and picked up a map and some food.

She settled back into the car and opened the map, pinpointing La Baie, knowing she would eventually need to find the place. After safely returning to the interstate, she popped open a soda and some chips and began munching away the mile markers. The further north she drove the thicker the appearance of snow became.

She stopped again in Presque Isle for gas, and once more, after the border patrol, in Jacksonville, before heading on to Les Treize Lunes in La Baie.

Taylor became weary as the drive north dragged on. She chugged down sodas just to stay awake. Then finally the sun began to kiss the horizon, and the dark night was lighting up. The deep blue began changing into a lighter hue of purple. Off in the distance, light blue clouds began appearing out of the dark, and the shadowy passing of trees on the side of the road turned into a snowy blanket of pines and furs.

Taylor spotted a sign with some words, which looked like La Baie, but she wasn't sure because half of it was covered in snow powder. She pulled out her road map and glanced at it, still driving, and watched for more signs. As the turn got closer, so should another sign to direct her.

While she was watching the signs, she noticed that everything was written in both English and French. She remembered that she had taken a French class once upon a time but wasn't sure how much she would remember. Hopefully everyone up here, or at least everyone she needed to speak with, understood English.

She quickly found the turn and drove off toward the town. The scenery was beautiful. The drive was along a large river, which was frozen in most places. Pine trees and furs cluttered the surrounding terrain, and little houses were scattered among the trees, with smoke drifting out of the chimneys. She could see large mountains far off in the distance, but everything was pillowed with white powder, blending the terrain together.

She watched out for an inn. She needed to find The Thirteen Moons. For some reason, a man named Jacque is going to be able to help her, and she needed to find him there.

"Les Treize Lunes," she read a sign out loud. "Wait isn't that The Thirteen hmm, Lunes could that mean Moons?" Taylor thought, and then decided to stop and ask at least.

She pulled into the driveway and thought that it looked like a nice little inn. She parked the car and crunched through the snow up to the front door.

She rapped on the door. No one answered, and so she let herself in, deciding she might try to see if anyone was there.

The place was very nice. The front room opened up into a great room, where she could see the beautiful river of ice outside. There were some comfortable sofas facing the windows and a breakfast table in the corner.

"Hello, anyone there?" Taylor yelled, shuffling through some magazines spread out on a coffee table in front of the sofas.

"Hi, just a moment. . ."

Taylor jumped, as a voice came from the stairs.

She waited for a few moments and then a tall younger looking woman came down the stairs holding some blankets folded in a stack.

"Hi, I'm Jill. Can I help you with anything?" She set down the blankets on a small table and then reached out her hand.

"Taylor," she said promptly grabbing her hand in response with a brief shake. "Actually, I'm looking for Jacque; do you know where I can find him?" Taylor responded.

"Depends, who told you, you could find him here?" She asked a little suspiciously.

"My friend Tim, Tim Ambler. He said I could find out what I needed to know up here. He said that Jacque can help me." Taylor replied, a bit frustrated that she wasn't getting a straight answer.

"What kind of help are we talking about?" Jill asked again.

"To be honest, I'm not exactly sure, but I do think it has something to do with this stone that I found. . ." she was interrupted.

"A stone you say?" A man appeared around the corner at the top of the stairs and asked curiously.

"That'll be all Jill, thank you dear." He said to Jill. He walked down the stairs, leaned over the young woman, gave her a kiss on the forehead, and then politely motioned her to leave. The man motioned Taylor to follow, exiting the main floor, and out onto the patio, overlooking the river. Taylor promptly followed, assuming that the old man was Jacque.

"Tell me some more about this stone that you found, if you wouldn't mind." He asked Taylor.

"Am I to assume that you are Jacque, the Jacque that Tim sent me to find?" She replied.

"Ah, yes, and that is my lovely daughter Jill, you've just met inside." He motioned toward the window.

"Okay, well I guess everything started when I found this stone in Lake Crescent."

"Do you still have it, can I see it?" He interrupted her. She could hear the excitement in his voice.

"Uh, no, you'll just have to listen to find out what happened." She commented and watched as a frown stretched across the old man's face. She could tell that he was disappointed.

"Anyway, it looked like a very large diamond, so I kept it, but then my friends and I got into trouble on the lake and some park rangers stopped us. I swallowed the stone thinking I would, you know," she paused. "Poop it out." She whispered, flushing with embarrassment. "But when I swallowed it, a weird pulsing feeling went through my body and then I felt sick. I threw up and then I was arrested, and then I was put in juvenile hall, and then I was moved to Maine, and then I began having strange dreams, and then I broke my leg," she began flying through her words as if she were unloading years of stress onto the man. "And then my leg healed that week, and the news crew came and cut me on television and then that healed while we were in the house."

"Slow down, slow down." He urged her. She stopped and took a large breath in, then calmed herself. Tears had already begun to well up in her eyes and she felt embarrassed that the stress was so overwhelming. Usually, stress was easy for her to deal with, considering all the stuff she used to have to put up with in foster care. She exhaled and started again this time slower.

"Well, then I was plastered all over the news as a Devil Child and I hadn't even started school yet. Oh yeah, and I had a dream, or at least I thought it was a dream, until recently, where I thought I turned into a gargoyle. And then I flew along the river in town, and then found a church and went inside. There was a boy inside. That was Tim I guess, but I couldn't really tell until later at school." She stopped for a moment.

"What is it?" Jacque asked.

"Well, I guess, I always assumed I was dreaming, but if I wasn't, then what happened next, was really strange. Somebody barged into the church and shot me with something that knocked me out, and when I woke up, I was back in my room." She paused.

"Did anyone follow you up here?"

"Not that I know of, why, do you think Major Bradshaw knows where I am?" She cringed.

"Actually yes, but I don't think that that was his men at the church. I don't think he would have returned you home. Sounds like someone else is following you . . . any idea who?" He sounded genuinely concerned.

"Not really, your nephew's the one who told me all this stuff in the first place. He said I needed to find you before anything else happened." She replied.

"Okay, that makes sense. So, tell me, what else happened?" He asked, leaning against the rail.

"Well, something pretty bad happened at school. I changed into a gargoyle again, but this time some kids saw me and attacked my grandparent's last night. They burned it down thinking I was inside, but my grandparents were." She choked on her words, "that's when Tim sent me up here. He said I'd be safe here and that you could help me." She finished her story and wiped her eyes trying desperately to hold back a barrage of tears.

"Well dear it seems like you've had a tough journey." He motioned for her to go inside. "I think Jill has breakfast almost done, you're welcome to join us and have a bit of a break. We can continue this conversation later this afternoon. You can get yourself a good bath and some fresh clothes, I'm sure Jill has some old ones you can wear." He finished talking and walked back into the house.

Taylor followed behind him. He walked to the far end of the room and around a corner. There was a large kitchen with beautiful maple cabinetry. She watched as Jacque washed his hands in a sink under a large bay window, she did the same. Jill was slicing some fresh baked bread and placing the slices in the toaster. Taylor dried her hands on a towel hanging below the window next to the sink.

"Can I help you with anything?" Taylor offered Jill.

Jill finished buttering some toast and placed them on a plate. "Sure, you can carry these out to the table." She handed the plate of toast to Taylor and a jar of jam.

Taylor marched into the dining room, placing the toast and some jam on the table and then sat down across from Jacque. Jill soon joined them and sat near her father at the other side of the table.

"Dig in, there's toast, bacon, eggs, and fries. Please enjoy." Jill announced, spooning herself some fries that looked more like hash browns.

Taylor was exhausted and said very little during breakfast. It gave her a chance to recollect her thoughts. She was watching Jacque and couldn't help but notice the striking resemblance that Jill had of him. They both had ultra light blond hair, thin and wavy. Jacque's hair was much shorter than Jill's, but still long enough to see the waves wrap around his ears. They both had clear blue eyes, the blue you would find on the northern part of the Pacific Ocean which reminded Taylor of swimming in Lake Crescent. They had the same nose, narrow and to the point and high cheek bones. The only real difference was the lips. Jacque had large normally proportioned lips for a man, but Jill had dainty little lips. Her upper lip almost hidden by her small lower lip, she guessed those came from her mother. Their skin was lighter, but not pale like Taylor's, it seemed like they got a lot of sun, but in this cold, their color was drained. But all in all, she could tell that Jill was most definitely related to Jacque.

"Taylor is going to be staying with us for a while. If you could set her up with a room and I thought maybe some of your old clothes might fit her, it'd be much appreciated." Jacque explained.

"Sure thing, dad," she responded and then looked at Taylor. "I'll get you all set up, just try and keep tidy around here and mind your manners. We get lots of guests that come and go, and we don't want to upset any of them." She added, finishing up her breakfast.

"Come with me, and I'll get you all fixed up. Don't worry about the table. Dad will get it." Jill escorted Taylor upstairs to a large bedroom on the left end of the hallway.

"Here are some clothes that you can wear, towels are in there. Go ahead and clean up, I'm sure dad is going to want to talk to you some more after you're all settled." Jill handed Taylor a stack of clothes and pointed out a cabinet under the sink with some towels and bathing supplies, adjacent to the room.

After Jill left, Taylor pulled out a towel and relaxed into a nice warm bath. She cleared her head of any nonsense and listened to the wind howling by the window in the bedroom. Time passed by as she enjoyed the warm bath, until she heard a faint conversation between Jill and Jacque coming from a vent.

"Don't get too comfortable, with all that press she's been getting we might have to leave before any government officials arrive. You'd better bet they've been watching her." Jacque's deeper voice boomed.

"But don't they think she burned down in the fire. Wouldn't that have kept them distracted?" Jill's more delicate voice responded.

"Maybe, but it won't be long before they don't find her body in the house and go looking for her. And you better bet they'll think she's come to me. I was after all, the head of research and development for the Major's old team. And even though they may not know where I am, you better bet they're going to try and find me. None of us are safe here." Jacque continued, but was interrupted by a knocking at the front door.

Taylor was already on edge listening to their conversation, but when someone knocked at the door, she jumped. She got up out of the tub and dried off quickly. She heard some more talking as the third party entered the house and the conversation was continued.

"Did she make it safely, Professor?" The third voice asked. It was obviously male by the deep tones but not as deep as Jacque's voice. It sounded kind of familiar.

As Taylor was listening, she suddenly felt a strange tingling feeling run up the back of her spine and her heart began to beat more rapidly. This was a new feeling; it was strange, as if her body recognized the third person downstairs without even seeing him. It felt like hundreds of years of yearning all pressed into one little moment, a moment that was far to brief, but could last forever.

"Yes, but I think we may have to leave soon." Jacque's words snapped Taylor back into reality.

"That would be wise; I've seen three large black sedans heading north about two hours south of here. One of the men was Major Bradshaw, I'm certain they know she came to you, and someone must have tipped them off on your location," informed the third voice.

"Thanks, we'll get packed and head out within the hour. Will you go ahead and ready the Chateau Le Cache? Notify the grounds we're coming and try and delay Bradshaw if you can. Buy us some time." Jacque finished up, bidding good luck to the stranger.

"I'll do what I can." The voice finished and then the man stormed off outside and the door was closed behind him.

Taylor was frantic. She threw some of Jill's old clothes on and ran down the stairs and to the door. She swung it open to see who was there, but no one was outside. The cold air blew in causing a shiver to run down her spine. She stepped back into the house and closed the door. Both Jill and Jacque acted alarmed when she flew to the door.

"Who was here just a minute ago?" Taylor asked Jacque with an accusing look on her face.

"No one of any importance, but we must pack. Get together anything you brought up here we don't want to leave proof that you were here. We must be leaving within the hour so hurry." Jacque ordered.

"Yes, Sir," she promptly responded with no quarrels because she had heard the conversation from upstairs, so she already understood why they needed to leave.

Jacque was a little surprised that she had not questioned him or argued back, but he was also glad because he needed to pack quite a bit of gear and high-end technology and had little time to do so. He brought all sorts of boxes and cases up from the basement and piled them next to the door. Once Taylor and Jill had packed some clothes, Jacque reversed a hummer out of the garage and they all started stacking the gear into the back.

"Should I drive my car?" Taylor asked, as they were stacking the last of the gear.

"It's not yours, right?" He responded.

"No, Tim lent it to me." She replied.

"Right, well we are going to have to leave it here. Just, park it in the garage and make sure all of your stuff is out of it." He told Taylor.

They just finished packing and Jacque pulled the hummer further out of the driveway as Taylor moved the Lexus into the garage. They all piled into the hummer and Jacque pressed a button that made the garage door close.

"House is locked?" He questioned Jill.

"Yes, and everything is secured inside." She replied and handed him the house keys. He placed them into his jacket pocket and backed the hummer onto the street and pulled forward.

"What is the Chateau Le Cache?" Taylor asked as they drove off.

"So, you heard our conversation, did you?" He replied, keeping his head facing the street.

"Some of it, I heard that you are a professor and you used to work for the government. But that's about all really." She commented through a long yawn. She realized that through all the commotion the last day or two, she hadn't really slept for a while and was no longer able to fight off the sleep deprivation.

"It sounds like you might be tired, try and get some sleep. You'll see soon enough what Chateau Le Cache is." Jacque replied, and then began talking to Jill.

"The good news is that he is going to try and slow Bradshaw down, Will . . ." she listened with intensity trying to follow the conversation but drifted off into a heavy sleep and began dreaming.

○ ○ ○

Chapter XII: Chateau Le Cache

"Ahh," Taylor released a long yawn that triggered everyone in the hummer to yawn in response.

"Are we there yet?" She asked the Professor, slowly waking from a long-needed slumber.

"We're just pulling in now. . ." He stopped and pointed past some trees outside.

There were several feet of snow outside and Taylor could feel the tires crunching over the thick blankets of white on the ground. As they drove between the trees, plumes of snow were knocked off the branches and forced to fall to the ground, uncovering the thick evergreen trees beneath. Taylor's eyes followed Jacque's finger, as she gazed past the trees at the scene in front of her.

"Wow!" She gasped, as the most incredible sight she had ever dreamed of, unfolded.

The trees parted, revealing a pathway that led up to a Castle. The snow was stacked in layers on each side of the pavement, but the pavement itself had been cleared. The long driveway led up to a shiny black gate.

"Welcome to the Chateau Le Cache." He said, watching her surprised face.

Once inside the gate, there was a circular driveway, surrounding a large garden, quilted with snow. Several large buildings stood in front of Taylor, all made out of the same large stones. The largest building had three towers and long corridors that drifted backward. The towers had openings on top, which, she assumed were probably used for guards in the old days. There were two other buildings, but not as large as the first, arranged one behind the other. They were made of the same stone, but one looked like a stable, and the other a hotel. The Castle was magnificent, strewn with elaborate balconies and sky-high stain glass windows.

"It's so beautiful?" Taylor commented.

"Thank you, but shall we unpack, and I'll tell you everything you want to know, inside?" He responded, shutting off the car.

"Sounds good," Taylor replied.

A butler walked out to the driveway and greeted them.

"Willem informed us you were coming. Everything should be to your satisfaction, Sir." The butler said with a very monotonous voice.

Taylor paused for a moment, wondering about who this Willem was. Based on the conversation she heard earlier, he must be the guy that was at the Inn.

The butler hastily carried some luggage inside the castle. Taylor picked up a couple of items as well and followed him.

"Please leave your stuff here. I will take care of it and show you to your room later." The butler told Taylor.

"Thank you, Philip." Jacque replied, nodding to the butler. "We'll be having lunch in the kitchen." He added. "Let Madeline know please."

Taylor followed Jacque past a long room with green marble floors and several elegant light fixtures, into another room with a long mahogany table and matching symmetrical chairs. Jacque disappeared into another room with Taylor following shortly behind. At last, they were in the kitchen. The kitchen was fantastically large. Any chef would feel privileged to use such a kitchen, with its ceiling to floor oak cabinets, high end appliances, and large island.

"I'm glad you're here sir, I've made some food for you." A woman standing over the sink commented. Taylor assumed that she was the cook, with a white apron tied around her waist and hair net covering her head.

"Thank you, Madeline." Jacque replied. "We'll need some privacy for a while, if you don't mind." He added.

"Sure thing, Sir," she smiled, placing steaming bowls of soup in front of them, while they made themselves comfortable, and then returned with a platter of sandwiches.

"Well, where should I start?" Jacque huffed, reaching for a sandwich.

"How about the beginning, like how you got involved in all of this." Taylor replied.

"Okay will do." He tasted the soup and then dipped the sandwich into the steaming bowl. Taylor followed his lead, picking out a sandwich and began eating, while listening intently to his story.

"It all began about fifty years ago. I was only about twelve. . ."

"I was accepted early to the Massachusetts Institute of Technology, very early. And my mother was extremely happy for me, as was I, but that didn't mean the four years I spent there were easy or forgiving.

"The students found that having a child compete for the highest grade in their classes was a serious threat. Not only did I make many of the student feel intimidated by my genius, but I also made the school look like a breeze, flying through the advanced courses my first year, and working on my master's degree in the third year.

"As you can imagine, I was not a favorite among students, but still, I excelled, finding every means possible to further my studies.

"When I finally graduated, with the highest honors, I was one of the youngest students ever, to graduate at MIT with a doctorate in bioengineering. I was considered quite a prodigy in my time. But anyway, at graduation one of the most promising offers of a lifetime was made to me, by Second Lieutenant Bradshaw." He explained.

"Wow, he's really gone through the ranks over the years, and he's been in for a long time." Taylor commented. "But sorry, go ahead."

"At sixteen, I was very excited to join such a prestigious research team, as was my mother, granting me her best wishes in my future career. Only back then, I was naïve, and didn't realize how manipulative the military can be, even though I was a civilian partisan.

"Youthful, excited, and naïve, I eagerly began research for Lt. Bradshaw, working with some basic protein bonds to reconstitute DNA helical structures. I flew through the processes, creating new combinations with astounding results, which must have impressed Lt. Bradshaw, and before I was nineteen, he moved me to a top-secret lab. Only some of the most prominent names in protein bond science worked in the labs and I was beyond thrilled to be placed in charge of the scientists who'd been working there, some for nearly twenty years."

"That's crazy, I bet you got a lot of crap from them, being so young and all." Taylor interrupted, finishing her sandwich and slurping on some soup.

"Maybe a little," he replied, cocking an eye at her. "But anyway, the research was the key. The military accidentally stumbled upon a stone fragment during WWII, while they were building bunkers on the Western Coast. The man who found it, had gotten injured during an accident, and when he stumbled upon the stone, he was able to heal himself. The military instantly covered up the event, stationing the man on the U.S.S. Lusitania, and buried the accident under a mountain of red tape. To anyone who knew anything about it, that was the end of the stone. But what they didn't know was that was actually only the beginning. The lab I was placed in charge of had been doing research and experiments on the stone for several years.

"The research was fascinating; it was as if the stone was alive. Using first, guinea pigs and lab rats, we discovered a protein serum, that when paired with a catalyst, or host, reconstituted DNA, causing significant changes in the host's makeup. Only one problem kept occurring. We really couldn't discover the stones true capabilities using rodents. Eventually, at that time, Captain Bradshaw approved human subjects for the testing, and began bringing them in. At first it was all on a volunteer basis, using people with significant sensory deprivations.

"Although difficult on the host's body, the protein serum reared amazing results, fixing and enhancing the targeted sensory loss. It was almost as if they developed super-senses," he waved his hands around excitedly.

"It sounds like you guys made some really cool medical breakthroughs." Taylor butted in again. "So why are you up here then?" She added, dampening Jacque's mood.

"Well, sadly it got out of hand. We had become so comfortable, that we decided to try injecting already affected subjects with different strains of the protein bonds, and at first it was magnificent. Some of the subjects began showing signs of supernatural powers. One could read minds, and another could see through objects, one could even move things with his mind. But we got too excited.

"We began putting additives in the serum to see if we could manipulate the causes more to our liking. And that's when it all began going downhill. Captain Bradshaw decided that some of the abilities we had created were useful in combat. He had us combine all the strains together and inject them into four of his best men. I refused to do it. I told him that we had no clue what that could do to the subjects and that it could possibly kill them. He ignored my warning and went ahead with it anyway."

"So did they die then?" Taylor interrupted again.

"Just let me get there. At first, it seemed like it was going to be too much for their bodies to take, their hearts were racing, and their blood pressure was off the charts. Then suddenly they all flat lined, just as I had suspected their bodies couldn't handle it. The injections were very tough on the subjects' bodies, even the single strain injections.

"We watched, as the monitor displayed a lone unmoving line across the screen, but then almost in sync, their heart beats came back. Weak at first but then the beats got stronger. Two of the men began changing. Claws jutted out of one man's hands, long bat like wings from another. They had transformed into very evil looking gargoyles, bony and clawed. Then one by one they busted out of the restraints, holding them on the medical beds. The one with claws knocked me back against the wall; another one picked up a bed and launched it at the window in the lab. All four of them climbed through the window with amazing agility and barreled through the long corridor knocking down scientists in their way.

"They were out of control and dangerous, but Captain Bradshaw didn't seem disturbed in the least bit by what had just happened. Instead, he sent some men out to find them, and ordered me back to work. He wanted more work done with the stone, but what he really wanted was an army of soldiers. After watching those men, destroy the lab as they left, I knew that this was not what the purpose of the stone was for.

"I began working on a treatment that would reverse the effects caused from the serum and acted like I was making progress for the captain. He didn't have a clue, at first, but eventually he caught on. I found that if I placed the stone in between a ray gun and the subject the result was a cancelation of the protein strains in the subject. I used this method on a couple of the subjects until Captain Bradshaw found out what I was doing, and boy you better believe he was angry.

"I knew I didn't have much time before he came down to fire me or more likely kill me. I released all of the subjects from the labs, set fire to the place, and before I left, I wanted to destroy the stone. I didn't want him to continue any of the research. I entered the safe code to the containment lab, but the captain had caught up with me. When I was in the containment center, I reached for the stone, but the captain pulled a gun out, pointing it at me. Without hesitation, I threw the container at the captain and darted for the door. He dropped his gun to catch the container, but it smashed against the side of a table in the lab and the stone fell to the ground. As I was headed out the door I turned, out of sheer luck, and a piece of the stone slid across the floor and stopped at the edge of my foot. I reached down snatched it and then sealed the room, with the captain inside. That gave me enough time to escape. I fled the lab, with most of the patients, and we set up headquarters here, at my parent's old summer house. Now most all of them call this home. Basically, all the kids you meet around here, used to be test subjects from the lab. Unfortunately, I didn't escape with all of the stone and so I'm sure the Captain or I guess Major now, has probably been continuing his research on the stone and has possibly got a fairly large army of superhuman drones."

"So, what are you going to do if he finds you?" Taylor asked.

"Well fortunately I've been doing my own research as well. I've found a way using my portion of the stone to reverse most of the effects of the stone; however, it only works up to a degree. I would be able to reverse more if I had more of the stone, but I only have this half. I also discovered that the portion of the stone that Major Bradshaw found so long ago was in fact only half of a whole stone in the first place. So, what I'm saying is that there is another half of the stone out there somewhere." He explained, tilting his head at Taylor.

"You mean the other half, the one that I found then, right?" Taylor asked.

"Yes, most likely." He responded. He looked at Taylor curiously and then finished off the glass of water he had with his meal.

"I will need to run some tests to confirm my feelings, but I suspect that indeed you and the stone have become one. I have seen what someone can do holding the stone, but to have the power of the stone inside of you, part of you, which altogether is a new discovery that I never imagined." He remarked. "I bet the possibilities are endless." He added.

Taylor sat at the counter for a moment staring off into space. She had finished eating and was momentarily distracted. "Um, Jacque. . ."

"Oh, you can call me Professor, like everyone else. It's just easier." He interrupted.

"Okay, Professor . . . can you tell me who was at the inn earlier?" She finally asked.

"Why do you care so much?" The professor responded.

"It's just that, there was this feeling, no. . ." she wrinkled her brow, "connection more like, when he was there. And I've never felt anything like it before." She hesitated.

"Curious, very curious," he commented. "That was Willem. You might get a chance to meet him some other time, but for right now I think we are done here. I've got lots of work to catch up on, so go on ahead and Philip will show you your room, we'll meet up again later." He finished, calling to the butler.

"You called, Sir?" Philip popped into the room.

"Will you please escort Taylor, to her room and. . ." the professor leaned over to Philip and gave him some inaudible instructions to follow.

"Yes, Sir that will be fine." The butler responded.

"Right this way Miss Taylor." He motioned to her, leading Taylor back the way she'd come in. Once in the main room, they marched up a grand spiral staircase and around an overhang, down through a dark corridor. At the end was Taylor's room.

"Make yourself comfortable, you'll find your bags are beside the dresser. While you are staying with us, please remember, there are other guests, so refrain from loud noises after dusk." He explained, handing her a skeleton key, before leaving.

Taylor took a deep breath, soaking in the surreal atmosphere. The room was far too elaborate for her to feel at home. All she wanted was her old bed at her grandparent's house. Peering out of the magnificent window, in her room, depression began to settle in, as she realized that she may never see them again. If only she'd never gone drinking that day, then she never would have found the stone, and none of this ever would have happened.

"It's all, my fault," the words escaped her mouth, as silent tears trickled down her cheeks. She gazed off into the milky white abyss of the lifeless courtyard, until she was disturbed, by a light tapping on the door. Using her sleeve as a handkerchief, she checked her face in the mirror and then answered the door.

"Oh, hi Jill," she forced a smile.

"Hey Taylor, just thought I'd let you know I'm in the room across the hall from you, okay." Jill responded. "Is everything okay?" She added.

"Oh, yeah. . . I just had something in my eye, that's all. Taylor replied, rubbing her face.

"Sorry about your family," Jill offered, leaning against the doorframe.

"You heard about it?" Taylor said, wondering if the professor said something to Jill.

"Yeah, it's been on the news most of the day. They've been calling it a high school prank gone seriously wrong, but they wont release names or anything like that." She explained.

"I wish I knew what happened to my grandparents." Taylor mumbled, "It was all my fault."

"I'm sure they'll be okay." Jill wearily added with a smile.

Taylor forced another in return. "I hope so. . . So, what's up?" Taylor added, figuring Jill had some other purpose of coming over.

"Oh, I just wanted to let you know that Dad. . . I mean the professor, wants you to join him in the lab downstairs. I think he just wants to take some x-rays for tonight." She finished. "Just get me when you're ready, and I'll take you down there."

"Okay thanks," Taylor responded, watching Jill disappear into her room, across the hall.

Taylor decided to empty out the bags that Jill packed for her at the Inn. Philip had piled them neatly in the far-right hand corner of the room. After she was finished, she found a hair-tie and messed with her hair for a while before settling on a simple ponytail.

Jill's door was cracked, and so she lightly tapped on the doorframe, before popping her head inside and glancing around the room and spotting Jill, crouched down in front of a big chest.

"Hey, ready to go downstairs," Jill looked up.

"Yeah, if you're not busy," Taylor responded.

"Nope, just fiddling with some clothes, might as well get comfortable, if you know what I mean. Probably gonna be here a while. Dad . . . I mean the professor; sorry I keep forgetting, said that the Inn was burned down. These guys really don't want people to know you exist. The good news is that they'll never find this place, he's got it hidden very well, it doesn't even show up on maps, plus there are hidden cameras and silent security alarms everywhere." Jill watched as Taylor's face displayed signs of alarm. "Oh, don't fret we'll be fine here." She finished explaining and closed the lid to the chest.

Taylor followed Jill, paying close attention, as they marched past the grand stairwell, down a smaller set of stairs and finished at a large room downstairs, another long dark corridor.

"This room seems like it's right under our rooms," Taylor commented.

● ● ●

"It basically is, but there's no staircase that leads down on these ends of the castle, so we have to walk the long way." Jill replied and then greeted her father who was fidgeting with a box hanging on the wall. "Hi dad, do you need some help with that?"

"Nope just a sec," he hit the side of the box and then it began to glow. Taylor realized that it was the same kind of light that the doctors used, to look at her leg x-rays.

"Okay Taylor if you will come with me into this room over here. I will take some x-rays, and then we can be done for the night." The professor said, with Taylor following him into a small room adjacent to the main lab. "Here, put this jacket over your body. I'll get your head, first." He placed a heavy lead jacket over her shoulders, and then disappeared behind a little protected niche in the room.

"Hold still for a moment," his voice echoed from the niche. The room went dark, and then a machine whirred around Taylor's head, pausing briefly, while making little clicking noises.

"Okay, now lift your arms like this, and hold still again," the professor popped out, pushing her arms up like a scarecrow, and then disappeared into his little operating room again.

The machine made several stops, before it was finished. The professor came out of his room just a few more times, repositioning Taylor's arms and legs, in order to finish the x-rays, and then finally stopped. When the lights flicked back on in the room, the professor popped out of his little room and dismissed Taylor.

It was about fifteen minutes before the professor rejoined Taylor and Jill, waiting in the main lab. He carried a large folder, and inside were the x-rays.

"Everything looks normal, except for a growing area around your heart." He explained, pulling her chest x-ray out and placing it on the light box.

"This is your heart, and this is the abnormal area." He pointed to the large cloudy spot on her chest. "If you swallowed the stone, and it never exited, then I would have found it in your stomach or bowels. But there's nothing there. The heart is the only abnormal area I can find in your body, and if you asked me, I'd bet it has become a part of you and has basically encased your heart in some sort of bone hard case. A good protection mechanism, I think." He remarked; arms crossed around his chest, staring fascinated, at the x-ray. "It's really rather incredible."

"So . . . I'm like this forever?" Taylor asked.

"Quite possibly, also it doesn't look like I'll be able to get the other half of that stone in order to completely reverse the effects of the protein strains." The professor sadly commented and then plopped down onto a chair in the lab and began sulking. "There is most definitely going to be a war now, and I'm gonna have to do some things I've always dreaded," he mumbled, too low for anyone to hear.

"Don't worry Professor; I'm sure it'll all work out just fine." Jill encouraged, with her usual unrealistic optimism. "Come on Taylor, let's go turn in for the night, and we can talk some more tomorrow." Jill nudged her and then whispered as they walked out of the room. "I think he needs some time alone right now; he's got a lot to think about."

The professor waited for the girls to leave the room and then walked over to a small T.V. and turned it on.

". . . Swine flu. . . Is it the pandemic we've feared, Don Reese, acting director of the Federal Center for Disease Control says; 'I fully expect we will see deaths from this infection' as the count raises to 3,049 infected confirmed accounts from yesterday's 1,020. Already 159 deaths in Mexico are confirmed to be from swine flu and another 2,500 infected. Pandemic alert has been raised from level 4 to level 5 as we now confirm the spread of the disease in more than two countries. Schools everywhere are being shut down and residents are being urged to avoid highly congested areas and stay home if they're sick. . . Next Director John Pablo of the Federal Bureau of Investigation makes a comment on the disappearance of children in elementary schools all around the country. Later, another attack on the white house, who is doing it, and what do they want?"

Chapter XIII: Gym

"Professor," Philip called as he stepped into the lab.

"Oh, yes, just a moment. . ." He startled, when Philip woke him up. Looking down he noticed that he had fallen asleep watching the news in the lab.

"What is it, Philip?" The professor asked, once he was coherent enough.

"I just wanted to let you know that Willem has returned, Sir. He came in around three o'clock this morning and I believe he is in the courtyard. He heard that Taylor made it here safely and wanted to meet with her. I told him that he ought to let her rest she's been running on very little sleep for days now, and that you had quite a busy schedule for her later, so he'd have to wait, Sir." Philip informed him. He glanced around the laboratory and then commented quietly. "I really wish you would let me have this place cleaned Sir."

The professor raised an eyebrow to Philip and then glanced around the lab. He noticed that it was indeed very messy and unorganized. "Very well Philip, but only because Will has been working in here for a while, without my presence and I would agree that this place is a terrible mess. Oh, and by the way did, he mention anything about Major Bradshaw?" He asked, checking his wristwatch. "Four thirty-five," he commented and then asked the butler, "You said he got in at three?"

"Yes, Sir, three o'clock, and I believe he has some information on Major Bradshaw. Will that be all, Sir?" Philip finished talking. The professor nodded to him as he walked around the lab and picked up several glasses and a couple of plates scattered about.

"Oh, and try and have the lab ready by noon. I'd like to continue my research with Taylor later." The professor added, watching as Philip left with a pile of dishes. He didn't notice the terrible condition of the lab, the night before, because he had been too excited, trying to get Taylor's x-rays done. Usually, he didn't let Philip or any of the maids clean the lab because things could easily be broken or misplaced, but in order to get any work done later, he needed the lab to be in usable condition and at the moment it was not. He had no choice, he needed the lab clean, and he did not have time to clean it.

● ● ●

He walked down the long corridor, all the while glancing at the moonlit stain glass windows, covering the walls, until he had found his way out into the courtyard. He remembered, playing as a young boy in the trees, when his parents threw balls inside. It was nice being a child, he never had to worry about anything, and his parents always took care of him. But now, he had a war to fight, and he had to take care of the kids that lived with him.

The professor's thoughts were interrupted as he heard a shaking of some branches and his eyes averted in the direction of the noise. Once his eyes adjusted to dim light, he was not surprised in the least to find Will, standing on a large branch hanging toward the East Wing of the Chateau. His long silver tail, almost like a third arm, twisted around the tree trunk, bracing him, while he leaned outside a window.

"Will," the professor yelled at him. "What on earth are you doing?"

Will startled, releasing his grip on the trunk, and leapt down from the branch, silently landing in the snow beneath.

"Sorry, I was just trying to see if she changes in her sleep like I do sometimes. Your nephew, Tim, said that she might have once. He caught her off guard in a church and was hoping to retrieve the stone piece, but he said that she didn't have it. She's not like me, I think she has far more power than any of us realize. When I'm carrying the stone, I can find her anywhere. That's how I found out she was in Maine. It pulses anytime it gets near her. She was just lucky I'd been following her when she got hurt on the tracks because after I gave you the stone back, I couldn't track her. She's almost like a honing beacon for the stone; the closer it gets to her, the stronger it pulses. Crazy I know, but maybe it's saying something." He explained, wrapping his long silver wings around his shoulders.

"Keep your voice down you're gonna wake her and she needs the sleep. I'm planning a lot of work for her later. There are things I need explained, and I need her for most of them." The professor shushed him.

"Oh, don't worry she's in a deep sleep right now, she won't hear anything. She's having a strange dream about the stone. I think maybe she feels its closeness, and it's calling to her in her sleep." Will explained.

○ ◎ ○

"Hey, I know I've warned you about looking into people's minds, plus it's an invasion of privacy. If you don't behave better, I'll return you to Major Bradshaw." The professor teased. He would never truly intend to put any of the kids he'd rescued years ago into danger. "But speaking of the stone, where is it?" He asked.

"Don't fret," Will commented, reaching down into a money pouch attached to his belt, pulling out a little quarter inch piece of stone that looked like a diamond. "See what I mean," He added as he pointed to the small glowing stone piece.

Both the professor and Will watched as the stone piece released a dim glow that barely lit Will's silvery hands, in a slow pulsing rhythm. "Watch this," Will said, holding out his hand, with the stone inside, and stepping closer to the window. The glow in the stone became just a little brighter and the rhythm of the pulse quickened with each step. "It's calling to her, I swear." He said.

The professor watched, and sure enough with each step the stone grew brighter. The professor hadn't really seen Will very much as a gargoyle and remembered how impressive he could be. Once Will was close to the building the professor noticed that he practically disappeared into the snow. Were it not for his clothing or obscure shape, Will's silver color, shadowed by the moonlight, it made him look just like the snow. He could lie down into the snow and vanish, if he wanted, but probably only in the night.

"How do you think I get by unnoticed so well?" Will asked, catching the professor off guard.

"Stay out of my head and get back here. I want you to keep the stone for right now. At this point in time, I'm pretty sure the other piece is indefinitely a part of her heart. If I remove it, I will kill her and that's not necessary. Let's get inside and talk some more. I don't like talking outside, and you know that. There are always ears listening." The professor finished and then led Will back inside.

"We might as well grab something to eat while we're catching up. Cook should be awake." The professor remarked. Will agreed and stopped in the dining room. He was about to sit at the table before he realized that he needed to make a change.

"Can you bring me a glass of water?" He caught the professor before he disappeared into the kitchen.

"Sure, what do you want for . . ." the professor stopped mid-sentence and shuddered, as the remarkable, but also disturbing sight

● ● ●

of Will phasing back into a human began. First, his silver embossment of leather skin began to sport a Mediterranean tan, and then the ridge that ran from the nape of his neck to the end of his tail began shriveling up and sinking back into his body. The large silver wings that were wrapped around his body sank into his back, and his tail sucked into his rear end, leaving a tall, medium tanned boy, with a gentle muscle build, standing in a pair of loose pants.

"Derek Ralph Willem, you have seriously got to be more private about that. The sight of your change can ruin an appetite, you know." The professor scalded.

"Sorry," he snickered. "I just can't eat at the table like that, and I wouldn't mind hanging around for a while to catch up with Taylor. I would love to see what she knows about her abilities. Or if she even knows she has any. Last time that I saw her, it was just for a brief moment, and I was trying to give her something to do, to keep busy at school. I was hoping that she wouldn't get caught up in all this so quickly, but that whole fiasco at the game happened, and then Tim sent her up here." Will explained.

"Just a sec," the professor said, disappearing into the kitchen and then returning with two large glasses, one with water and the other with milk. He handed the water to Will, who was now sitting at the table, and joined him on the opposite side. "Okay, so how is Tim doing anyway?" The professor asked, drinking some milk. Will paused while the cook carried in two plates smothered with some sort of egg scramble and then thanked her.

"You boys are up early this morning," the cook commented, distributing the plates.

"The early bird catches the worm, or so to speak," the professor reminded her.

"Well, I'm not complaining. It gives me something to do. You boys enjoy." She stated and returned to the kitchen.

Will began, "Tim's fine, but I'm not sure he's on our side. I mean he sent Taylor to the Inn where you were hiding out and I'm pretty sure he knew she had a tail on her. I know he's family and all but I'm not sure we should trust him right now; I don't know if Major Bradshaw has gotten to him."

"So, what is Major Bradshaw up to right now?"

"I'm not sure. I thought he was part of the caravan tailing Taylor, but when I returned to slow them down, he was gone. I led

○ ○ ○

them off on a faulty trail back toward the west coast. I'm not sure how long his men will follow it, but they won't find us here. Shyla's tailing them. She'll let me know if they change their course. The good news is that I don't think Major Bradshaw knows that she swallowed the stone." Will explained.

"Well let's hope you're right for now." The professor grunted. "You sure Shyla is okay?" He added.

"She'll be fine. Aren't there more important things we should be worrying about right now anyway? I caught a glimpse of the news last night, and I've been meaning to ask, why does the Major need so many young kids?"

"So, you think he's been kidnapping them too?" He pushed back in his seat and groaned again.

"Undoubtedly, who else can pull so many children out of school without anyone questioning the act?" He replied.

"I know. I've just feared that it was him. One thing we did discover about the protein strain injection, was that the younger the host, the more it affected the brain, and the less it affected their appearances. So little kids, like the ones he's probably been kidnapping, would be prime subjects for intense psychic abilities. And at such an influential age, who knows what he might be preparing them for." He explained.

"Oh god, that sounds horrible. We've got to stop him. What if he experiments on them like he did us? I mean look what he did to his own daughter." Will paused, thinking about poor Shyla and her permanent tiger-like transformation.

"Did you catch the part on the news about the White House attack?" The professor asked, finishing up the last portion of his egg scramble.

"Yeah, I see he made another staged attack, only this time he's targeted the U.S. If he keeps these supposed terrorist attacks up, he's going to win quite a bit of support by the United Nations to make his research public, and possibly begin regular injections of the army, to create a super powerful army of gargoyle drones. And who knows, maybe he's brainwashing the children so that he can use them to control his army." The professor sighed, slapping his hand against his forehead, and rubbing away the wrinkles formed from his scowl.

The professor sat thinking for a moment and then finished eating. He stood up and gestured for Will to follow. Although Will was not quite done eating, he knew that the professor had some serious issues bothering him and decided it was imperative to follow. He followed him into the lab and watched as he fumbled through some paperwork. The professor twitched his finger at Will, signaling him to come closer, and then pointed at some locations on a map.

"This is the Cyndac Oil Refinery, Northeast of Hughes, Alaska; it's in the Kokrine Hills. I've been there once before, for a research project with Major Bradshaw. It's not really an oil refinery but rather a prison. We were able to experiment freely without risk of inspection or anything else on whomever we wanted. The refinery was rather secret, but I'll bet that's where he's taking the children, if he's behind their disappearances. Anyhow, I want you to fly out there and poke your nose around. Find out what you can about the children and what he's up to. I need to know if he plans to experiment on them. Call Shyla back and take Kam with you, I would prefer that you work with a team out there in case anything goes wrong."

"What about Taylor?" Will inquired.

"Don't worry about her. I've got other plans for her. Take the stone with you, but keep it safe, just in case you need it." The professor added, "Now get going!"

"Guess I'm not catching up with Taylor after all." Will grumbled under his breath.

"What's that?" asked the professor.

Will responded agitatedly, "Don't worry, I'm leaving." And with that, he stood, scowling, and despite the professors scalding earlier, began phasing back into a gargoyle as he was exiting the laboratory.

The professor observed the final changes as Will disappeared into the corridor. His silver wings jutted out of his back and the ridged tail sliced through the air just as it slid out the door. The meticulous control that Will had over his abilities stressed the professor.

"Now if only I could get Taylor to do that," he mumbled, wondering what kind of work it would take to teach Taylor control over her abilities.

After Will had left he noticed that Philip was in the lab with two maids organizing and washing materials.

"Philip, if you think that you guys are nearly finished in here, I could use some help in the gym. Do you think you could rustle up a couple of kids to help me out, and then send Taylor in later?" He popped his head into the lab, catching Philip's attention.

● ● ●

"Yes Sir, that shouldn't be a problem." He replied.

"Also, can you make sure she gets breakfast, before you send her over?"

"Certainly Sir," the butler added.

The professor's eyes wandered the lab searching for an item he had used in the past to induce transformation in Will and Shyla. He wasn't sure exactly how he was planning on training Taylor; she was young, much younger than the other kids he had worked with, and he had been working with them for many, many years. She only had a little bit of time.

Taylor needed to learn what they had learned, control, calmness, sense of self, strategy, and teamwork, but quickly, and he had no time for her to rebel like a few of the others did. Will for instance, had gotten so frustrated with his inability to control mind reading that he ran away for several years. The professor had sent Anisa to look for him, but in his rebellion, he was not to be found. He mastered blocking out other's from entering his mind. The professor was so relieved when Will finally returned, that he didn't even pester him about his amazing control over his mind channeling ability. But that was then, and this is now, and Taylor had no time for such nonsense. She needed to learn how to hone every detail of all the abilities she possessed.

"Ahh, there it is," the professor cheered, reaching for a small machine with two prongs and a little dial. He placed it in a little pouch and fumbled around for some papers. Once he was finished in the lab he headed out to the other end of the castle and out to the hotel looking building.

He crunched his way step by step through the pathway outside, until he was met by a large, locked door. He pulled out a set of keys; they jingled while he fussed with the door, and then propped it open, heading inside.

Once inside the professor flicked on a set of lights and turned down a long empty hallway. He stopped outside two large plain doors and pushed both open, stopping them with a door jam, fully open. He waited near the doors while the large fluorescent lights flickered on around the enormous room. Once the lights were on, he walked down the left side of the gym and into his office.

"This will have to do," he mumbled, tossing the small pouch onto a desk, and stepping over to a shelf that held a big stereo, turning it on. In the back of the office were a couple of counters, one with a sink and another with a coffee pot. He turned on the sink washed the pot out and set up a pot of coffee to brew, while he waited for some kids to appear.

The professor sat in his leather office chair for about ten minutes before the first two boys appeared. One had long scraggly black hair and the other shorter spiked blond hair with white frosted tips. Both boys had very similar features, high chiseled cheek bones, olive skin tones, and muscular builds. The professor knew right away that the only two, truly related kids of his unorthodox family had arrived, always eager to help. Both Wolfe brothers stood at ease, against the office door, full of confidence, and beaming with anticipation.

"Philip said you wanted some help?" Ranulf, the slightly taller one, with the long scraggly black hair commented.

"Yeah, I hear we get to help train the new addition to the family." Arnulf chimed in with enthusiasm.

"Rumor is going around that she's the one who's caused all the tumult in the states. Is it true that she found the other part of the stone, professor?" A third, delicate voice questioned as the professor saw Esa Rosa, one of the youngest kids he'd ever had to experiment on, pass between the two brothers in the doorway, holding in her hands a rolled-up stack of newspapers. She stepped over to the desk that the professor was sitting at and plopped the pile in front of him. "Here, I've been collecting all the stories that appear to be connected, ever since that strange pulse back during the autumn months, while you were gone. I just had this feeling like it was important."

"Thank you Esa," the professor remarked, as he quickly shuffled through a couple of the top papers reading the headlines.

Swine Flu Inoculations or Defensive Concoctions: Is the military really making a big fuss over a simple flu shot or is it something more.

Smart Kids Smartly Gone: 3 more top elementary students gone missing in Alabama, totaling 79 students across the nation. Is there a connection between the disappearances?

Terrorists Drop Bomb outside White House: Is Al Qaeda striking back at the U.S. for infiltrating their bases, or is this a new terrorist group, with a bigger purpose?

Where Are They? 5 more students randomly swiped during school hours. Is this the making of a large underground sex trade brewing in the United States?

Teens out of Control: Several students rallied the day after a bad game and set fire to a fellow student's home. This terrible prank went seriously wrong when people were trapped inside.

"These headlines really make it look like the world is in some serious trouble right now." He commented.

"Yeah, pretty scary huh, especially since I think the Flu Inoculation the headlines are referring to, is actually the protein strain serum that Major Bradshaw is trying to push onto the armed forces. I bet he and the president are trying to get it approved and then once everyone has experienced its effects the military will be forced to hush it up and strictly control the media to prevent a nationwide panic. It's a perfect plan, because the Major is the only one who knows how to train and control them. That's probably why he's jacking all of those smart children from school. He'll use their psychic abilities to control them. I think he is behind the attacks in Iraq and on the White House as well." She explained.

"Yeah, that's what Will was thinking too. I guess we are running out of time, and we should probably get started." He waved his hand over the stack of newspapers. "And as much as I don't believe in fighting, we should probably consider making an attack on Major Bradshaw, before he does one on us." He added.

The professor sprung up, out of his seat and motioned for everyone to follow. He looked around the gym and noticed that no one else had shown up just the two brothers and Esa. "Where is everyone else?" He asked?

"You've been gone for a while, and Connor decided he was in charge. He took Anisa and Bryan with him. We didn't want to be a part of his plan, not without your permission. They are trying to steal the stone away from Major Bradshaw, and maybe destroy his research. I told them it was going to be way too dangerous. And then Will, Shyla, and Kam left early this morning. I don't know where they are going." Ranulf, the older of the two brothers replied.

"They're okay. I sent them on a trip, but Connor, err. . ." the professor scowled. "If any of them get hurt, I'm going to kill him myself." He grumbled. Struggling to rid his mind of worry for Connor's makeshift team, he concentrated on the task at hand.

"Here's what we need to do. First, we need to trigger Taylor's transformation. It's not really clear what causes it, from what I understand she's only changed two or three times. Let's try the typical physical stress trigger that usually worked for you guys. Once we've figured that out, then we can move onto the mental challenges.

"Once we've figured all that out then we can set up the ropes and the dark room. Work on her agility and response time. Then once I think she's ready we can move outdoors to the woods and set up all out tactical attacks on her and see how she both evades and defends herself. Once I feel comfortable with her self-control then I think we can start testing for any special abilities she might have, got it?" He explained "But let's get the transformation down first."

Ranulf and Esa nodded, heading towards the back of the gym and disappeared into a room for a brief minute and then stepped back into the gym with a large, tangled pile of ropes. Ranulf fumbled through the pile until he found an end to a rope and then began weaving it in and out until all of the ropes were untangled.

Esa pulled out many large bars, poles, bases, and connections from the same room, and then began connecting them together in a separate part of the gym. Arnulf stayed with the professor to help set up the springboard floor used in floor routines by gymnasts.

"While you were gone, I did some research." Arnulf managed to say as he pulled out a large plywood sheet loaded with springs.

The professor picked up the opposite end of the springboard, helping Arnulf carry it down the gym, until it was in the correct position for set up.

"Yeah, on what?" he replied.

"I had to dig pretty deep, but I found sort of a myth, about the stone. Several of the ancient tribes in Washington, and Canada, used to tell it as a sort of a motivational story to convince children to work hard, and not to cheat. Nowadays very few even know the story, but those who do, would tell you it's just a stupid folktale. I'd believe them except for the fact that I'm direct proof that the stone is real." Arnulf explained, as they placed several more boards from the closet, in line with the first one, and then began a second row attached to the first.

"Go on," the professor urged.

"Well, the guy I talked to said; once there was so much fighting amongst the tribes that the tribal leaders left on a journey together. He said they were gone for a full harvest season. They hiked to the tallest mountain, with offerings from each tribe, and prayed to the Gods for enough power to end all the fighting.

"He said that while they were on the mountain, a stone was crafted from the earth and sky, but the gods could see that the men were not ready for the power, fighting amongst themselves, leaving spilt blood on their precious mountain.

"The Gods were so angry the stone was cast away and broke into two halves, one landing in a river, and the other on the coast. The tribal men were confused, some thought it was a test of will, believing they had to abandon their homes and search for the stone. But others believed it was a lesson, because they weren't ready for such a gift from the Gods, and immediately returned home, working harder than ever before to keep peace in the tribes.

"The legend says that the man who finds the stone will wield the power to rule the world, but whether he rules with evil or goodness, will be only that man's choice." He paused.

"And. . ." the professor waited.

"I think it all kind of makes sense. He said the reason no one believes the legend anymore, is that supposedly the stone was lost thousands of years ago. And when it broke, its power was lost, and as time passed, people stopped looking for it, and it became a myth. Two halves; can you believe that?" He commented, "What if the half the military found in the forties is the first half, and Taylor has the second? Only now you have a quarter of that half and Major Bradshaw has a quarter of it." He hesitated, before adding, "But that means no matter what happens here, Major Bradshaw can never get Taylor, or our piece of the stone. If he unites that thing, I don't even want to think what might happen." Arnulf stressed, as they finished placing all the springboards in a large square floor formation.

The professor followed Arnulf back to the closet, where they retrieved all the springboards, and pulled out a long rolled up mat with Velcro attached to one side. He helped tow the long mat down to the far end of the springboard floor and lined up the edge of it with the end of the boards.

"Who else knows about this?" The professor asked, glancing around the room, before unraveling the mat over the boards.

"Just Will for now, and he's not going to say anything, unless you want him to. It's not like you can keep a secret from him." Arnulf added.

○ ○ ○

"Let's just keep this between the three of us, for now, as a precaution. I don't want Major Bradshaw getting news of this, just in case he hasn't found out. I would imagine that if he had known he would be trying much harder to capture Taylor?" He finished with the subject and browsed over the gym making sure that all the equipment was set up properly and ready for use.

"Right now, err. . . Can someone go wake Taylor? I think we're ready to begin training." The professor shouted.

Chapter XIV: Kokrine Hills

Will left the castle a little disheartened. He was hoping for a chance to speak with Taylor, to let her know that everything was going to be all right. He wanted to apologize for leaving her by herself at the basketball game and apologize for making her go to the game in the first place.

He spread out his silver wings, like an eagle ready to spring from its nest, and began sprinting through the snow, like a cheetah in the savannah, until he had enough momentum to spring into the air. Once he was in the air and on his way west, toward Alaska, he began worrying about Taylor some more.

Other than the first day, he didn't really get a chance to know her. Even after he found her, using the stone, and the professor stationed him there to keep an eye on her, he never imagined she would get into so much trouble so quickly. In no way had he ever imagined that his butting into her personal life would have resulted in the trigger of events that led to the complete destruction of her new life.

How could he ever make things right, right for her again? She lost everything that ever meant anything to her. Could things ever be completely better for her again or was she left to wander alone as they all do now? Each one of them was left to their own strange transformations from the stone's resulting protein strain injection, years ago. None of them had aged a single day since their forcible injections. Granted they all seemed to have unusual gifts that had become more powerful over the last few decades, most of them felt very alone. Aside from the Wolfe brothers, Arnulf and Ranulf, who always had each other, everyone else was orphaned at one point or another. The professor was the only real connection between all of them, well that and the stone, and only because he offered them freedom from the horrifying experiments that Major Bradshaw wanted to continue on them.

Will broke his thoughts, needing to figure out how close he was getting. Kam was following silently on the ground underneath racing at incredible speeds. If it weren't for the heightened senses of Will's transformation, he may never have noticed the silent, ivory stone, against the white pillows of snow, gliding through the forest bellow, but he knew all too well that Kam couldn't fly and preferred the silence, that traveling on the ground presented him.

Will pinpointed a large green sign, half dusted with snow covering some of both the English and French words, approximately two miles out, reading Saskatoon in large white letters. The numbers were on the side of the sign, dusted by the snow and therefore unreadable, but he knew that it was probably time to call Shyla. She needed ample time to catch up with them, before they meet in Alaska.

"Shyla, the professor has a mission for us. Can you hear me?" Will sent his thoughts into her mind, hoping that she had not been too far, or too distracted to hear. He waited patiently while her thoughts shifted from a black Sedan on an interstate, to a blank state with blurry fragments of words popping in.

"What," the words formed clearly into her mind.

"We have a reconnaissance mission. Turns out Major Bradshaw might be responsible for the disappearances of the children. The professor wants us to stake out and gather information. He'd like to know exactly what they are doing with those children and whether they are at the Cyndac Oil Refinery or not." He sent a long stream of word flow into her mind because he couldn't actually say anything into other minds, only send images, and words seemed to be easiest for most people to understand.

He watched as her thoughts twisted, with images of missing children, he'd seen on the television and in newspapers, shifting around in her mind. He could tell immediately that she was worried for the children. He could feel the sorrow in her thoughts as she procured each image of a child's picture she remembered, and then he watched as it screamed out in pain and then faded behind the memories of her own experiences in the labs.

He remembered with her, the dripping wet face, from tears of pain, attached to her thrashing body, strapped to a table, while men sliced and prodded through different sections of her body, and it sent a sudden panic through him. She was right; they could be doing that to the children.

He knew that she was tormented, and now more than ever he was glad that she'd get to help him with this mission. He had sat through many years of watching her nightmares, with her, while she slept. Before he had learned how to control his ability to read and speak to minds, he was an airport for thoughts, they came and went from anyone anywhere, but they were especially difficult to ignore the closer they were to him, and Shyla has been near him since they escaped the laboratories in 1987. He knew only too well, how badly Shyla had been treated. None of them were subjected to the repetitive torturous dissections that Shyla had been submitted to, week after week. It was no wonder that her final transformation became permanent with all the scars and strangely colored patches of abused skin on her body.

Will became furious thinking about Shyla, and Major Bradshaw. How could a father let such terrible things happen to his own child?

The poor girl would never know a normal life. After her mother passed away, the Major blamed it on Shyla, and resented her. He saw Shyla happy with her new husband, and because he was in the military, the Major had him transferred to Iraq, where he was lost during a cargo hijacking. When he started subjecting Shyla, involuntarily to the tests, she begged for mercy, pleading that they do not harm her baby. But the Major, filled with contempt, forced the scientists to take the child, and claimed it had been a stillborn, crushing any possibility she would ever have of having a happy life, ever again.

After that they simply kept her isolated from everyone else and began torturous experiments on her hoping that they might lose her as well. But rather than kill her it only made her what she is today, and full of hate and rage for her own terrible father. She would give her soul to crush the men that killed her baby and tortured her so fervently. With such hatred towards Major Bradshaw and all of his scientists, she was sure to help Will protect the children, if they were there at the prison so crudely disguised as an oil refinery.

The professor wanted this to be a simple reconnaissance mission, but Will had never intended to leave the children there, alone, if they found them, and he knew that he would be able to count on Shyla to rescue them.

He could feel the anger welling in Shyla as the tortured memories of her past swirled around into a raging red vortex of thoughts. He decided now would be a good time to interrupt her thoughts, if anything he might be able to distract her just enough to help calm her down, put her in a tranquil peace of mind, only because he could feel how much it tortured her to be reminded.

● ● ●

"Can you meet us in the Kokrine hills just northeast of the Hughes? We'll make camp there and wait until you've joined us to continue forming plans." He directed the stream of words into her mind.

"Sure thing, maybe two hours," her thoughts responded quickly.

He hesitantly pulled his mind away from her thoughts making sure that she was no longer suffering the misery of her previous memories. Once he was freed from her mind, he realized that he hadn't spoken to Kam, other than to drag him along, on the mission.

Will knew that if they found the children at the Cyndac Oil Refinery, both he and Shyla would be planning an assault, possibly risking their lives. He knew that Shyla would defend the children with her life, but he could not say the same for Kam. Kam rarely spoke to anyone and hardly shared his feelings. Even though Will could read everyone's mind, he had a difficult time understanding Kam's thoughts clearly, and as a result rarely listened.

There was something mysterious about Kam, and the silence that he frequently demonstrated among the household confused and frustrated him. However, everyone had their tragic requisitioning and horrific torture anecdotes of the experimentations, and if one among them chooses to maintain silence and keep hidden the incident that brought them thus far, no one pestered for more information.

Kam was the only candidate seized, in which no one knew the story of how they found him, or where he came from. The professor wasn't involved in his capture, and unless he was on the appropriations team for the candidates, he wasn't informed of their mysterious appearances, nor did he ask. It was only until later, when he had escaped with several of the youths that they revealed their own grievous abduction stories to him and others on their own time.

Kam never revealed his story, and his mind was often processed using an ancient language and old thoughts, thoughts that didn't make sense for a person his age to have. Will had been able to discover that the language was rooted in Latin, and many of the thought pools he watched were of things he couldn't understand. People on horseback, villages burning, villages without cars and technology, women screaming, holding their babies, wrapped in dirty old rags, and gothic type clothing.

Will couldn't watch Kam's thoughts more than he had to; he resented ever having peered into his mind in the first place. Most evenings while everyone drifted away, fitfully into restless sleep, back before Will had total control of his mind reading ability, he sat outside, as he often did, in the courtyard, and peered into the minds of each of them. One by one, he'd try to practice blocking and accepting their thoughts. One particular evening he felt Kam's mind more strongly than the others and decided to use his for the practice.

As he opened up his mind, and peered deeply into Kam's subconscious, he was repulsed by the hazy fading inward vision reeling in his head, like a movie on a wide leather screen. A young man, tall, handsome, and stunning, but icy and pallid in complexion, with short earth brown hair and crystal blue eyes, dreamily drifted over the snow, much the same as he was doing now, following Will, only he wasn't following anyone, but appeared to be leading a small band of mercenaries. The three men and two women, following behind him, were dressed in the same elegant gold and black embroidered gothic coats and gowns that lightly concealed the same pasty white complexion that the first young man had, only their eyes were glowing red, and they seemed all too impatient to arrive at their destination.

Will assumed, while watching the memory, that maybe the man leading the group was a distant relative of Kam's because of the astounding similarities in their features, and that maybe this was a memory passed on from his relatives. If it were, he could most certainly understand why it haunts Kam so frequently.

As he watched further, the posse silently drifted over the deep snow, into a small village where a large crowd had formed, confronting them. The villagers appeared very angry and hostile towards the beautifully cold statues, drifting to greet them. A man walked forward, out of the crowd, bearing a smelting hammer at his side, and a trinket wrapped in one hand, dripping with blood.

The man shouted something at the icy figure, which Will couldn't understand, and held open the hand, carrying the trinket, in front of the elegantly composed icy statue. The possible ancestor of Kam muttered a few incomprehensible words to the man in a sharp accusing voice, and then, from out of the village crowd, a woman ran at the handsome man with a dagger.

In a blurred moment, one of the gowned women, from behind the leader, slid beside him, and reached out for the woman's arm. She wrenched the wrist carrying the dagger, and twisted her body around in such a way, that it shifted her neck between the icy woman's cold grasp, and then with a quick snap, the limp body fell, lifeless to the snowy ground.

The man carrying the bloodied trinket furrowed his brow in anger and clenched the hammer at his side tightly. He roared a vicious command out, and then all the men and women in the snowy village brought to arms the poorly assembled weapons they had clearly struggled to find.

In one quick instant, all mayhem had broken loose. The elegantly dressed posse that had accompanied Kam's ancestor, unleashed a furry of bloodlust. As if it were almost too easy for them, they delicately, but swiftly danced around the pool of villagers, literally eating the life out of them. Screams were mixed with roars of furry, as jugulars were torn out and throats ripped at.

The icy statues flowed from person to person unscathed, peeling back their lips and ravaging into the convulsing bodies of every last living being. Only one person stood by and watched callously the slaughter of the village. He hovered over the man with the trinket in hand, who had fallen to the ground on his knees beside his wife. As he gazed down at the weakened man, the man tossed the bloodied trinket at his feet and cursed him violently in the unidentified language, and then groped his wife into his arms and sobbed hysterically.

The handsomely tall figure brushed aside his embroidered coat, to reveal the golden and silver hilt of a sword, poking out past the sheath. In on graceful movement, he reached his hand down to the grip, drew the sword out, and sliced it straight through the space where the man's head was sobbing over his dead wife's body. The expression on the man's face went blank and then his head rolled over his neck and off the back of his body, crunching into the blood-stained snow below.

The cruel but handsome man barked some orders to the posse that had accompanied him, in the same incomprehensible language, and then turned away from the village and began to glide off. He stopped briefly to cleanse his sword in the earth, and then swiftly replaced it. He turned only once, after drifting away from the city, and Will could feel the sincerity of the sorrow that filled Kam's thoughts, as the icy cold statue watched billows of smoke, funnel out of the cottages and shops, and a poignant stench fill the air, as the bodies of the villagers were hurled on top, of an already decent pile of burning carcasses.

It was then that Will had gained almost irrevocable control of his ability to block out Kam's thoughts. And although he struggled greatly, to keep out the images and thoughts that haunted everyone else around him, he no longer had any fathomable desire to ever perceive Kam's mind again. Ever since that disturbing night, he never attempted to infiltrate Kam's conscious. As a matter of fact, he only ever uncomfortably spoke to Kam when he had an urgent question or needed to collaborate with him. Kam was a very private person, and although Will didn't understand a thing about him, he respected his privacy and allowed him his peace and quiet. Whatever troubled Kam was darker and more deeply rooted than any of the other kid's darkest secrets, and Will didn't want to know more than he had to, but unfortunately, he needed to talk to Kam.

Cautiously, Will opened up his mind and reached into the protective sheen of conscious, gliding far below him underneath a deep thicket of evergreen trees, and briefly watched the images forming inside. It was apparent that Kam was reminiscing in the past again.

He stood just inside the door of a nicely built log cabin hidden in the woods. Nestled inside his pale icy hand, was a dainty white wrist, bent forward as he reached his face down to kiss it. The woman's hand receded and then she nodded her head in approval, dropping her deep brown curly locks of hair forward, brushing against the sides of her face, and then gazed directly into his eyes. She muttered something, in that language Will didn't understand, and Kam responded.

He was stunned, fixating on her cyan eyes. Little clouds of magnolia rolled around her irises, hazing the delicate cyan, and leaving a sensual mystery to her presence. A finely chiseled nose dropped down below her two perfectly placed eyes, and two luscious puce lips beautifully formed together, complementing the delicate features of her face, all accenting the pale pearl color of her skin. All her features so absolutely perfect, were still no comparison to the swirling magnolia mists shrouding her cyan blue eyes.

Now was the time to interrupt his thoughts, now before anything became violent and unnatural.

○ ○ ○

"Kam," Will interrupted, breaking the trance that had held Kam's thoughts in a lifeless suspension.

"Why don't you get out of my head and speak to me on the ground, man to man." Kam hissed.

"Calm down man," Will replied.

"What?" Kam's thoughts formed into a recognizable response clouded with resentment.

"Shyla will be joining us in the Kokrine hills, realistically she'll probably make camp before we get there, and we'll have to keep a watch for her. I'm sure she'll hide us in a cave or something safe from aerial view.

"Now I know I haven't given you very much information on the assignment, so I'll do my best to fill you in. The professor wants me, you, and Shyla to scout out the Cyndac Oil Refinery. He'd like a head count of the guards and the scientists. He'd also like us to inspect the facility. If we find any children, he'd like a count on them and their health statuses, along with an account for any of the experimentations." There was a pause in the flow of Will's thoughts as he directed them to Kam.

"The professor doesn't want us interfering in any way, only gathering information. That is why he wanted Shyla to join us. With her ability to create invisible shields, we should be able to stay completely hidden from any cameras or guards. But. . . the thing is, if we find any children there, I have no intention of leaving them there, and I can't speak for Shyla but I'm sure she can't either. We both know how she feels about children, and how much she hates Major Bradshaw." There was another pause in the flow of his thoughts again, giving Kam a moment to process the information.

He watched the images fade one by one, over each other as they quickly slid out of Kam's mind. First an aerial view of the facility. Strangely a fairly accurate view of the facility, but Will was under the impression that none of them had ever been out this way, and so Kam's thoughts of the facility boggled him.

After the aerial view spun around the facility, giving a distant outline of the metal and stone structure, it was veiled under the next image of several men in white lab coats, cluttered together holding syringes and griping little squirming arms, arms of little children, children that were flailing and sobbing, crying for their parents, parents that had no idea where their beautiful little children had gone.

Then the thought was gone shadowed by guards in military uniforms, storming past gates and through doors wielding firearms and shouting fierce words to each other. The next vision made Will uneasy, knowing that the possibility was out there.

The guards swarmed around three people, the first with blood-stained tiger striped fur, and the fury of a tigress after her kill, was clutching a child, possibly no older than ten or eleven. The frail delicate little child, numb to the world around her, noticed absolutely nothing in the commotion, only gazing off as if she were stuck in a better place trapped within her mind.

The other was grasping at the floor, trying to stand up, as a guard pinned the end of his rifle directly over one of the battered light-tanned arms of the victim. Seconds later the rifle ricocheted back from the recoil and a bullet splattered traces of skin and blood away from the newly shredded hole in the arm. The man gave up struggling on the floor, and grasped the freshly injured arm, scooting closer to what he now knew was Shyla clutching one of the children.

It was only moments before another image joined the unsettling one already lingering inside Kam's mind. A picture of Major Bradshaw stepped into the other one, joining the two together and he saw as the guards parted around the Major, allowing him to present himself before the three bodies crouching together on the floor.

"Lock those two with the others," Major Bradshaw commanded, as three men tightly gripped Shyla, unable to pry the child from her arms, and towed her away, away from the thought, outside the range in which Will could see.

"And so," the major placed one of his feet, over the gaping bloodied hole of the arm, of the already badly battered man, struggling to sit up.

"Derek Ralph Willem, subject number 2 5 7, you've got something I want." The Major's words gushed with victory, as if he'd just won a bet and was owed a great deal of money.

"I don't know what you're talking about." Will tilted his blooded head up, spitting at the Major. The major glared at him for a moment, and then smashed down his foot hard on the injured arm, grinding it painfully into the floor. Will groaned in pain, struggling to bring about enough strength to fight back, but failed horribly.

The thought vanished away, covered neatly by a visual image of the snow-covered ground and the dusted trees outside, as Kam swiftly passed around them, rapidly gliding below Will.

"Kam please keep those kinds of thoughts to yourself, I'm already very anxious. Anyway, I'm not forcing you to stay, but if we find the children, I will hope that you might choose to help. I'm not going to make you decide anything right now, just think about it please?" And then Will released his mind, never soon enough, closing the sheen of conscious, regaining control of his own observations, fully settling back into his flying, completely aware of his surroundings.

Will flew through the air with immense speed, utilizing every last gust of wind that might save him a beat or two with his enormous silver wings, much the way a crow would utilize the updrafts coming off of a forest fire to soar for pray. He barely rose above the glinting white treetops of the snow-covered evergreens, making every effort to conceal being spotted in the air of the morning light. The sun was in a nine o'clock position, slowly rising to greet the day, it would only be too soon before the three of them were together, in the hills and setting up camp for the night. Luckily for all of them, they would have plenty of daylight to get comfortable, before the evening sun set.

He quickly tried to clear away the uneasy thoughts that preoccupied Kam, remembering back to the intense and inhuman mesmerizing gaze of the woman he originally saw in his thoughts. Who was she and why was Kam so hypnotized by her, he wondered? He'd remembered when Kam's head was full of blood and lust and pure evil, and the way he had wanted so absolutely to be rid of his mind, but now he was intrigued. He was just as intrigued by the woman of Kam's thoughts as Kam had been, but also terrified by the bloody pessimistic turns that his thoughts often took.

Will considered sneaking another look into Kam's mind, but knowing how utterly fuming Kam would become, and unsure of the images that might be clouding his mind now; he decided that peering into his mind with his nerves already as agitated as they were, was a bad idea and could wait another time.

Will was confused and alarmed, with all of the negativity that encompassed Kam it was a wonder people didn't like him. He'd realized that no one in the Chateau ever gave Kam a moment's notice. It was usual to ignore him, allowing him to go about his day, as if he didn't exist, but that could probably explain his latent hostility and lack of desire to confide in any of the other affected. Aside from the strange but close connection Kam formed over the years with Esa Rosa, he might as well have never existed.

Of course, Esa was a very considerate darling girl, and the years of torture and experimentations didn't make her an angry resentful type of character, as it did the rest of them, and as a result the kindness and sincere relationships that she built with all of them, it was no surprise when she formed a close connection with Kam. And although Kam appeared irritated and annoyed by the presence of most of the affected, slightly less so by the professor, he really did appreciate Esa's company and must have confided quite a great deal in her, this of course irritated Will. Of all the people that Will absolutely couldn't read, Esa had to be the one. The one person who would have all the information he needed on any one of them, easily being able to explain Kam's strange and pessimistic thoughts, and she had to be the closed mind, sealed like a book. She might as well have been a bank vault to him, for whatever reason he couldn't read her mind.

Will paused for a brief moment, browsing the rough terrain ahead, interrupting the natural flow of thoughts streaming through his head, to realize that Kam had disappeared. He knew that Kam wasn't crazy about going against the professor's orders, and that he'd much prefer if they just scouted out the prison center, but he never imagined that Kam would ditch out on them.

As silent and mysterious as Kam was, Will always considered him a fighting warrior type, protect and defend sort, not a cowardly sniveling dog, running away with its tail between its legs. Something was wrong, and although he couldn't quite put his finger on it, he wasn't practiced with Kam's mind enough to find out where he'd gone. All those years of practicing keeping out of Kam's mind, ignoring its every thought flow, and now he wasn't familiar enough with it to find it.

Unsure of what to do, he reached out for the most familiar and most welcoming mind he'd ever viewed and spoke to, Shyla.

"He's gone," he alarmed Shyla, watching as a swirly haze of confusion swept over her mind.

"Gone, what do you mean gone?" The words formed across the haze of confusion.

"I was drifting deep into thought and when I browsed around, I'd lost sight of him." He sent the words into her mind.

● ● ●

"Well, can't you just find his mind and figure out from there, where he's gone?" The words sped through her mind again.

"Normally I'd say yes, but in his case I'm not familiar with his mind, the fact of the matter is, I've been sort of training myself for years to ignore it, and now I can't find him." He answered, annoyed at himself now, more than at Kam for leaving them.

He could see the hesitation form in Shyla's mind, the words "why have you been, never mind," flowed quickly through her mind and then faded out.

"It'll be fine, let's just meet up like we planned and move from there. Who knows, maybe he'll turn up, it's not like he doesn't know where we're meeting." She clearly thought, as Will read her mind.

"Alright, I'm not far off from there anyway." He explained, the comment drifting effortlessly into Shyla's all too familiar mind, and then added. "How about you, where are you at?"

As he was soaring silently, above a range of blue and white mountain caps, he watched in a half daze, both focusing on his flying and focusing in Shyla's mind. A snicker rolled through her thoughts, and then a cliff side blurred into view. First, a cave popped into view, and then a distant view of the Cyndac Oil Refinery slid into her mind.

"What's this, you're already there?" He asked, surprised.

"Of course, silly, we both know that I'm fast, and with my invisibility, I can take the most direct paths, without concern of being noticed by humans." He read the words as they moved around inside her head, fading in as quickly as they faded out, leaving the clearly painted picture of her location as if he were looking through her eyes at the scene around.

Shyla and Will had always been very close friends, directly resulting from the painfully clear memories that haunted Shyla both day and night. Willem understood Shyla and suffered alongside her reoccurring memories always watching as they attacked her sleep. She found comfort in his knowing, and he ardently reassured her, always finding ways to make her feel loved. They loved each other greatly, but it was a love that a brother would share with a sister, only the deepest compassion and feelings of protection overwhelmed him.

As a result of their closeness, Shyla was extremely familiar with how Will read minds, and knew that he didn't exactly hear what was being said in the mind, but that he saw the images better and could read what was being thought more clearly, if it was being thought into streams of legible writing. That's why she would often imagine the words and streams of sentences when she responded to the thoughts, in his inquiring mind. Rather than struggling to listen to her thoughts, as quietly whispered sentences, barely understandable, he simply had to read the words she produced in her mind, making his job easier, as he found that some people naturally did.

"Well, I guess I'll see you there then." The words sort of muttered into Shyla's mind as if he were mumbling in thought. Kam better show up, he thought, worried that what he saw in his mind, might have urged him to flee, and then decided that there was no sense in dwelling.

Will was getting close; he could tell by the familiarity of the terrain he saw in Shyla's mind. He browsed the hillsides, scouting out his position, from where he had seen Shyla's base camp. Even though he wasn't worried about the townspeople accidentally catching a view of him, he decided he'd better play it safe, and hit the ground for the rest of the run. If anyone from the facility suspected that they were being watched, they'd check the air. It'd be the first place they'd look, so landing on the ground and running the rest of the way was safest for him.

He folded his long wings back and arched his body into a dive, like an eagle aiming for a fish, and then just as he passed below the tips of the treetops, he swung his tail forward, pulling with it both his legs. He stretched out both wings, wide and graceful, slowing his dive into a calculated precise landing that only birds manage with such ease. His two large raptor shaped feet crunched into the snow and his wings folded together, just enough so that he could clasp them around his chest, like a cape, and then began running rapidly through the snow hoping to make camp before noon.

Chapter XV: Hughes Estate

"Can't anyone tell me what the hell has happened to Taylor?" Jake shouted in a loud demanding voice, at the police officers scattered about the room in the station. Two were chitchatting across from each other, and a third sat in a swivel chair rolled up beside them.

"Boy, watch your mouth, or we're gonna kick you out of here!" A fourth police officer shouted from inside a room. Jake didn't realize it, but the Chief was watching him through a large glass window, of his office. "Kid what are you fussing about anyway." He motioned for Jake to enter his office.

Jake turned to an officer sitting legs kicked up, on a desktop and snuffed at him. "Thanks for nothing, jackass," mumbling the last word under his breath as he walked off towards the Chief's office.

"Now tell me kid, why are you down here again, causing a scene?" The Chief asked.

"I just want to know what's happened to Taylor. Everyone knows about that house burning prank in Maine, but that was where she moved. I mean, she was all over the news for a while with that whole healing thing, and then her house burnt down. . . I mean what is this all about, and why can't anyone tell me a damn thing?" Jake nearly screamed at the Police Chief.

"Kid, it's not that we don't care or anything like that, it's just that it's not our district. It's not even our state. Even if we wanted to help out, we can't. Just let it go, I'm sure someone will give you a call in the future. Quit worrying." He stressed, not particularly interested in the boy's fit.

"Quit worrying? What the hell are you talking about, both her grandparents are at the hospital and in bad enough condition that the doctors won't let me talk to them, and no one will comment on her disappearance. They won't even say if she died in the fire or what? I mean, isn't this state kind of responsible for her anyway, if her grandparents can't take care of her. Doesn't the whole foster care system have to reclaim responsibility for her if the place that they sent her to, fails?" Jake shouted some more, pacing back and forth in the office refusing to sit or calm down. "I just want to know if she's alive, damn-it." He slammed a tightly balled fist down on the desk, startling the Chief.

"I don't know kid, but if you think the state has some sort of responsibility for her then you might want to talk to someone down at the courthouse. They probably know more about custody issues. If it'll shut you up, I can make some phone calls and see what I can find out, okay?" He assured Jake, hoping that a phone call here or there might shut him up enough to get him out of the office, not to mention the silent curiosity nagging at the back of his head. It did appear that the kid might be onto something. The girl on the news had seemed to be pretty popular there for a while, with that old Major coming in, looking for her and then the odd arsine prank, who knows, maybe something was up, or maybe he was just getting a little senile in his old age, but there was no harm in making a few phone calls especially if it would shut the boy up.

"Alright, but I'll be back tomorrow to see if you've found anything out." He threatened, hoping that it would put a little haste in the Chief's inquiries.

He watched as Jake left the room, making sure he didn't hassle any more of the police officers on his way out. Once he was gone, he rolled open a drawer in his desk, and pulled out a small white card with the name Major James Bradshaw, United States Army, traced onto the white card in gold leaf scroll and on the flip side of the card two phone numbers, printed in black ink. He picked up the phone and dialed the first number, listening to the phone ringing on the other end, until someone finally answered it.

"This is my private line, who is this?" A deep masculine voice answered, agitated.

"Hey this is Chief Patrick, at the Port Angeles Police Station. You told me if I needed to get a hold of you for anything to just call and you gave me your card." The Chief said.

"Right, well, what do you need?" Major Bradshaw confidently forced the words out.

"There's been this kid in the office, and he won't quit bugging us. I'm starting to wonder if he's on to something. Did you ever find Taylor Saskia, after you left here? I know you were looking for her, and I figure if you ever found her you would probably know best where she is right now or whether she was caught up in the fire." He asked cautiously.

"I'm sorry; I'm not sure who you are talking about, who's been asking again?" Major Bradshaw lied.

"Just some kid, claims to know her. He's been an awful pain in the ass." Chief Patrick responded but hesitated to say Jake's name. The Major had obviously known something and was hiding it, so something was seriously up. That left the Chief a bit worried for Jake's safety, and hesitant to tell him anymore information.

"Well, get that boy's name and call me back when you have it, if you please. I'm sure I can talk some common sense into him. Otherwise, please don't call me at this number again." Major Bradshaw stated and then quickly hung up the phone, leaving him listening to a buzzing noise at the other end of the line. The Chief was quite the opposite of pleased with the phone call. He'd called hoping to get a simple answer about the health status of Taylor Saskia, but instead hung up, wondering if there was some sort of large-scale government cover-up going on, and whether Major Bradshaw was at the head of it. Unsure of where that left him, he decided to make a few phone calls, possibly contacting the hospital where the girl's grandparents were being held. If he was lucky, one of the doctors would know some more information and at the least, whether or not Taylor was in the fire.

The Chief spun around in his chair facing the front door of his office, startled to find Jake staring at him. The boy must have forgotten something, how long was he standing there? He thought to himself.

"Sorry I forgot. . . I have the hospital's phone number - thought maybe it would help. I've tried calling but they won't release any information to me, maybe you would have more luck." Jake paused for a minute. "Was that the military guy that was trying to question me and Joe a while ago?" Jake asked curious, but in a much calmer fashion than his only minutes earlier confrontation. "I don't think he's gonna be much help, he seems to want more information than he gives. He wouldn't answer any of my questions when he was here a while ago." Jake offered, fumbling with a paper weight on the Chief's desk and then placing it down, alongside a piece of paper he had with the hospital's phone number and a few other ones scribbled in nearly illegible script, along with their names and addresses.

"Yeah, I noticed. He wasn't particularly helpful. These will be more helpful," he said looking at the piece of paper, briefly reading through the names. "Randolph Police Station, Gardiner Police Station, Fire Department, Augusta Hospital, Dr. Mathews. . . Yeah I'll try some of these, thanks kid." He commented, giving Jake a mild half smile as if something was still bothering him underneath the halfhearted efforts to appear thankful.

Jake turned and made his way out the door just before the Chief gave him one last quick comment.

"Do me a favor and stay out of trouble for a while, will ya kid?" He hollered to him in the hallway, hoping that Jake caught the comment.

To his surprise Jake turned and responded, "Sure, don't worry about me, and just figure out what's up with Taylor, okay?" And then Jake flipped his head around and continued out the door.

Jake wondered what was up with the Chief, he seemed so uneasy, and he had a hint of anxiety lingering in his voice, when he stepped back into the room. Of course, he considered that he might feel the same way after talking with Major Bradshaw, that guy was the embodiment of fear. Something about the Major made everyone feel inferior and nervous, like no matter how many years something was right, he could come along, tell a person it was wrong, and then they would begin to doubt themselves, and everything they believed in.

At least the Chief was going to try and help, no one else would even listen to him, not at the school, or down at the courthouse, or even at the department of social and health services. Jake was glad that the Chief appeared nervous, maybe he had found out something that would motivate him to find more information about Taylor. After all, he was just a kid and probably an annoying one, the way he'd been harassing all of the authority figures, but at least it paid off, and now the Police Chief was going to help him out, at least a little.

He left the police station on foot, heading back to his house, but decided to stop off at the Safeway on Lincoln Street, and pick up a snack before heading home. He'd normally drive but ever since he was arrested at the police station last month, both his parents had been in agreement on the punishment; sadly, the first thing they'd agreed on since the divorce, and decided to remove his driving privileges for the rest of the school year.

He walked up the large, paved parking lot, past the little gas station on the downhill side, and then up to the front of the store. He caught a glimpse of some of the vehicles parked in the lot, three or four Toyotas, a couple Fords, several Chevy trucks, and a large black Sedan pulling through the lot. He didn't see the more expensive vehicles often; most people had energy efficient cars or gas guzzling trucks, but once in a while he'd see an expensive Denali or Yukon or something like that, often driven by the older women that didn't want to be identified as soccer mom types in the town.

Jake ignored the cars, and small group of kids, kicking a hacky sack out front, and went inside for some doughnuts. Once he'd collected a couple of Boston Creams and a sour cream glazed doughnut, he headed for the cash register. He pulled out a soda from one of the cashiers stand mini fridges and tossed it onto the conveyor belt.

"How you doing?" The cashier brushed the comment out as if he'd said it a million times in the last hour.

"Fine," Jake responded, and then something caught his attention from the corner of his eyes.

"Four and seventy-eight cents," the cashier said.

Jake fumbled through his pocket and handed a five to the cashier keeping his eyes focused on the distraction. The large black Sedan had stopped outside the store, and a man in a nice black and white business suit was holding a square piece of paper and asking the kids with the hacky sack some questions.

"Thanks," Jake naturally responded to the cashier, as he handed him his twenty-two cents back and grabbed his snack to exit the doors.

Curious but wanting to keep a distance, Jake took the doors on the further side of the store, hoping to avoid any bothering questions, like the kids playing sac were getting, but as he stepped outside and turned nonchalantly towards the scene one of the kids pointed towards him and said, "sure that's him over there. I just saw him go in there a minute ago."

It happened so quickly Jake wasn't even sure if it really happened. The nicely dressed man pointed directly at him and hollered, "There, now."

The large black Sedan sped over to the curbside, simultaneously both the front and rear passenger doors opened and something sharp and painful smacked him, hard and deep directly under his chin. A haze of cloudiness began to saturate his visions and thoughts, and then he passed out just before watching two men surround him, catching his limp body before it hit the ground.

He didn't know how much time had passed, but Jake began to feel the stinging sensation that was left after the tranquillizer bullet had been removed from his neck. He found his body feeling normal, other than the stinging pain and a kink in his neck, usually caused from sleeping in a strange position. He couldn't quite open his eyes, but sat and listened, finding that someone was talking.

"Hey, I think he's coming to," one raspy voice commented.

"That's good; I think he'll really be able to help us find Taylor, especially given the proper means." Another gentler voice responded.

Jake rather curious now, found the strength to open his eyes and look around the room. He was slumped over, in a large brown leather chair, which would explain the cramp in his neck, arranged along with two large leather brown sofas and another chair around a coffee table. The room was large with an old den style fireplace, and tanned walls supporting various hunting trophies, including a large five-point buck head hanging above the mantle. The carpets were deep red, tying the room together, giving it that after dinner retire to the men's parlor for drinks and smokes, feel.

There were three men gathered in the room, one on a sofa, one in the other chair, and one standing beside a window.

"Jacob Anthony Stevens? Am I correct?" The man sitting in the chair asked.

Unwilling to argue, and not entirely sure what had happened, or what was going on around him, he answered the older man, politely. "Yes, that's me. May I ask what this is all about?" Jake fumbled with his question, unsure of whether he had any right to ask questions in the first place.

"We'll get to that in a minute, I'm Mike O'Neal," the man standing by one of the windows butted in, moving over towards the couch, where one of the other men were sitting, and continued to speak with the raspy voice he'd heard earlier. "This here's Jim, and the man over on the chair is Russet." He pointed at the man, lounging in the brown leather chair, smoking a cigar. He stepped over to Jake with a glass of water and some pills, which he'd lifted off the coffee table.

"Take these please, they'll help ease the stinging in your neck." He waved his hand forward opening his palm, revealing the two pills that looked exactly like extra strength Tylenol that his mom always took around that time of the month to relieve cramps, or at least that's what she'd say.

Jake glanced up and down at the man, acting as if inspecting the man's features would trigger some form of trust, or at least quell the distrust that shuddered through his mind. The man was tall and pronounced, carrying himself with the utmost confidence. He had a military high and tight hair cut, keeping his receding brown hair close to his head and matching brown eyes of no ordinary brilliance. His face was featured naturally, and if the man was younger and they were friends, they would always have had to compete to get girls, but the man was much older with lines of experience displayed on his face and knuckles.

With no sudden bursts of trust flowing into Jake's mind, he snatched the pills and chased them down his throat with the glass of water, fearing that ignoring the man's gesture might cause extra avoidable tension in the room. Once he was finished with the water the man reached over to the coffee table, picking up a folder from a small pile and dropped it onto Jake's lap.

"Taylor Saskia," he commented, dusting off a place on the couch and then sitting down against the side arm. "What do you know about her?" He asked?

Jake flipped open the folder and browsed through all the paperwork nestled inside. He found records of Taylor's birth, school's she attended, personal incidents that occurred with her parents that put her into foster care, which he'd never known, and paused to read more specifically through the information.

Date March 1st, 1999: Police arrived responding to house call at 3:45 am. No one answered the door, officer entered house, found mother: Eleanor Mandy Trevor – maiden name, behind couch dead on arrival, with large puncture wound on chest and kitchen knife coated in blood beside body. Young child was found name: Taylor Saskia; age eight, grasping the body, with a large bruise along forehead and several others found along the arms and inner thighs. Child was given to the on sight EMT and later tested for rape. Continued search on house and found in back room, father: Paul Martin Saskia, dead on arrival as well. Found large empty bottle of whisky on reading table beside empty bottle of sleeping pills.

Wow, that's horrible, he thought to himself. He'd never known anything as detailed about Taylor as this, she always told everyone that her parents died in a car accident when she was little and that she didn't remember much about it. Both him and Joe considered that enough information, and never bothered with troubling questions about her parents, but this police report was much worse.

As if a light just clicked on in his head, he suddenly understood why Taylor was so hard to read, why every time he looked into those beautiful black eyes of hers, he would see a hollowed pit of pain; such an unfathomable pain that it would cast a shadow over her soul to hide the very essence of her being. She was hiding the pain of her life, the murder of her mother and the evil crimes of her father, and she was probably hiding them so that she could endure her life, empty and alone.

Jake interrupted his own thoughts and closed the folder sprawled on his lap. He looked up to the man, now sitting on one side of the couch, Mike was his name, and asked, "all this stuff, um, personal information" he paused. "What does it have to do with me?" He was confused and began to wonder how angry Taylor would be if she ever found out that he knew about her parents.

"Well, boy," the man in the chair, Russet, responded. "Taylor has gotten mixed up into some pretty serious business, bad sort of business, you see. She's come into possession of a very powerful object, one that she stole from our labs. It's extremely powerful and ultimately very dangerous, especially in the hands of a kid who is just trying to sell it for some money."

"What? Steal something so she can sell it for money. What kind of crap is this? Maybe she's gotten into trouble for drinking a couple of times, but she doesn't steal." Jake responded defensively, taken aback by the possibility that Taylor might have changed a little, maybe gotten desperate, and resorted to stealing for money. Would she really do that? He wondered.

"Just listen Jacob," the man on the other side of the couch insisted. He remembered his name was Jim, calming back down, and listened to the rest, desperately trying to figure out the changes, if indeed they had occurred, that had transformed Taylor's personality so much that she would steal, and not only steal, but steal something so important to these guys that they would go to great lengths to get it back.

"She's a good kid. Don't get me wrong, just mixed up with the wrong crowd, understand? Regardless, we need help finding her, and retrieving the stone." Russet explained, in his deeper toned voice.

"Can't you just snatch her up, like you did me, and take it back, no harm done?" Jake asked.

"It's not that simple. She doesn't know, but the man she's hiding with is a dangerous renegade. A well-known killer, and on the FBI's most wanted list. He lures younger men and women into doing his biding for him, such as stealing from the government, and then once their task is done, he disposes of them, once and for all, destroying all evidence of their existence or their connection to his crime. If she is as easily coaxed as the others, then she'll already have been tricked into a false sense of security with the man, and we'll have a hard time getting her to reveal any useful information, if we are even lucky enough to pry her away from his yet to be found location." Russet strategically lied to Jake. The goal was to win his confidence so that they could use him to lure Taylor away from Dr. Ambler and into their clutches. Once they have her, then they can take the stone from her, by any means necessary, and rejoin it with the rest of the stone.

"Honestly," Jim commented, "We're a little concerned about Taylor's safety. She's only useful to the man until he gets what she has, so she must be keeping it safely from him, and we need to find her before he gets it."

"Kills her, someone is going to kill Taylor?" Jake fumed. "Of course, I'll help you, if it means helping Taylor." He declared, with all traces of distrust washed away like a sandcastle under the ocean's high tide. The imminent possibility of his best friend and secret crush's death sent a burning sensation of purpose through his blood boiling body. He was now suddenly ready to die for Taylor, die to save her life, die, if he had too.

"So how will I be able to help?" He asked, curious of what they had in store, completely unaware of the evil trap he'd just become part of.

"If you are willing to help us, then I would prefer you get cleaned up and fed before we continue this conversation. After you eat, we'll take you down to the labs and explain everything along with some of the intricate details we left out and you'll need to know." Russet stated, obviously pleased that they'd gained Jake's allegiance.

All three men nodded to each other in agreement to some unspoken comment, and then Jim and Russet left the room together, leaving the anxious and worried Jake, alone with the overconfident and exceptionally energetic older man, Mike.

"Now, Jake, if you'll come with me, I can set you up into a comfortable room where you can stay for a while. Russet spoke with your parents, and they have agreed to comply. They are sworn to confidence and mustn't speak with you while you're working for us. It's imperative that no one know about the work we do here. It's strictly classified, besides what you'll find out, and the men you see working with us, and the president, very few have any idea that we even exist, and it must remain that way, understand?" Mike changed the tone of his raspy voice to one of questioning.

"Yes," Jake hesitated, "Sir," he said cutting off his comment. Mike's presence seemed to demand a certain level of respect in addressing him, even though Jake wasn't used to speaking so formally.

They left the comfortable parlor room and walked down a wide hallway with the same familiar bachelor atmosphere. Instead of light airy colors and paintings with flowers or landscapes, the top half of the wall was painted in a sodden blue and the bottom half in a rustic red. Halfway down the hall, they stopped at a cream-colored door.

"You can stay in this room, shower and dress, and make sure to eat. You have an hour before I come back to get you so make it snappy." Mike said, turning away from the door and continuing down the hall, until he disappeared.

Jake stepped into the room, quickly pulling off his tacky brown and green long-sleeved shirt and pulling off his pants. He ran the facet in the adjacent bathroom tub, until the water was warm enough to start a shower. After shuffling through some cabinets in the bathroom to find a towel, he jumped into the shower, and soaped up as quickly as possible.

He was glad to know that Taylor wasn't dead and didn't get caught in the house fire. That's more than he'd ever expected to find out, he wondered how he was supposed to find her. If they didn't know where she was, then how was he supposed to find her? He finished showering while he was thinking about the possibilities. What would he say to her, after he finds her? How would he warn her about the man she's been living with? Being as stubborn as she was, would she even listen?

Finishing his shower, and draping the towel around his waist, he rubbed off his hair, staring into a mirror above the sink, watching as his golden-brown hairs, tightly spun back into small curls clinging closely to his head. Would Taylor even care about him anymore? Or had she changed so much, that it wouldn't matter if he tried to talk to her? He wondered, wiping away some steam built up on the mirror, and glanced into the cold blue eyes of his reflection. She'd been caught up with such a bad crowd that she didn't even seem like the same person anymore, from what he could understand, anyway.

He walked over to the dresser, pulling open a drawer to see if there might be anything he can wear. The top drawer was full of socks. The second one surprised him, full of neatly folded jeans on one side, and simple single colored polo shirts on the other, and they were all just his size. He pulled out a green polo and pair of jeans from the second drawer and paired them with some white socks from the first. After quickly dressing, he caught a glimpse of the clock, and sat down on the bed, pulling an old pair of sneakers on, until Mike had returned.

"You ready in there, kid?" He asked outside the door.

"Yeah, hold on a sec," he shouted out, tying the remaining shoe.

Jake leapt off of the bed and swung open the door, finding himself, nose to knuckles, just as Mike was about to knock on the door again.

"A little impatient, are we?" Jake exclaimed.

"No, just in a hurry, the longer we wait the more people are put in danger." Mike harshly corrected.

"Oh, sorry," Jake finished.

"Did you eat something," Mike looked at Jake, watching for a response. Jake shook his head no, wondering when on earth Mike thought he might have had time to eat.

"Didn't think so, I picked up some food on my way back here, you can eat it in the car ride to the labs." Mike said, and then silently escorted Jake out of the estate. As they left the oddly comfortable bachelor pad, they were joined by two other men; one was easily recognizable as Russet, but the other wasn't familiar at all.

They left the estate together, and the nameless man opened the rear passenger door to another large black sedan, motioning Jake to take a seat. He climbed inside, sitting silently, while everyone else finished slamming the doors closed, and then the driver quickly pulled a couple of miles down a road along the estate.

"Jake, you need to understand a few things before we go into the lab, okay?" Mike interrupted.

"Sure. I'm committed until Taylor is safe, so you don't have to worry about me backing out." Jake exclaimed, browsing out the window at the approaching white cement building. It reminded him of a prison, only there was a large patch of transformers in one corner of the building outside and 'dangerous high voltage' signs on the fencing. Everything was covered in snow, not like in Port Angeles, were everything was wet and overcast, but here, the sky was clear, and the sun shone, but there was a chill outside and the ground was blanketed with layers of snow.

"First, I'd like to remind you that everything you see in the labs is top secret and that you must take a confidentiality oath before entering. Nothing you see here exists, okay?" Mike said, smirking, which made Jake feel a little excited.

"In the labs you will see, umm, what should I call it, genetic engineering at its best? The government came across a specimen some sixty years ago, a stone specimen, similar to a large diamond, but with extraordinary genetic manipulation abilities. We've been enhancing human aspects to make us perfect. With the use of the stone, we have been able to restore broken bones, regenerate lost limbs, and cure fatal diseases, even cancers in all of our patients. I'll let you see for yourself but the medicinal uses from this stone are endless." Mike thickly disguised his well laid out lie with hopeful hints of a bright new future for humans, one without sickness and disease, and Jake readily ate it up, like a mouse eating rat poison.

"That sounds amazing, so why is it dangerous then?" Jake asked, as the sedan was pulling up alongside the facility. He noticed a large wooden sign that was pounded into the ground a few feet from the front of the vehicle with large, engraved letters stating, 'Welcome to the Hughes Cyndac Oil Refinery, Refining some of the purest oil in the country.' He thought it was quite clever that the labs were disguised as an oil refinery.

"Don't be alarmed by the – side effects – we'll say, most are reversible with a special treatment," he continued his clever and complicated, completely made-up lie. "And as you will be able to see for yourself, there are potentially very dangerous side effects. You will understand more when you see them, trust me."

"Okay . . ." Jake hesitated, somewhat confused by the mixed messages he was picking up. "How will I be able to help, I mean suppose we can't even find Taylor, then what?"

"I don't think that will be a problem, the stone that she has is like a honing beacon, and with the piece that we have, we can use it to target her position more specifically."

"So why haven't you done that already than?" Jake asked, again confused by their need for his presence.

"Like I already said, delicacy is needed in this situation. She may not have the stone on her person and in any means may be unwilling to help us if she has in fact been persuaded by Dr. Ambler. We need you to find her and coax her back to us, safely and secretly. If he finds out someone is helping her, you both might be in danger." Jake could sense the irritation in Mike's tone of voice; maybe he would finish asking questions for now.

Jake watched as a series of numbers were pushed into a small panel attached to the main door. Once the doors unlocked, and finished sliding open, they all went inside and waited until the doors slammed closed again. Two men sitting in chairs, glanced up at them and then back down, systematically, left to right, looking at what must have been security monitors. Past the reception desk were several large doors along the back wall, they were all closed with little keypads implanted in the wall beside each, similar to the main entrance.

They waited for an elevator inside the main lobby, but then only Mike and Jake entered. The other two men that accompanied them inside, continued down the corridor, both splitting off into different sides of the reception desk, disappearing as the elevator doors closed.

"Where are they going?" Jake asked, forgetting that he wasn't going to ask any more questions for a while.

"They've got some work to manage in the holding suites. As for us, Major Bradshaw is awaiting us down in the number two blue room lab. I believe you have spoken to the Major before, am I correct?" Mike asked, while watching the elevator levels pass by.

The elevator dropped six levels underground before it finally stopped at the B level.

"Yes, um, he questioned me a while ago about some strange power surge, but I really had no idea what he was talking about. I was really only in trouble for drinking." Jake volunteered the information, more than Mike cared to hear.

Jake got the impression that Mike was forcing the small talk, not particularly interested in anything Jake had to say, as if this was just another job for him, another job to locate and entertain some random kid. The idea sent a chill down Jake's back. It seemed odd that someone could become so callous.

"What's the B stand for?" Jake asked.

The doors slid open and no more than eight feet in front of Jake was a large white wall with a huge two-foot blue horizontal stripe painted all the way down it, and in large blue letters above the stripe were the words 'Blue Sector.'

"Oh, never mind," he blushed and quickly mumbled loud enough so that Mike wouldn't respond to his obviously stupid question.

They immediately turned left down the hallway. It was a hallway among many hallways it seemed, and then continued until they found a room with a blue painted steel door and keypad implanted in the wall next to it, with the number four inscribed on the heavy metal door.

"Boy, security is really tight around here," Jake hinted at a joke, which apparently was not funny to Mike, because he looked down at Jake with disapproving eyes.

"Security is no laughing matter here, as your presence being required to obtain something already stolen from us, proves. Please contain yourself in the presence of Major Bradshaw, he will consider you a soldier, and as such, you must act like one." Mike's dawning presence suddenly changed to a more confident soldiering one as he punched in the pass code on the keypad.

Jake sighed, wondering if Mike would always be so unpleasant, and then tried diligently like a good little boy to pull a more serious face, hoping to ease Mike's edgy temperament.

The large metal door echoed a click from behind, and then began whirring as it slid open, disappearing into the wall. Jake took all of about half a second to make certain of the figures inside the room and then jumped back, slamming with fright into the door across the hall.

"What the hell?" Jake yelled, absolutely alarmed, his heart racing. He stood plastered to the door for more than a minute forcing his body to obey his mind, trying desperately to calm down. When finally, he felt the blood rushing back to his fingertips and toes, he swallowed hard and just starred at the six, straight from hell, gargoyle like creatures gathered around the table inside the room, hardly making notice of Mike or Major Bradshaw, calmly standing just inside the doorway greeting each other warmly.

Chapter XVI: Cyndac Oil Refinery

After a few moments, Mike quickly returned to Jake, leaning close to his ear and whispered, "I thought I asked you to keep it under control? Remember I was telling you about the side effects?" He stressed.

Jake swallowed hard, realizing that he hadn't prepared for something this massive, something so gruesome. Eyes still locked on the six figures in front of him he searched through his memory for the conversation he had with Mike and found the one he was looking for. "I – uh – thought you said the side effects were reversible?" He choked out the words as calmly as possible, taking deep long breaths, hoping to slow his heartbeat.

After a few moments he regained enough self awareness that he was able to pull away from the door he had plastered himself to.

"There are, only we need the stolen portion of the stone to reverse them. These were six of my best men, injured in battle years ago, when they finally volunteered for the experiments, we gladly excepted them knowing that injured war heroes deserve proper, if not the best care possible." Mike explained while Jake cautiously stepped into the number four blue room lab, keeping a close proximity to the wall.

He browsed over each figure first, taken aback by the all too familiar humanlike features each creature contained, noting the distinctions silently in his head, between the colors of the skin, if you could call it skin, and the shapes of the wings, wild and elegant, and or course who could forget the tails, strangely familiar, but not something you would find on a human, as Major Bradshaw made the introductions.

"Jacob Stevens, good to meet you again," Major Bradshaw caught Jake off guard with a handshake and then quickly released it motioning to the other bodies in the room.

"You've been getting acquainted with my old friend Mike here," he commented, throwing a hand over Mike's shoulder roughly patting him like a good dog.

Jake nodded.

"Now you will get the pleasure of meeting some of the best fighters I've ever had the satisfaction of working with." The Major bragged, as if he were showing off all the old trophies he'd won.

"First Lieutenant Rachel Dawson," the first gargoyle at the left side of the table tipped its spiny bone notched head forward, in acknowledgment. Her teal green eyes glaring directly at Jake, slightly shadowed by her bone etched brows that protruded like crowns over each eye, made him feel uncomfortable. And although she was horrifying, there was also small traces of human features that made her distinctly woman, and frightfully beautiful, in a nonhuman sort of way.

"Nice . . . to meet you," she hissed, like a snake, and then returned to her stance at attention behind the table.

"Second Lieutenant Matt Marshall," the Major motioned to the next figure, vastly similar to the first, minus the female attributes.

"Pleasure, I'm sure," he hissed as well, making no other acknowledgment of his presence, never breaking his stance at attention. He too like Lt. Dawson, appeared bone carved and spiky, with bones protruding from strange areas, like the eyebrows, and shoulders. His body was the same teal green color as Lt. Dawson, but rather than scales, his skin appeared to be a very rich leather, and just slightly deeper toned that Lt. Dawson.

Before Major Bradshaw made anymore introductions Jake peered quickly to the others and noticed one thing, they all had in common, their skin tones matched the tones of their eyes only separated from the gray tone that would normally be the whites of someone's eyes. They all seemed to have wings and tails, although he couldn't see them on the ones hidden behind the table. And although their eyes matched their skin tones, none of them had the same exact skin tone or texture, like he'd already noticed with Lt. Dawson and Marshall with the differences being that of scale or velvet leather.

"Captains, Sean Paul, and Seth Paul, brothers of course," the Major Continued, noticing little of the changes of Jakes face as he fixated on each strangely unique gargoyle in front of him.

"Watch out, I bite," the one on the right lurched at him. Jake could only assume it was Sean, by the order of the introduction. Jake stepped back startled by the gesture, gasping for a breath.

"Ha ha ha, he's only kidding kid," the second one broke down in laughter, which must have been Seth, obviously pleased with his brother's act.

"Oh, ha ha, yeah. . . that was funny," Jake forced out a weak laugh, glancing first at the gray leather body of Sean and then back to the splotched silver and white body of Seth, hopefully not blushing from the embarrassment. This broke the ice, a little, easing the tension in the room. Because although Jake was staring at six basically well mannered, obedient and somewhat normal soldiers, something about their boned crowned foreheads, vibrant colored and oddly textured skins, and gargoyle wings and tails, gave off a very inhuman hell bound feeling of dread, and that was tough to get over. But fortunately, the little joke gave the room a slightly more human undertone and put Jake at ease.

"Sergeant Mathews and Lieutenant Gordon," Major Bradshaw interrupted his thoughts, finishing the introductions. "Lt. Gordon is in charge of the team, and you will report to him with any issues or concerns."

"Welcome to the team kid," Lt. Gordon surprised Jake with his very warm, welcoming tone, that seemed out of place coming from a large reddish-brown gargoyle, tattered with scales and large bone claws. The other, Sergeant Mathews, was covered in a bumpy lizard like texture that appeared at first to be a cream color but then after Lt. Gordon made his welcome a strange ripple ran over his body, and it changed into a browner color as if his skin was in agreement with Lt. Gordon's welcome.

"Glad to be of assistance, I think." Jake mumbled, settling his nerves more comfortably in the scene around him.

"This is the Viper Task Force which you are now a part of, your mission is to locate and persuade Taylor Saskia to hand over the stone. Once she and the stone are safely in custody you are to inform me immediately. I thank you for joining our team and hope that you will not disappoint me, or our great nation, in bringing the stone back into the right hands. If you run into any deserters, our policy is to kill them on the spot." Major Bradshaw cut down to business, stating the obvious, but once he was finished, he turned the command over to Lt. Gordon and was out of the room at once.

"Deserter list," Jake looked up at Lt. Gordon's deep red-brown eyes, "what is he talking about?"

"Don't get yourself worked up about it too much, just know that some of our old buddies basically followed Dr. Ambler when he took off with the stone, leaving us horribly figured like we are now, and they are wanted for treason. They shouldn't be a problem though, don't you fret, our concern is Taylor, and don't forget it." Lt. Gordon warmly and calmly assured Jake.

"We've got some training to do, let's go kid." Lt. Gordon ushered him, and the rest of the team followed out the hall door and back to the elevator.

Feeling more comfortable with the six gargoyle soldiers at his side, Jake became inquisitive while they rode up the elevator and walked out of the building, marching rapidly through the snow, back towards the Estate.

"So, what happened to you guys, if you don't mind me asking?" Jake commented.

"What do you mean?" Seth replied, more at ease in conversation with Jake then any of the rest, aside from Lt. Gordon who had a father like commanding presence.

"I mean like, why did you need to volunteer for the experiment trials, what happened to you guys?" He explained his question more clearly.

"Oh, well, Lt. Dawson, I know, lost both of her legs on a supply run in Kuwait. A band of refugees attacked her convoy killing everyone on the supply run and taking all the supplies. They must have thought she was dead when they left, because usually they capture prisoners for negotiations, but she was left there, so they must have thought she was dead. My team showed up on a medical chopper to assist, but she was the only person alive when we arrived, and we had to amputate both her legs. I mean they were practically hanging by strings anyway, but with this new technology, both her legs grew back. It was really awesome at first but then this happened." He motioned at his body and then the others.

"I'm not saying it isn't really awesome, it's just strange, and we have no control over our appearance. There are definitely some benefits to this though," Seth was drawn off topic, indulging in the niceties of being a gargoyle.

"For instance, these wings," he stretched open his large, splotched silver and white wings, bursting them open, showing off their unique elegance. "They're great for flying and you wouldn't believe how awesome it feels to sore through the air, as a single unit, like a bird." He reminisced.

He leapt almost ten feet to a nearby snow covered evergreen tree, and quickly worked his way towards the top, like a cat, and then in an instant threw the whole of his body off the side of the tree and the large silver and white splotched wings caught the air. Like shaking out linens, his wings echoed downward while he took six or seven large flaps and climbed the air, until he was just above the treetops, easing into a glide.

Jake picked up his pace, wrapping his arms tightly around his chest, clenching to the warmth of his body, only wearing jeans and a shirt. Staggering through the thick cold snow, falling only a little behind the rest, he glanced around hoping they were getting near the estate, he had no idea why they wanted him to walk. They all moved so easily in the snow, with their large, padded feet for grip and long tails for balance, he wasn't sure why they dragged him along outside when he could have just taken a car back, and it probably would have been quicker, without him stumbling through the snow and all.

"Pretty cool don't you think?" Seth shouted back.

"So aren't you guys cold," Jake asked, stumbling up beside Lt. Dawson.

She glared at him briefly catching a glimpse of white steam puffing out of his mouth as he talked. "Ha," she laughed at him, "Not really. I mean, it's cold out here for us, but it kind of feels like a chilly day in April that's all really, not freezing as it is for you."

He was surprised by her answer, assuming that she was more hostile towards him then the others but was pleased that she was talking to him as well.

They could see the estate only half a mile or so ahead of them, and Jake was relieved because he was starting to lose feeling in his fingertips. Before they were maybe a quarter mile from the estate, they all turned off the road and walked less than an eighth of a mile, before the trees around them revealed a large conventional gym looking building.

The five gargoyles on the ground bounded ahead to the main entrance, closing the distance in nearly seconds, and the sixth one dived down toward the roof of the building, landing perfectly in the snow.

"Come on inside, you've got a choice to make." Lt. Gordon waved to him.

"R-r-right," Jake stuttered, shivering from the cold. At least they were going to be inside now, he was bitter that they couldn't feel how cold outside it was, and that they made him walk the entire distance, which must have been around four or five miles.

He walked inside; a heavy sigh of relief escaped his mouth when he was greeted by a burst of warm air, surging through the building. He walked around the room, observing the warm lounge-like appearance. The room was large and thickly carpeted in a coarse brown and cream speckled pattern. There were two long wooden cherry tables with several matching chairs in this room and a large wood burning fireplace roaring in one corner. The lighting was good, probably for the reading, and along the walls were built in bookcases, overflowing with books, which appeared to be in no particular order. Aside from the two tables, there were two large sofas arranged back-to-back and several chairs scattered about the room. The room was clearly for reading or research but was very much out of place with what was on the other side of the room.

At the far end of the room, directly across from the main entrance, were two large sliding glass double doors and a large window on each side which displayed the finely constructed gym, clearly organized for obstacle training on the other side. Jake wasn't even sure what most of the obstacles were for, but he didn't question any of the items he saw and drew his attention towards Lt. Gordon, who obviously had something to talk to Jake about.

Jake, more relaxed in the reading room, with the warm air flowing about, sat down in one of the wooden chairs beside Lt. Gordon at the table.

"Okay I'm all ears," he commented, watching as Sean and Seth disappeared into the gym like little kids ready for gymnastics, they both began tearing through the gym hitting each obstacle before moving on to the next.

"We need to find Taylor," he hesitated, "but there's only one way to do that. One of us could do it, but there is no guarantee that she would listen to us. You could do it, but . . . it will mean change."

Jake stopped staring at Seth gliding from one rope to the next in midair, clutching tightly to each and allowing it to swing high before releasing to glide over to the next. "Change, you mean change like you guys, am I right?" He asked, now looking into Lt. Gordon's earthen reddish-brown eyes.

"Well, yes and no. We all have had the fifty-six fifty-four protein strain serum injections, which have recovered us from our injuries and granted us unique abilities, along with these changes, but we won't be giving you injections, that is if you agree to do this. There is a quicker more precise and powerful way do attain the changes and unique abilities, it's my understanding that you would have better control of them as well, and although we cannot confirm it, we believe you would be able to change from gargoyle to human freely, rather than be stuck like we are. The reason for doing this is that it is the only way to find Taylor." Lt. Gordon explained as coolly as she could.

"What is so special about it that it will help you find Taylor?" Jake asked, not sure what to make of the conversation yet.

"The stone . . . it, it calls to itself, and with it one is naturally drawn to the rest of it. We are sure Taylor has the stone on her, and as a result, know that with the part we have we can find her." Lt. Gordon continued to explain.

"Okay so give me the stone and I will find her, sounds simple enough." Jake triumphed at his idea.

"No, it's not that simple. We have to insert the stone into you. It has to be a part of you in order to use it and not only that, but it will change you, and we need to train you how to use your abilities if you choose to comply. Granted, with the stone directly a part of you, you'll be much easier to train. Anyhow, the decision is yours to make. Will you take the stone or not? You can mull over it for the night. We'll meet here again tomorrow in the morning. This is the research room and that's the training gym, if you choose to do it, we'll get started right away. Okay Kid." Lt. Gordon finished. He pushed his chair to the side and stood up, reaching over, he roughly patted Jake on the back with his reddish-brown hand. "Just think about it kid," he said and then walked over to a sofa and collapsed, sprawling one leg over an arm and tossing his wings, like blankets, covering half the couch, and leaving an arm hanging out onto the floor.

"Tell me, will I be able to be normal again?" Jake asked concerned.

"Yeah, as long as you don't mind us taking the stone out, it would probably be a minor surgery, no big deal." Lt. Gordon lied, knowing full hardy that once the stone was a part of you, death was

● ● ●

the only way to remove it, but of course Major Bradshaw had no intentions of keeping Jake around after they got Taylor, he wanted the whole stone united and alone, only the stone and nothing else. It would mean killing Taylor once they had her as well, Lt. Gordon knew this, and didn't care. He was under Major Bradshaw's explicit control, he and three others, the four original soldiers that Major Bradshaw injected the combined fifty-six fifty-four protein strain injection into.

Jake kicked back in one of the recliner chairs, taking note of Lt. Gordon's actions and relaxed, figuring on some sleep before they got training, knowing full heartedly what his decision already was. Of course, he'd do it, take the change, and save Taylor. He didn't need the night to think about it, before he met Taylor, his life was empty and boring, his parents always fighting, forgetting about his very existence, too caught up in their financial and emotional altercations to even bother feeding him most nights. He fell asleep on the recliner thinking about the first time he'd met Taylor, and how much of a relief she was.

"Mom, Dad, please stop arguing, you're embarrassing me." Jake urged his parents, trying to quiet yet another fight they began, while walking down Front Street browsing at the different art displays and enjoying the musical talents of local bands during the arts festival in downtown Port Angeles. Jake caught a girl maybe a year younger than himself, with beautiful long black hair, dangling on her shoulders and matching jet-black eyes, staring over at him with a small smile on her face, almost as if mocking him.

He'd seen her a couple times at school off and on, she was a freshman, he thought. She was hard to miss, with her tattered torn up jeans and faded long sleeve shirts with little holes ripped into the wrists so that she could push her thumbs out through her shirt sleeves, almost wearing them like gloves, if that was the sort of thing that caught your eye. Yet he'd never paid any attention to her before.

He looked over at her, sitting on the side of an old rusted headless and armless naked metal woman sculpture, one of many among the downtown streets of Port Angeles, and she wasn't mocking him, she was giggling at him. More curious than anything else, he left the side of his parents and crossed the street over to where she was slouched, sitting against the fixture.

"What's so funny," he huffed at her.

"You, and your parents," she said, nodding in their direction.

● ○ ●

"There fighting in public again, that's not funny it's embarrassing." He exclaimed.

"Yeah, but at least you get to be embarrassed by your parents." She said.

"What, your parents don't embarrass you?" He doubted that was possible.

"No, I don't have any." She surprised him with this response, her face unchanged as if she'd no real emotions on the subject.

"Oh, I'm sorry." Jake felt that awkward silence of saying the wrong thing at the wrong time cover the atmosphere around them.

"Nah, it's not a big deal, I just like watching other people hate the parts of life, which they don't even realize other people wish they had." She explained in an uppity out of place tone.

Jake fell silent unsure of what to say, still awkward from the previous comment and now, sorrier that he took for granted what this girl in front of him wished, she had.

"I'm Taylor, and you are?" She interrupted Jakes uneasy silence.

"Jake, so what are you doing out here?" He asked.

"Same thing you are, enjoying the arts festival, right? I mean who doesn't come down here and look around." She said presumptuously. "That and my foster parents are playing in that band by the water. They don't trust me at the house alone, so here I am." She grimaced.

"Oh, yeah, my parents always insist that I go with them to look at some paintings and what not, make it a family thing. I'm not even sure they know what that means. They fight too much if you ask me. As much as I hate to say it, I've been thinking they might be better off apart, you know, divorced." He looked down, ashamed of the idea. "Anyhow, wanna ditch the folks and come hang out with me, we could catch a movie or something?" He pointed up the way at the theater which was only a few blocks from where they stood and easily within eyesight of both their parents.

"Sure, I'd love a break." She pushed off the sculpture, shook her head enough to toss her long black hair behind her shoulders and off her face where he could more easily see her mysterious dark eyes. "Oh, and don't be so hard on your parents, believe it or not you really would miss them if they were gone." She tossed in the last comment as they walked together up the sidewalk, toward the theater.

Jake woke up to a nudging feeling on his shoulder. Lt. Dawson was tapping him, trying patiently to wake him up.

"Hey kid, we need to head back to the Estate, so you can get some sleep and some food in, before it gets any later." She stepped back, giving Jake a chance to stretch out, slowly waking up.

As Jake prepared his body for the freezing temperatures outside, he noticed that aside from Lt. Gordon and Dawson everyone else had left, which left him wondering how long he'd been asleep for. The sun was already setting behind the trees and the cool blue of the sky was rapidly diming into a darker grey. They hastily led him back to the Estate, quickly correcting him as he tripped in the unevenly packed snow, making rather hasty efforts to get out of the dark, a little too hasty for these hell-like guardians. As if something would threaten them; the idea seeming entirely impossibly.

"I d-don't know i-if you need the-the answer now, but I-I'll do it. The st-stone, I-I'll do it," Jake stammered, freezing from the cold chill outside, announcing his position to Lt. Gordon.

"Great, well if you want, we can get started tonight." Lt. Gordon sounded pleased with the decision. "I'll let Major Bradshaw know the instant we get back.

"Okay," Jake sighed not sure if he was ready for what was to come or not, but regardless of his courage, he was willing to try, and better sooner than later. That's what Taylor always used to tell him, better to get it over with sooner rather than build up the anxiety for later. She always was one to leap before looking, he thought to himself, especially the first time she jumped off the Devil's Punch Bowl.

He briefly remembered cringing as she nearly grated her body along the Cliffside because she barely jumped out far enough to avoid hitting the sides of the cliff - of course it was his fault for not warning her. No one in their right mind would need to be reminded to jump away from the cliff rather than straight down, if they'd only looked down before they jumped off the ledge, but of course Taylor, completely careless of the risks, just sprang forward, without hesitation and it was with fortunes grace that she survived with little but a nick on her hand where it brushed some rock on her way down.

Lt. Gordon took two long lunges ahead and peeled open the door at the Estate, allowing for Jake to stumble inside, stiff and shuttering from the cold. Once again, the nice warm air of the roaring fires in the great room billowed around his body, helping to ease the tension built up from his tightly clenched arms across his chest, allowing him to relax. Jake ruffled his body and stamped the ground shaking lose any remaining clumps of snow that had gripped to him, while walking there, and then hurried over to the fireplace at the far end of the room rubbing his hands over the warm glow.

He hadn't even noticed that Lt. Gordon had disappeared, but once he was beginning to feel the tingling sensation of his warmed blood, flowing through his body again, he noticed that Lt. Gordon returned with a doctor. The man was dressed in a white lab coat, like a scientist, but carried a stethoscope around his neck, and a large black bag in one hand, which he tossed onto a coffee table and sat down.

"This is one of our onsite surgeons. If you will sit here on the couch, he can quickly stitch the stone into you." Lt. Gordon announced.

Jake's throat got dry as he tried to swallow, a little panicky from the word stitch. But obediently he left the warm glow of the fire, and sat down beside the doctor on the couch, hoping the cooperation would get this done faster.

"I'll need you to remove your shirt." The doctor stated, pulling out a bottle of iodine and a cotton swab, dowsing it.

Jake pulled his shirt over his curly hair revealing a chiseled set of abbs. A cold icy feeling startled Jake, as the doctor wiped a patched of his chest right above the sternum with the iodine and then flicked at a syringe. Jake cringed as the doctor plunged the syringe into his chest, injecting the clear fluid into his skin.

"Just a local anesthetic to ease the pain," the doctor informed.

Jake was nervous now, afraid of what was about to come. He was prepared to risk his life to save Taylor, experience the most horrifying changes that would make him look like a gargoyle, but to have a doctor slice his skin open, and stitch something inside of him, right now, that was the most horrifying thing possible.

Then before Jake could oppose another move, the doctor pulled out a long thin scalpel and pierced his skin, just below his collar bone and pulled the knife nearly two inches, exposing the rib bones beneath.

Jake, prepared for the most horrifying pain. He nearly went white as he watched the doctor peel open his now bleeding chest, only to discover little discomfort, mostly a tugging feeling.

"That doesn't hurt, does it?" The doctor asked.

● ○ ●

"Uh, no, n-not really," Jake stuttered, relieved by the ease of the cut.

Jake watched, as the doctor pulled out a small stone, rough and thin, but magnificent in brilliance, and diamond-like in appearance, holding it up to his chest.

"Put your finger on this, and don't move it, until I ask you," the doctor said, placing Jake's finger on the stone holding it in place, just inside the cut on his chest. The doctor pulled out a needle and some wire that looked much like fishing line and began threading the edges of his skin back together.

"Okay, you can let go now," the doctor told Jake, pulling together another stitch. Once he was finished, he taped a large piece of gauze over the stitched up cut and then cleaned his tools and put them back in his bag.

"Because we've never really done this before, I can't tell you how long it will be before that heals, but I'd wager it won't be long. If anything goes wrong, just have me paged." The doctor announced to both Jake and Lt. Gordon and then made his way back out of the room and disappeared somewhere in the Estate, most of which Jake had not toured.

"Never done this before, what is he talking about? You guys made it out like you've done this plenty. I'm a first?" Jake freaked out, storming around the room in a ball of anger. "What if something goes wrong? What if this thing kills me, what then? How do you propose I help Taylor then? Hmm," Jake angrily cast words at Lt. Gordon, pacing back and forth along the fire.

Then suddenly he jerked upright, as his chest heaved forward, causing one large convulsion to surge through his body. He reached an arm forward, catching the mantle of the fireplace, steadying his body from the seizure, and grabbed at his chest with the other. Jake, suddenly very conscious of the gauze covering the stitched area on his chest, throbbing with pain, tore away the gauze. He was staring at the cut as the pain began to pulsate through his veins, flowing out into the very tips of his fingers and toes. As he watched, still clenching the mantle, the stitches disintegrated and the skin sealed closed leaving a large, dimly shadowed scar, and where the small bulge from the stone had appeared moments before, was now a flat slightly sunken in patch of skin along the line of the scar. The pain surged through his body even greater than moments before, like someone was turning up the voltage on an electrifying chair and then the feeling erupted away from his body and surged through the room causing the lights to flicker, and then singularly vanished. He could feel the immense surge of power dwindle away, until he was left with a nauseated feeling in the pit of his stomach that caused him to lean over and vomit.

Chapter XVII: Mysterious Night

"Oh my god," Taylor shouted, so absolutely distracted that she failed to dodge Ranulf's oncoming punch, which smashed her right between the eyes, sending her backwards from a fall that was already coming.

"Did you feel that?" Taylor placed her hand on her forehead, but not her nose, gasping for breath trying to find a way to explain what she just felt.

"Yeah, and I'm sure you did too," Ranulf commented, rolling his wrist around, shaking off the blow. Taylor, too distracted, failed to acknowledge that Ranulf hadn't successfully landed a punch on her yet today, which, as a result, left him far more frustrated than her. He was unsuccessfully drawing out her strong emotions which the professor had said were needed in order to cause the change.

"No, you bullheaded sledgehammer," Taylor jeered, glaring at Ranulf, while finally patting down her sore nose, "the explosion?"

"I'm sure that's what it felt like when I hit your nose," Ranulf sneered, very pleased with the description she used.

"No," she shook her head frustrated with Ranulf's stupidity. "You're telling me you didn't feel that burst of power, like someone just blew up a room full of C-4?" Taylor threw out a hand, silently requesting Ranulf to help her stand up. She looked over to the professor. "Professor, you didn't feel that?"

"No Taylor, we didn't feel anything, but maybe you're getting upset. Maybe you're feeling those emotions that will trigger the change. If that's the case, try and harness those feelings. Physical stress hasn't appeared to do anything for you. You've already ran five miles, struggled through the obstacle course, jumped several stories into a pool, and swam two miles, not to mention the beating that Ranulf has been trying to give you. It's obvious that we have to find a trigger some other way." The professor explained, exhausted from the long day. "Maybe we should call it a night and try again tomorrow."

"Come on, I just got one hit on her, and you want to stop for the night?" Ranulf whined.

"Sure, I gotta go repair this nose anyway." Taylor glared at Ranulf, tilting her head back, keeping the little red speckles forming, from dripping down her face. She didn't know what she felt, but it most certainly wasn't the change, that the professor wanted her to feel.

Ranulf followed Taylor from the gym, whining in the background about stopping for the night. Taylor didn't respond to his annoying jeers, deeply held in thought, but instead, wondered what could trigger such a strong power surge that no one else felt. It reminded her of the first day she found the stone. She felt a strong, pulsating feeling, surge through her body and then burst away, apparently causing a power surge, which the professor had told her was probably an effect of the stone becoming one with the body. But that would mean that someone else had just become one with the stone, and Taylor didn't know how that would be possible with Major Bradshaw safely controlling one portion and the Professor controlling the other.

"Can I just get a sandwich," Taylor asked Madeline, the cook. "I'm tired and want to go to bed."

"Sure, I've already made up several on the counter over there," Madeline pointed to the bar side of the island. "When the professor has everyone doing trainings for the night, usually no one is that hungry, so I just make sandwiches in advance. Seems to keep everyone happy," she explained in her polite calm voice, keeping a half smile across her face.

"Thank you," Taylor exclaimed, grabbing one of the sandwiches. She guzzled down a glass of water and then retreated to her room with the sandwich, nibbling away at it on the way.

"Hmm, ham with melted cheese on rye. Pretty good," Taylor whispered to herself, grinning at the simplicity of the delicious sandwich.

"Night Jill," Taylor peeped her head inside Jill's bedroom giving her a brief goodnight. "Oops, sorry, night," she whispered silently realizing that she had startled Jill in her sleep. Jill turned her head over on her pillow glancing at the door with a groan, and then shoved her head back into her pillow tossing another one over her head. Taylor slowly ducked out of the door, closing it carefully, so as not to make any more noise, and then retreated into her bedroom across the hall.

She pulled off her pants and tossed them into a little pile in a corner near the door, apparently someone comes through the rooms daily, to clean them up and do laundry. It was kind of cool, Taylor thought, the way she didn't have to bother with the meddlesome tasks of everyday life. She finished off her sandwich, while peering outside her window into the garden below.

With the dark swallowing the night she wondered about how late it must have been and glanced over her shoulder at the clock hanging on the wall, an analog, that read ten thirty. So it wasn't that late, it must just feel like it because of the long day. She knew the next day was going to be even longer, waking up early in the morning, and decided to tuck in for the night. She crawled into bed, and laid her head down on her pillow, closing her eyes, to think about the strange pulse she felt earlier, before swiftly falling into a dreamy sleep.

"Mom, Dad, please stop arguing, you're embarrassing me." Strangely she began dreaming about the first time she met her old and best friend Jake. She watched as this older, much taller boy, with the body of a soccer player, lean but cut, desperately tried to hush his parents. He was pulling a picture out of his dad's hand and placing it back onto one of the artist's podiums, displaying their talented work along the sidewalk of downtown Port Angeles.

Taylor's new foster parents were playing in a hippie band, with casual but not too hip music, a block or two down the street and didn't want to leave her at the house, so she was chilling outside the shops watching the tourists run around like chickens with their heads cut off, buying and critiquing all the various art displays.

The boy was looking at her, almost glaring. She couldn't help but laugh at him. He looked so embarrassed, like a turnip, face beat red, a frightful look for such a lightly tanned complexion.

Uh oh, she didn't know what to do, he was coming towards her. He'd brushed both his parents off and was cutting across the street locking eyes with her.

"What's so funny?" He hollered, not quite an arm's length away from her. He finished closing the gap between them, and then coolly slid his hand through his tightly wound, golden brown curls.

"You, and your parents," she replied, still with a little laughter in her voice, relieved that he wasn't going to comment on the way she looked or anything like that.

"They're fighting in public again, that's not funny it's embarrassing," he exclaimed, still red in the face, but now trying to appear cooler and more confident.

"Yeah, but at least you get to be embarrassed by your parents." She tried painfully to hide any emotion in her face while spitting out the words.

"What, your parents don't embarrass you?" He pulled a questioning look on his face probably doubting that someone couldn't be embarrassed by their parents.

"No, I don't have any." She quickly replied, hoping that she hadn't revealed too much information to a perfect stranger, but also keeping back the tears, from the thought.

"Oh, I'm sorry." The boy's face changed quickly, surprised maybe, or ashamed. He fell silent, probably embarrassed by the question like many people would be. They never seem to expect that kind of an answer.

"Nah, it's not a big deal, I just like watching other people hate the parts of life, which they don't even realize other people wish they had." She explained to him, trying to express her feelings without being to mushy, which would probably frighten away a boy, and to quickly fill in the silence that obviously made the boy nervous.

"I'm Taylor, and you are?" She quickly changed the subject, hoping that this would keep the handsome boy talking to her. She didn't have many friends and wouldn't mind one.

"Jake, so what are you doing out here?" He replied.

"Same thing you are, enjoying the arts festival, right? I mean who doesn't come down here and look around." She said presumptuously. "That and my foster parents are playing in that band by the water; they don't trust me at the house alone, so here I am." She grimaced, hoping the word foster didn't scare him off. If she hadn't lost him at parent's are dead, she most certainly would at claiming to be a foster kid, that's where she lost most people.

"Oh, yeah, my parents always insist that I go with them to look at some paintings and what not, make it a family thing. I'm not even sure they know what that means. They fight too much if you ask me. As much as I hate to say it, I've been thinking they might be better off apart, you know, divorced." He looked down. "Anyhow, wanna ditch the folks and come hang out with me, we could catch a movie or something?" He pointed up the way at the theater. She thought about it for a minute, relieved that he hadn't flaked out yet, and then agreed.

"Sure, I'd love a break." She shook her hair out of her face while getting up and caught a glimpse of Jake's handsome blue eyes starring

● ● ●

right into hers. A strange fluttery feeling formed in her stomach. "Oh, and don't be so hard on your parents, believe it or not you really would miss them if they were gone." She commented, to distract herself from the butterflies in her stomach.

And together they both walked up the block to the theater, until everything went black and all that remained was her and Jake. She watched as the dream turned dark and the feelings of happiness and ease quickly washed away into fear and sorrow.

Right before her eyes, Jake transformed, transformed into a gargoyle, much like the one she had seen herself turn into. Only he was pure white, white from the daunting tail, and elegant wingspan, to the ridges that formed a crown over his head and the once sky-blue eyes. Everything on him was white, all except for a dark purplish bruise on his chest, above his sternum.

He turned his gargoyle looking head towards hers and gazed directly into her dark black eyes, and said, "I will save you." The words struck her like a knife, piercing deep in her chest, pounding out the very feelings of loss she had locked away inside, from her mother's death. And then he was pulled away by some unseen force, dragged into the pit of the darkness.

She screamed out, waving her arms wildly to grab him. "Don't leave, Jake, Jake," she broke down in sobs, in the dream, no, in real life. She'd awoken, hands clutching her face, tears streaming from her eyes. "Jake, I'm so alone," she whispered out into the darkness of the night, slowly clearing away the tears that drenched her face.

She didn't realize how much she missed her best friend. They had even parted pretty badly, barely speaking as neither of them was any good at farewells. She wondered if she was ever going to see him again. If things had been different, if she had stayed in Port Angeles, who knows, maybe they would have been dating by now. She always knew he had a crush on her, and she wouldn't deny that he was handsome, and attractive. She just wasn't ready to date yet, and back in the day she would never have admitted to having feelings for him, yet alone anyone. But oh how she missed the comforts of her best friend. Even though he wasn't very good at saying the right thing, his very presence calmed her and often tamed the hidden sorrows that woke her early in the mornings.

She remembered when Jake used to come over early each morning, before school started to watch cartoons with her – it was the only time to catch them, but that was just an excuse to have him around, comforting her.

Exhausted from the day and worn from the strange nightmare Taylor passed out tightly clutching her pillow, and drifted back into a deep sleep, with small sniffling sobs breaking the slow steady rhythm of her snores.

Two weeks had passed with the same routine, eating breakfast at six thirty in the main dining hall with everyone else, and then joining the professor, the Wolfe brothers, Esa, and Jill in the gym for training. Training took up most of the day with only a few breaks for snacks and lunch. Half the morning consisted of Ranulf and Arnulf taking turns pounding Taylor into the ground, and then before the break for lunch, the professor forced Taylor to run ten miles or she wouldn't get to eat. This often took her close to two hours and she was spent by the end of the run.

She was toning up very well, for what she wasn't sure, but by the end of the two weeks she could run the ten miles in under an hour and a half, and aside from her good luck avoiding Ranulf's poundings the first day, she was getting better with her defense response time, and both Ranulf and Arnulf were landing shots less and less. She'd dealt with the mornings fairly well, but the afternoons were beginning to wear on her. Finally, she'd had enough.

"Stop it already," Taylor yelled at the professor. She was getting fed up with his little electric shock treatments, trying to stimulate the change, which he'd perform for several hours each afternoon.

"No, damn it. You need to change, everything depends on it," the professor stressed, the pleasantness of his voice long gone from his frustrations during training.

"But I need to heal, and I'm hurting, please," Taylor whined, slumping over in the small wooden chair she was strapped in. She took a deep breath and shook her head, causing the little electrode wires hanging over her face and chest to tangle together. She looked at her arms, small and large bruises alike were forming on her arms from Arnulf's earlier assault, and little burn marks were etched into her flesh from the electric shock machine that the professor was using. All the 'training' was beginning to show, and Taylor's ability to heal herself, was weakening. Each day she was awaking with more and more bruises remaining from the previous day and the burn marks from the electricity were not going away at all.

"What is he doing to me?" Taylor whispered the words she meant to think.

"Helping you, damnit – Now change." The professor shouted, and then turned up the dial on his machine to full throttle and watched Taylor. Her body tightened, each muscle balling into an uncontrollable Charlie-horse, teeth gritted tightly against a slice of leather propped into her mouth, and nails digging into the wooden armrests on either side of the chair. A small wisp of air escaped her mouth as she attempted to scream in desperation, but then disintegrated into midair, as she lost total control of her body.

The professor left the machine running longer than a minute, showing no signs of emotion towards Taylor, only watching with a straight and worn face.

"Stop it, you're killing her." Esa screamed at him. "You never did this to any of us," she declared, and then reached for the knob and turned it all the way down releasing Taylor from the involuntary tortuous electrocution.

Taylor grasped for breath, sucking in all the air she could, filling the painful stabs in her chest from the absence of air.

"If you can't deal with this than get out here, Esa." He shouted at her, knocking her back, away from the controller.

"She needs to learn the change, and gain control of her powers, and now." He exclaimed, "You've seen the news just as I have – more and more children are disappearing and Major Bradshaw is getting ready to make his move, without her under control, we will have already lost." He said, with anger welling in his voice.

"Now, either help, or get the hell out of here." He shouted, sending Esa into a fit of tears.

"Sorry, Taylor, I can't watch this." She said, tears drenching her face, and then stormed off, out of the gym.

"If either of you are going to short out, you'd better leave as well." The professor hissed at both the Wolfe brothers, looking each one up and down, like wrestlers – judging their strengths.

Although they were in disagreement with the professor's methods, both the Wolfe brothers understood what he was trying to do and knew of no better way to hurry up Taylor's transition, and therefore did not put up a fight with the professor.

"No, we're fine," Arnulf, spoke for himself and his brother, sharing a glance of fear.

"Good, now let's get back to work." He moved his hand back over the dial.

Still gasping and chocking for breath, Taylor whinnied out a small cry, "No more, please."

"Fine, I didn't want to do this, but it seems I have no choice. The professor quickly began un-strapping Taylor's arms from the chair. "Quickly, help me," he harked at Ranulf, pulling the electrodes from her head and arms.

The professor pulled one arm around his shoulder hoisting Taylor from her sitting position. Ranulf joined in supporting Taylor's other side with his shoulder.

"Hold her there," the professor instructed to Ranulf, "don't move."

He stepped back – Taylor lifted her head, eyes glazing over from the exhaustion, and looked at the professor as he drew from behind his back, under his shirt, a pistol.

"What are you doing," Arnulf shouted out, startling the professor.

"The only thing that's worked so far," he responded, nose flaring and teeth gritted.

He raised his hand up, directing the pistol at Taylor's head, placing his index finger on the trigger, and squeezed gently, mumbling under his breath. "Please work."

Silence filled the air as both Arnulf and Ranulf held their breaths sharing another look of fear and confusion. Neither one willing to stop the professor, in his determined spree of chaos, nor pretending to understand his methods anymore, held their places and made no sudden movements to stop him.

The ricochet of the bullet tore through the room, slicing through the air like a hot knife on butter, exposing the mixed screams of anger and fear, resentment and shock, alongside the gut-wrenching sound of the bullet splitting open her skull and nestling deep inside her brain, still and deadly, awaiting Taylor's timely death.

Taylor fell limp in Ranulf's arms. He fidgeted with her body keeping her from hitting the ground, and then slowly leaned her forward lying her limp lifeless body on the pale cold wooden floor of the gym.

"You killed her!" Ranulf said accusingly, wiping away a drizzle of blood where it formed at the bullet hole in her head.

"No," the professor screamed and then threw his body over hers frantically feeling for any sign of life – wrist, neck, airway – "wait," he hushed the boys. "She's breathing," he pointed to her chest. A slight but apparent rising and falling rhythm of breathing was occurring.

Almost instinctively the professor broke down into a stream of regretful tears. "Oh God, what have I done?" He began to question his own methods. Looking back at the sadistic turn he'd taken trying to transform Taylor.

Arnulf smacked the professor across the face. "Snap out of it, if she's breathing you can still do something to help her." He reminded the professor. Half afraid of the professor's response to the smack and half afraid that Taylor was going to die. Arnulf bolted across the room and into the office, where the professor kept his medical bag and retrieved it, quickly redirecting the professor's thoughts. He crouched down beside the professor and fumbled through the bag searching for something to remove the bullet with or at least something to stall the bleeding, until he was interrupted.

"Look, look at this," Ranulf pointed to the bullet hole where he was wiping away the trickling blood. The skin began to bulge outward like a thick layer of wrinkles piling up on an old man's face and then all of the blood that was trickling out, sucked back into the wrinkly bulge exposing a hard metallic bullet squishing its way back out of her head.

"Wow . . ." was all any of them could say, speechless from the miraculous scene unraveling before them.

The bullet finished working its way out of her skull until it rolled off her head and clinked coldly on the floor below. She gasped loudly as if she'd just regained the ability to breathe and then blinked. Where the pure black had once glistened inside the pearly white edges of her cold human eyes, the white was vanishing from her eyes. Like a thundercloud swiftly floating to cover a town, so too did the black billows fill her eyes, swirling around until not one ounce of any other color existed exposing two lustrous almond shapes barely recognizable as human.

Her skin began to shift color, slowly like the sky shifting from day into night, darkening into a shadowy black. She reached one arm back, one darkening glossy arm back, to part herself from the very ground she was laying on, and as if she were waking from an awkward sleep, she twisted her head around her shoulders, stretching. She then steadied herself allowing for two long and brilliant leathery wings to burst out of her shirt from between her now black shoulder blades and then finalize their position draped over her crouching body, as if she were an angel ready to spring for an attack. And then, as the minute details of her body were correcting themselves, her long glossy tail, emerged through the back end of her pants, ripping a hole in her jeans. She glared at the professor, with her razor black eyes, and a long gurgling growl rumbled from deep inside her throat.

"You tried to kill me," she hissed.

Everyone had stepped back from Taylor, while she was changing, surprised by her response, and the professor, slightly afraid of her, especially after shooting her, and rearmed himself with the pistol that he had earlier dropped on the ground.

"Um, just listen, please Taylor." The professor stammered, taking in a big gulp of air, a bit afraid of what stood before him. Never before, even with Will, had he seen something so majestic and frightening. She was beauty incarnate touched by the devil himself, both mesmerizing with her glorious grace and terrifying with her untamed spirit and wild fervor beating in her eyes.

"And you helped him," she looked first at Arnulf and then Ranulf, and then twisted her head back around staring into the professor's old worn eyes.

"I'm s – sorry Taylor, but I had too, look what it's done. You changed, look." He handed her a large mirror from his bag, placing the pistol into the bag carefully so as not to startle the newly changed gargoyle in front of him.

"You could have killed me," she uttered the words more deeply this time, never breaking her focus.

"But I didn't, and now we are one step closer to controlling your change." He explained, trying to calm her down, feeling the tension rise in the room. One wrong word and she would snap possibly killing everyone in the room and destroying anything in her path.

"We . . . are closer to controlling my change," she hissed. "Is that all I am to you, something you can control, something you can order around, to do your dirty work? Why should I trust you, what makes you better than, say, Major Bradshaw?" She hissed again, tilting her head side to side still maintaining focus on the professor's golden brown worn eyes.

"I don't want the stone for myself. I only want it to stop the Major from using it to rule the world. If he gets the stone, then he'll be sure to kill anyone opposed to his rulings and nothing and no one will be able to stop him." He desperately tried to settle Taylor's hostility, but only seemed to push her further into resentment.

"So, in order to stop him, I owe you, my allegiance. Why should I owe anything to anyone after all the hell I've been through?" She paused; glaring so evil a stare that medusa herself would have turned to stone. "I've lost my parents, my best friend, my grandparents, and now my life, why should I owe anyone anything?" She declared her true feelings, so passionately that the gym itself could not hold her overpowering emotions, and the wooden walls and floors began to quiver.

If only Jake was around, he would be able to settle her down. And then, as the thought became a harsh reminder of the things she had lost, she released a loud ear-splitting scream.

The windows in the building burst into powder and remained suspended in midair while she released her horrifying scream. The wooden floors began undulating from her body like the focal point of an earthquake and the springboard floor broke apart quickly followed by the various other obstacles set up inside the gym.

The professor and both the Wolfe brothers covered their ears, hiding from the painful scream of agony that Taylor bellowed out. They watched as she clenched both her clawed fists tightly together around her temples as if she were trying to forget something terrible, and she closed her eyes tightly, trembling with anger. The professor made a step towards her reaching out to place a hand on her shoulder, anything to stop her from screaming, and then. . . She was gone.

Like a burnt-out light bulb, rather than leaving a flash of light and disappearing, she simply disappeared, almost taking the very light that was present around her, leaving where she had stood, only a small wisp of dark mist that within seconds also dissipated, and with her went the chaos. The room fell silent, the floors stopped undulating, the walls ceased from bowing, and the shattered windows' fine mist fell to the ground leaving only an eerie silence, the room once full of overflowing emotion was now empty and hollow, as if all the water in the ocean just suddenly went dry.

"Taylor," a voice beckoned to her in the darkness of the night.

"Where am I," she asked, peering around the moonlit snow-covered forest. Nothing was familiar, not a sound nor smell, not even the trees were familiar. Glancing down at herself, she noticed she was still a gargoyle, with her jeans tightly pressed against her leather legs and her t-shirt stretching over her body, pulled tightly by the wings that had burst through the back part.

"Taylor," the voice beckoned again, this time more loudly as if it wasn't just a thought in her head, but a person searching, searching for her.

"Who is there," she whispered into the darkness, browsing past the shadowed brown trunks of the trees that poorly hide her black body against the white snow. There was no response, and she wasn't sure she was actually hearing anyone outside of her head anyway, and so she didn't respond again, and decided to figure out where she was instead.

She found a tree large enough to support her weight and with great feline dexterity, climbed to the top of the tree and leapt into the air, swishing her long black wings outwards catching the evening drafts, allowing her to climb the sky high enough to see that she was clearly lost.

Peering as far as she could see, hoping a small town or road or something might give away her location, she glided on.

"Taylor, where are you going?" The strange voice asked her, almost a familiar voice.

"Are you in my head?"

"Yes," the voice spoke again. The voice was becoming more and more familiar as if it were someone from her past, someone she used to know.

"Who are you, what do you want?" She hesitated. "How are you in my head?"

"I'm a friend. Let's just leave it at that. I'm in your head because we share something, something very important to people that are not us. Those people want it back, people that we can give it to, and then have a normal life back." She couldn't put her finger on the voice, but somehow it made her feel calm and secure, she wanted to trust the voice, prayed that she could trust it.

"Say I believe you, what do you want me to do?" She asked the voice without hesitation. The invitation of a normal life sounded appealing, too appealing. She never imagined that she could ever want to just be a regular foster kid again and move every few months into another home and resituate herself over and over again, but all this turmoil, rollercoaster of emotions, was wearing on her, and she wanted it all to end, all to go back to a regular old boring, nothing to do, nothing to change lifestyle.

The voice went quiet, with nothing more to say to her.

Despite her new appearance and her unknown strengths and abilities, Taylor felt more afraid and helpless than ever, with that voice pushing her over the edge of reason. She glided around the countryside looking for something small or abandoned a cottage or a shack, something where she could settle for the night and gather her bearings.

She wondered if she just jumped through space to get out here and wondered if this was one of the abilities the professor was talking about. Now she just had to figure out where here was. She spotted a large lake with a hut on one side – it appeared to be empty. Swiftly landing on the frozen ground behind the hut, she peered through some small single paned windows to make sure no one was present – it appeared to be abandoned, and that was fine, she wanted to get a fire going and find some food. She was ravishing, tired and cold.

So she could pass through space, which was kind of cool. She figured that meant she could go anywhere she wanted to. Maybe she would try it out a little, before making assumptions. She stopped her thoughts before they got too carried away, walked around to the front of the cabin, and tried the front door, but it was locked. Not wanting to disturb the hut in case the owners were just gone, she decided to try out her new ability.

Not knowing how she did it the first time, she pictured herself near a fireplace cozy and warm, eating biscuits with strawberry jam smeared on them. Once the image was clear enough inside her mind, she closed her eyes briefly, and a strange tingling feeling overwhelmed her senses.

"Oops, where am I now?" She looked around at the scene surrounding her. She was definitely not in the hut, not even in the same area, but standing in the middle of a street. A Street full of cars and trucks racing back and forth in the dark moonlight, with tall, tall buildings scrunched together, packed tightly into a small bay. "Is this New York?"

A car horn warned Taylor that she was in its way.

"Oh my god what is that?" Some woman screamed, accompanied by the hysterical screams of other random people on the streets.

"Crap I need to get out of here," Taylor quickly thought of leaving the city, away from the commotion and the hustle, and then closed her eyes again.

This time, less confident of her ability to control her space jump, she opened one eye and then the other, silently peering around hoping to be somewhere more useful.

"Oh, boy," she sighed. "Back where I started, guess that's better than in the city." She said, looking around at again nothing familiar in the dark night. There were different trees, new unaltered snow-covered hills and fields, and again no houses or signs of life anywhere. She scurried up another tree, tossing her graceful body into the night sky and began scanning the fields for another possible place to hide out.

"Okay, I guess I won't do that anytime soon, not unless I get it under control," she noted to herself. She scanned the ground some more. From what she knew of traveling she must still be in the Northern part of the country, maybe still Canada, hopefully. The night was cold, and the thick blanket of trees and random empty fields covered with snow suggested that she was in the northern hemisphere. It was mid February and most of the southern states, if they even got snow, had lost it by now. But up here, wherever here was, was thickly covered with heavy layers of snow and there was no real hint of the spring coming at all.

Taylor's eyes were beginning to strain from the intensive gazing through the cold air, but finally, after close to an hour of soaring around, keeping close to the trees for cover, she spotted what must be a little town, and where there was a town there was most definitely some place for shelter, and just in the nick of time too, because it was starting to snow out. First the snow lightly fluttered from above swirling around in delicate little dancing patterns, but then almost instantly the snowflakes quadrupled in number and size and the wind picked up, pouring them sideways against Taylor's flight, causing her to work twice as hard and blurring her vision.

The cold was finally starting to effect Taylor, with the wind blowing, the temperature must have been in the negatives, she could feel little icicles forming around her eyelids and nostrils, and the previous warmth that filled her vessels keeping her extremities comfortable in the minor cold, was replaced with a tingly pinching feeling that hurt as she slowly began to lose feeling in her fingers and toes, which had shredded the shoes she wore when she made her transformation back at the gym.

"Hmm, what's that?" Taylor felt something warm slowly and softly surge through her body causing her head to instinctively turn towards the direction it was coming from. She saw a dim glow off in the distance, one of the few things she could see in the blizzard. She changed direction and began flapping her long black wings, forcing her body against the wind, to find safety and shelter near the warm glow. As she got closer, she could see it more clearly. A large building, house, no, mansion of some sort, with open fields around it, and other buildings sporadically spaced among the trees in the surrounding area. But it, the warm glow, was a fire. A fire inside a large room, someplace where she could warm up and fall asleep.

She flew in closer until she was only meters away from the room with the roaring fire, exposed by a large open window. She noticed a cleft that ran along the entire outside of the mansion supporting various stone gargoyle statues at corner points among the building.

"That's so funny," she commented, picturing the gargoyle statues bursting alive and becoming like her. Snickering at the statues, she swung her legs forward, and grasped with her black claws, the cleft, landing ever so perfectly.

One by one, she placed each hand on the brickwork, scooting sideways, like a gecko in a terrarium moving along the plated glass, toward the window in order to get a better idea of how to get in and warm up, or to see whether the room was even empty in order to warm up.

She peered inside carefully, the warm fuzzy feeling more intensely surging through her body, and noticed a man, an older man standing inside. He looked a lot like the man in her old dreams, the one that had appeared at her hearing, dressed in a nice business suit accompanied by military types.

She wondered if that was Major Bradshaw, forgetting her caution, pressing her black cat like ear up against the window, listening closely to the chatter inside.

She couldn't hear well, but it sounded like someone was coming. It was a boy, someone roughly her age. She couldn't tell for sure, but it looked like Jake.

"No way," she paused, gazing at the figure more precisely. He had tight golden brown curly hair, icy blue eyes, a chiseled face, a soccer player body, lean masculine muscles, and his sensitive face. It had to be Jake.

"She's here," the words slipped out of his mouth, as he turned his gaze towards the window. "I can feel her." She managed to hear the words, muffled through the glass, as he kept his gaze.

Locked in a trance together, his sensitive baby blue eyes were melting away the cold she felt, smothering the fear and blowing away the sorrow trapped deep inside her soul. Gazing deep into his eyes, she could feel it all disappear, creating an almost tangible warm feeling pulsing through her body. There was no longer any doubt in her mind that this was Jake. It seemed that even her soul remembered him, connected by some ancient force, unexplainable, strong and bonding. They gazed at each other, while the other man, searching frantically through the glass, blinded by the crystalline facets in the window, stood silently by, until; "Crap. . ." She mumbled, ducking behind the wall disappearing away from the window realizing that she had just been seen.

Chapter XVIII: United

"Oh crap, crap, crap, crap ... I think he saw me - not me, but me – a gargoyle. . . Now what do I do?" She quickly scurried along the side of the building until she was far enough from the room that no one would be able to see her.

She glanced down at the ground, still heavily snowing outside, and found a spot clear of trees and then released the building landing in a crouch, two feet into the snow.

After getting up and shaking off the cold flecks that clung to various parts of her already damp clothing, icing over from the cold, she wrapped her wings around her chest again, and sped off towards a barn she remembered spying nearby, hoping to find a warm hideout.

"Stupid, stupid, stupid," Taylor kept repeating the words to herself, afraid of the consequences of being seen. She found the barn approximately a mile from the mansion, and noticed that nothing was open, except for a small shutter door, propped only inches open toward the top of the barn. She crawled up the side and allowed herself in through a shutter. It was a loft, perfect for the nap she needed. She crawled into the thick piles of hay, prickly but dry, above the animals and pulled close the shutter door, crouching in the fetal position, with wings tightly wrapped around her body, trying desperately to warm up.

Senses dulled from the bitter cold; Taylor couldn't hear much above the howling of the snow as it pounded the sides of the barn. Shuddering in the cold bundle of hay she found, she was left only with her imagination to connect the points that would draw Jake into the ensuing war.

"W-what are y-you doing out h-here Jake? H-he's gonna k-kill you." She stammered to herself, barely hearing her own thoughts, numbed from the cold. Her thoughts began to go black as the freezing cold began to drag Taylor deep into unconsciousness.

"Taylor . . . Come to me," the comforting familiar voice beckoned to her in the cold darkness she had fallen into. A misty shadow appeared in her mind motioning for her to follow.

She felt the pain in her body return as the cold became real again, but she ignored it and followed the dark shrouding figure. She rose from the huddled spot she'd passed out in, in the hay, and pushed open the small loft door looking out into the night, eyes closed as if she were following something in her sleep. The bitter cold brushed against her face as the howling wind pushed a flurry of snow into the barn, and sent a shudder down her already frozen spine, and in her dream made her cross her arms, holding in the little warmth she felt as she followed the mysterious figure.

She leapt into the air and began soaring, soaring to a destination she was unaware of, in a place she couldn't see. Her eyes still closed, in a walking sleep, she felt comfort as she followed the figure.

"Where are we going?" She asked, still following the figure, for what seemed like hours.

"Somewhere familiar, somewhere right, somewhere where we both belong, somewhere happy and real away from this bad dream." The voice echoed through her mind, as the dark light began to brighten into a warm glowing light, and the shrouded figure began to form into a person. She followed until it stopped, and she was finally able to catch up to it.

She landed gracefully outside a school, a darkened school, lights out and empty from the night.

The figure faded away as she began to open her eyes. She glanced around, noticing a green mountain sign with a cowboy and the name Roughriders underneath, suddenly feeling comfortable and calm in the familiar place and caught a glimpse of her hand as the last remnants of leathery skin on her claws shimmered and shifted into her familiar ivory fingers, and she relaxed, standing right outside the Port Angeles High School.

"You can have this all back," the familiar voice caught her off guard.

"Jake," she launched herself at him, wrapping her arms around his neck. Surprised to see him standing beside her outside of their old school, together and human, she broke down into a silent stream of tears.

"Hey, it's okay," he consoled her. "Come on," he placed an arm around her waist and guided her through the school. "Remember Mr. Cadine used to teach Math in there, his crazy hair. You still have to finish up that class this year." He pointed into one of the classrooms down the long corridor lined with lockers.

A smile formed across Taylor's teary face, "Yeah, he was a pretty cool teacher." She left the comfort of Jake's arm and crossed the hall to one of the lockers, placing her hand on the little dial of the lock spinning it around a couple of times. "This must be another one of my strange dreams." She mumbled, still fiddling with the lock on the locker.

Jake snickered, "Come on, I've got more to show you." He wrapped his arm around her waist again and escorted her out of the school down across the street to his very familiar old car. "Go on, get in girly." He popped open his door and shoved the keys into the ignition.

"Where are we going now?" Taylor asked, excited to be home.

"A surprise," Jake responded.

Content with the response, Taylor quieted herself, enjoying the peaceful ease of being in Jake's presence, neither of them bothered by the silence. Still sure that this was all a dream, Taylor traced the ridges of Jake's hand gently and smiled at the thought of being his girlfriend.

Jake seemed just as pleased with the idea that was silently drifting between them, but kept his attention on the road driving down a couple of different streets cluttered with everyday ordinary houses until he found one with a large multi-angled hillside wall. He parked on the road above the house and escorted her around the back of it, to a part that was level with a large cascade window.

He quietly pushed aside some bushes and crept up alongside the eccentric house.

"Shhh. . . Look," Jake pointed into a corner of the window at the old couple sleeping silently in bed. One had a long tube connected to his nose with the other end hooked up to a breathing machine at one side of the bed and the other had a large bandage covering most of her arm.

"Grandma, Grandpa," Taylor squealed, loud enough for the old women to toss in bed as a response to the nose outside.

"Shhhh, I said," Jake grabbed Taylor, holding her back, placing one hand over her mouth. "They moved up here as soon as the doctors released them from the hospital, they were hoping that if you ran away, then maybe you returned here. They've been hoping to find you, but you can't see them. Not unless you make a choice." He explained, holding Taylor dearly.

"But they're alive, they're okay, they're here, why can't I have them." She began tearing up again, this time difficultly holding back the sobs.

"You know you can't see them while your, um, dangerous," he paused looking down at Taylor. "Now, come on," he lightly whispered, as he helped Taylor up and walked her back to the car, stopping to wipe some of the tears away every few moments. Jake helped Taylor into the car. "I'm sorry, I didn't mean to upset you like this. I just want to let you know that they're not dead, and that you can have a normal life again. You can have everything back. You just have to make a decision." He finished starting the car and drove off in the night heading west, out of town.

"That's the second time you've said that Jake, what decision do I need to make? Whatever it is, I'll do it, if I can go back to my grandparents – they need me as much as I need them." The words spilled out her mouth as she was quieting her sobs and clearing up her face. Jake was beating around the bush, and it was annoying her. What was he leaving out, that she couldn't quite pick up on? As a matter of fact, how did he know she was going to be here, was he the person calling to her in her strange dream? The thoughts swarmed through her mind while they drove on. Jake refusing to comment more as he kept silent until they finally pulled onto the long dark road that winded around the back side of Lake Crescent.

"It's a nice night for a walk, you up for it?" He asked Taylor, breaking the silence. He parked the car against a mound of dirt near the trailhead and stepped out of the car, slamming the door behind him.

Taylor followed him, closing the door behind her, all the while keeping her eyes cautiously on Jake as he nonchalantly ambled down the trail. "Something's not right," she mumbled to herself. When she opened her eyes, Jake was standing right there, at the school. She had seen her own finishing changes, so unless she was dreaming, he had to have seen them too, which meant he was in on something. He was acting too casual, something wasn't right. The strange warning wandering around in her thoughts began to get stronger as she followed him in the dark out to the place she once knew as The Devil's Punch Bowl. When they finally arrived at the Cliffside, Jake crossed onto the bridge and hung his arms over the railing looking out over the glistening water, from the silvery light of the moon.

"Remember all the fun we used to have out here?" Jake rolled around leaning his back against the railing. "I remember when you first jumped off of that ledge. You scratched up your hand because you didn't even look when you made it to the top. You just ran off the edge fearless and stubborn, as always." A smile crossed his face, lighting up the moonlit baby blues, perched above his naturally flawless nose.

"Yeah, that was funny. I didn't realize you had to get some distance on the jump. Talk about an adrenaline rush." Taylor forgot herself for a moment, laughing about the good times. "Hey Jake," Taylor's face became more serious, drowning out her laughter, she pulled her black hair out of her face, glistening from the moonlight, and back into a ponytail. "What are you doing? I mean – how'd you know where to find me? What's going on?" She asked, picking up some pebbles and tossing them out onto the cool, shimmering lake, disturbing the shallow waves that brushed across the surface, in the gentle breeze.

"It's just that, well, I wanted you to know you're not alone. I'm here to help. I can save you." He said.

"Save me . . . save me from what, Jake? What are you talking about?" Taylor cocked her head, confused at the thought.

"Um," he didn't respond yet, carefully trying to correct his words.

"Save me from what. . . Jake?" Taylor demanded more impatiently. "Jake, save me from what? What's going on?" She was booming.

"Shh, shh, sorry, calm down, sorry I, uh, worded that wrong. Just, just give me a sec. Maybe its better I show you and then try to explain." He cuffed Taylor's shoulders, holding her still until she calmed down. Although he towered a good seven inches over Taylor, he starred down into her eyes piercing her soul. "Just watch."

Locked in his gaze, Taylor quickly loosened up, relaxing her thoughts. Her face twisted into confusion as his baby blues became saturated with a cloud of billowing white, quickly fading away any color that once existed. And then to her amazement the same cloudy white quickly replaced the lightly tanned tone of his skin. A bit taken aback, Taylor stepped back from Jake's grasp, and watched as his body began to take form of a shape ever more familiar to her.

Taylor fell to a knee as she tripped over a lose board on the bridge stepping back from Jake. Still baffled, she ignored the scratched knee and steadied herself as she watched Jake finish his change. Before the long white leathery wings could jut out from his back, Jake pulled his shirt off over his head, which was no longer covered in tightly knit little golden-brown curls and revealed the purple blue bruise that sat right above his sternum.

Taylor gasped, "What, what happened to you?" She reached out a hand and placed it on his scar, closing the gap between them, forgetting her caution from before. She flinched, when her hand touched his skin. It was colder than she could remember. She knew that when she was changed, she could withstand colder, but she didn't realize it was because her body was colder.

His still human hands reached up and grabbed her wrist pressing her hand firmly to his skin. He closed his eyes and filled his chest with the strong delicate smell of her hair which through the change became much stronger and ever more luring to him. Then he opened his eyes, finishing up the change, he released Taylor's hand, and stepped back as his fingers finally sharpened into deadly razor like bear claws, that could pierce titanium, and his tail slithered down and out past his legs and around Taylor pulling her in closer.

"I can show you how to control it," the words drifted out of his mouth catching Taylor in a trance.

She was no longer looking at Jake, but at a large white gargoyle, with glacier white eyes. Yet she felt just as calm with this gargoyle as she had with Jake. If angels had to look like demons, that is what Jake looked like. He was strong and pure and full of protection, his very essence felt overpowering.

"The only catch is that you may have to give it up. You would have to agree to one day give it all up. The power, the changes, the breathing underwater, the flying," his mouth wasn't moving the words were directed straight into her head, he was talking to her using telepathy.

He paused after each thing showing off the display of talents accumulated by the change. When he said breathing underwater, he arched his back and leapt up onto the railing and off into the water disappearing for several minutes. Taylor searched around the glistening surface of the lake for him, only to be surprised when he launched into the air like a dolphin jumping out of water, only instead of re-entering the water he spread out his wings and caught the air swooping down along the water's surface and around until he landed coolly beside Taylor again.

"The telepathy," he singularly shook his body in one motion causing the remaining droplets of water to fling off and then looked down again at Taylor, this time with a smile across his daunting white face, still not saying a word out loud.

"The stone," he said out loud. That caught Taylor's immediate attention, snapping her right out of her little trance.

"What do you know about the stone?" A worried look drew across her face. She wondered if he could possibly know what he was talking about. "I can't give up the stone, according to the professor that would kill me." Then she wondered if she really could give up the stone, maybe the professor was lying, he did shoot her, what else was he willing to do or not do, say or not say?

"I'm listening, for now." Taylor stated, quickly disregarding her first question, hopeful that there might still be a chance, a chance for her normal life back, and her grandparents back, and school, even never fun, ever so boring school back.

"This learning how to control my powers, it doesn't involve guns or electricity does it?" She handed Jake her hand allowing him to swiftly scoop her up into his large arms, cradling her like a baby. Almost instantly, he leapt off of the bridge and into the air soaring gracefully toward the heavens.

"No, why would it?" He asked her, baffled by the strange question.

"Um, no reason, just making sure," she smiled and held tightly around Jake's neck trying not to let go. She couldn't help but feel a little embarrassed. She didn't want to admit that she needed Jake's help, and being wrapped so tightly to his body made her feel very secure.

"So where are we going?" Taylor asked, curled into Jake's chest. It was getting colder as he continued to fly north. Luckily it wasn't snowing, and the sun was beginning to peek over the far eastern hills.

"I'm gonna take you to the Estates, try and teach you a thing or two," he paused. "I believe you were there earlier," the words lingered in the air.

"There earlier," she thought. "The mansion in the storm, you mean?" Taylor asked, surprised. "I didn't wasn't sure anyone noticed me."

"No one did, I could feel your presence though. The stone connects us." He replied.

She thought about what he said for a moment and then replied. "I think I know what you mean. I've felt the connection . . . before." She mumbled, and then slipped into a silent stream of comforting thoughts.

She wondered if none of this had happened, would she still be able to live with her grandparents, and who knew, maybe even date Jake. Long distance relationships don't work out very well but it'd be worth a try. Who could trade Saturday morning cartoons and long mindless conversations, while driving out to the lake for a mid morning freezing dunk, for all this crap? And after she graduated high school, Jake and she could go to the same college, and be the annoying mushy couple that started out back in high school. Everyone would say 'oh they'll never make it, those high school sweethearts never do,' but they would, and everyone would be so surprised. And then who knew, maybe even kids some . . ."

"Hey, I'm gonna bring us down for a landing now, I'm gonna bet that you're freezing in this snow." Jake interrupted her, swooping down close behind the back side of a very large three-story estate.

"It looks different without the blizzard whirling around," she commented, as Jake's large, clawed feet puffed into the newly white billows of snow, disturbing the fresh powder.

"Let's get you inside," he set her down onto the ground and rushed her into a back door of the estate. They moved quickly through a long faintly lit hallway and into a minimally decorated room.

"Sit there," he pointed to his bed and disappeared into the bathroom, adjacent to his room, reappearing with two towels. "Wrap up with these. I'll go find you something warmer." As he was speaking to her, she watched his glistening white body hurry out of the bedroom, scrambling around as if nothing was out of the ordinary.

"This is just too much," she sighed, and snuggled into the towels tossing her body back against the pillow pile on the bed. A couple minutes passed by, and she glanced around the room finding nothing particularly interesting. She watched the minutes flick by as she stared at an alarm clock standing on his dresser until close to fifteen minutes passed with no sign of Jake and then decided a bath sounded rather cozy.

● ● ●

Steam swirled around in the bathroom as the nearly scolding water filled the tub, and she quickly undressed tossing her partially damp clothes into a pile on the floor. Taylor shuffled through the drawers under the sink until she found a tie, and pulled her hair back hastily, wrapping her silky black hair loosely on top of her head.

A long sigh echoed through the air as she slowly sank into the deep tub, allowing the steaming hot bath water to warm the cockles of her heart.

She lingered in the tub until the water began to cool and then forced herself up, allowing the trickles of water to drain from her hair onto the floor. The mirror was steamy, so steamy that she wiped a hand over the glass, clearing a space off.

The reflection she saw in the mirror was familiar but so very different. She relaxed and took a deep breath as she realized that the little girl she once knew was growing up and changing. The whole world was changing; nothing would ever be the same for her, or for anyone. People were becoming greedy and hateful. Countries were fighting over material possessions just so that they could fuel the impersonal wars they were waging in the name of God. Technology had become so advanced that one person could kill thousands of people with a few clicks of a button and never feel the responsibility of those deaths because of how impersonal the fighting had become. The world she knew as a little girl was gone, and she of all people just might have the power to change that, but at the cost of what?

Just then the door opened in the bathroom and Jake stood, fully dressed and in his old human form, flushed with embarrassment. Taylor startled, quickly snatching a towel from the counter, and draped it around her naked body.

"Jake . . . a little privacy," she harked.

"Sorry, I, I just never, seen, oh . . . so sorry." He struggled with the words and backed away from the door, face completely red and walked over to the bed.

After a couple minutes had passed, Jake decided to say something, hoping to change the awkward silence in the room. "Sorry I took so long. I found you some warmer clothes and rustled up some food." The words drifted into the bathroom.

"Can you hand me the clothes?" She leaned out of the bathroom door, surprised to find Jake standing there with a pile of clothes in one hand.

She let go of the doorknob and stood up straight towel wrapped tightly around her body and became fixated in Jake's gaze.

"I never noticed how. . ."

"Shh," Jake placed a finger over her lips and then slid his hand down around her chin and delicately tilted it upward as he pressed his firm masculine lips against hers.

"Handsome you are," the thought dwindled out of Taylor's mind as Jake's strong lips caressed the small dainty creases of her own lips and sent a wave of tingling warmth all the way down to the bottom of her toes and caused her foot to lift slightly up, pushing her ever so slightly back into the long-awaited kiss. The kiss lasted only a few seconds, but the chemically jolting atmosphere lingered for what seemed like a lifetime. She was completely entranced by Jake's strong, guarding, blue eyes, until he broke the silence.

"Here," he handed Taylor the clothes and then quickly left the room.

"Oh my God, that was amazing. What am I doing? What is he doing? Oh. . ." Taylor squealed with excitement. "Calm down, calm down," she repeated over to herself, as she pulled on the oddly perfect fitting clothes that Jake brought her.

Jake left a bowl of soup on the dresser and a couple of rolls. Taylor quietly gobbled them down and drank the soup up, she was excited and nervous and hungry all at the same time, but the soup helped ease the tension.

After Taylor finished eating, Jake returned, and his more childish slightly less charming attitude had returned with him.

"Good, they're not too small," he said, pointing at the sweater and jeans he'd given Taylor. "Hope you're feeling warmer now," he winked at her.

"So, tell me about this secret to control the transformation." Taylor unfolded a blanket at the edge of the bed, and wrapped herself in it, then leaned back against the headboard.

"Well, it's much easier than you would think, but I'm guessing that one has to experience it to understand completely." Jake began to explain. "I think the transformation is connected to your emotions, but not just everyday emotions. It takes an intensely strong emotion to trigger the energy required for your body to make the change. It doesn't appear to matter whether it's a really angry emotion or a really happy emotion or even a very sad emotion as long as it's extremely powerful, then the emotion appears to trigger a rise in adrenaline which stimulates the energy required for transformation. That combined with a powerful focus on changing drives the body to begin changing. That's pretty much all it takes. Some people have a harder time with it then others, but I think that's just because they probably haven't experienced something so powerful that they can't reproduce the strong emotion."

"Others, you mean you know about the others?" Taylor asked.

"Yeah, how do you think I learned all this in the last few weeks? They've been teaching me." He commented.

"But aren't you working with Major Bradshaw?" Taylor asked confused.

"Yes, and he's a really great guy. . ."

"Really great guy," Taylor's voice strained. "Do you realize what you're saying? He's supposed to be the enemy. He's been kidnapping little children from school and performing all sorts of torturous experiments on them. He's also supposedly behind many of the missile attacks in Iraq, and China, and the assassination attempt on the president. Him and his monster strike force team." She said accusingly. By now Taylor was standing beside the bed pacing frantically back and forth nearly shouting at Jake.

"No, he's not, he's a good guy. He gave me this power to help save you. He said that if I brought you here, he would be able to get the other piece of the stone, and then you could have your normal life back, otherwise you were in serious danger." Jake began shouting back at Taylor defensively.

"Danger? Getting back the stone? Do you realize what bringing me here has done?" Finally, all the information and advise that the professor was telling Taylor fit into place and she realized that although the professor was a little cruel and demanding he probably realized that Major Bradshaw had been concocting a plan to bring her into his grasp.

"Jake," Taylor grabbed his hand. "Listen to me, removing the stone will kill me, same as it would you." She swallowed the anger trembling in her voice and covered up the fear.

"No, he said, he can remove it safely and we can have our normal lives back." Jake desperately tried to argue.

"No, he won't, he doesn't care about us. He just wants the stone and its power. He just used you to get to me, do you understand? He used you." She forced the words upon him.

"No, you're wrong Taylor and you're in danger, just listen to me."

An alarm began screaming through the entire Cyndac site, drowning out the words of their argument.

Taylor clasped her ears and moved closer to Jake frantically. "What's going on?"

"It's an alarm, intruders. I have to go." He released her hands and ran off towards the door.

"No wait Jake, don't go, this is all wrong, something is very wrong." She cried after him, but he didn't hesitate and before she knew it, he was gone unlike the blaring sound of the alarm ricocheting off the walls.

Chapter XIX: Viper Task Force

Meanwhile as Taylor was getting reacquainted with Jake up until they were separated by the alarm at the facility, Shyla and Will had met up in the Kokrine hills and begun preparations to bust into the facility and free the kidnapped children suspected to be stashed somewhere on the facility's grounds.

"Have you noticed anything new?" Will directed his thoughts to Shyla, who was silently and invisibly patrolling the northern and eastern sides of the Cyndac Oil Refinery.

"I haven't seen much commotion since they brought in the boy. Although, there has been a steady stream of scientists, coming and going from the eastern entrance, no sign of any children though." She responded in thought.

"I haven't seen any children either, but I did pick up a steady stream of thoughts focused on Taylor coming from that boy they brought in. I think he must have known her before she found the stone. What he's doing up here, I'm not sure, but he does seem to have some sort of self-righteous idea that he's going to save her or something like that. I'm not sure how he fits in to all this though." He explained to Shyla, perched quietly in a large snow-covered evergreen, only meters from the base's perimeter, blending in perfectly with his snowy blue-hued color as a gargoyle. "Well sit tight and keep watching something is bound to change." He finished, settling back down into a slow steady search through the various minds scattered about the facility hoping to find a glimpse of any one of the missing children.

A couple hours passed as Shyla and Will patrolled the sides of the facility, Shyla at the northern and eastern walls and Will at the southern and western walls.

"Another scientist is exiting the eastern door. He's the one that came in two days ago. See if he's seen anything." Shyla alerted Will.

Will pushed past the wall of thoughts waving around the outer structures of the main facility and singularly directed his penetration into the lone scientist leaving the facility at the eastern wall. He peeled past the protective sheen of consciousness and into the mind of the scientist. As he began to ruffle through the thoughts and memories of the scientist, as he usually does, to read into the persons past, he was slammed with a blank slate. It was almost like a billow of clouds completely shrouded each memory. He moved from one to the next only to be blinded with more cloudy unreadable memories. Each memory of the scientist was either hidden or destroyed and it left Will completely helpless.

"Shyla, something's wrong?" He shouted into her mind frantically. "I can't get a read on his thoughts." He explained.

"Just tell me what you're seeing, I'm sure I can explain the picture, I know words are easier for you but maybe I can help." She harmlessly suggested.

"No, you don't understand, there are no pictures. His mind, it's completely shrouded by something and unreadable. I can't tell what's causing it." He sent back the thought with a feeling of hurt in it, ashamed that he could be losing control of his power.

"You're going to be fine. I'm mean you're still reading my mind just fine. It's probably not you," Shyla tried to calm him down.

"You're right. I can still read your mind. That means something is wrong with the scientist, but what could do that to him. What on earth could be so powerful that it could possibly keep, ME, out?" Shyla could sense a bit of ego gushing over into his thoughts as he spoke.

"Okay, let's just put aside your little haughty attitude for a minute and think. What do we know that can block your mindreading?" At first, she teased, but then got serious with Will.

"Well, nothing that I can think of. There's nothing and no one that I can't read." He huffed.

"That's not true, are you forgetting one key person?" She paused giving Will a brief moment to put together his thoughts. "Esa . . . Duh! You can't read her. You can't read anything about her, you can't even speak to her with your mind. Maybe there is a connection there."

"Well unfortunately I can't read her mind, nor can I send thoughts to her so that doesn't really help us now, does it?" Will respond angrily.

"Don't get flip with me, I'm just trying to help." She scolded.

"Sorry, let's just keep an eye . . . Wait someone is coming on the road near the southern gate. Ooh I think I've got something." He stopped arguing with Shyla and focused on the armor-clad jeep pulling up to the southern gate of the facility.

Shyla ran full speed through the snow, all the while holding her focus of invisibility, like second nature around herself, until she too could see the armor-clad jeep pulling up to the southern gate. The window in the jeep rolled down revealing an old man with a pass and I.D. badge, stunning both Shyla and Will.

"Major Bradshaw," the words echoed through both of their minds at the same time.

"There in the back, did you see? It looked like a little kid." Shyla thought allowing Will to pick it up.

"Yeah, it was a kid, only I'm trying to read his thought and I can't get anything. Both he and Major Bradshaw are shrouded by those same cloudy auras. I don't know what it is. That must be why I didn't pick up on him sooner. His mind is protected by something." Will explained.

They both watched as the jeep continued down the snowy road that circled around the inside perimeter of the facility. It passed several different buildings, before it stopped at the far northern building on the east side where the scientist had exited earlier. The child stepped out, followed by Major Bradshaw, who then brushed his coat off, and gave a suspicious preview of the visible tree line outside the facility's perimeter. The child stood, statuesquely still until Major Bradshaw roughly sounded an order to the child and disappeared inside the building's eastern entrance with the child robotically following behind.

"Protected by something, or someone?" Shyla questioned suspiciously; eyes still locked on the door where the two had disappeared.

"Have you ever seen anything like that before? It's as if that child was under his total control." Will pointed out.

"I've seen that kind of behavior before. Its brainwashing! That child is brainwashed and he's in charge." There was a break in her thoughts momentarily. "Do you think that child is what is blocking your thoughts? Maybe he's some sort of shield for him?" Shyla asked hesitantly, afraid of the response.

"That would explain why he's shadowing Major Bradshaw, keeping him off my radar." Will mumbled.

"Is that what he's doing with them? Brainwashing them into submission, after he's done with whatever horrible experiments, he has planned for them?" Shyla gulped to hold back the tears that would accompany the anger she was containing.

"Well, that kid was clearly guarding his mind, and if he has more of them like that, down there, with abilities like that kid, then it would explain why I'm not picking up any thoughts of kids or odd experiments at all." Will responded. "It's almost morning, we should probably head back for the night. I can keep a decent enough watch on the area with my mind, we need to decide what we are going to do, especially without Kam." He leapt down from his perch in the evergreen and sped off towards the Kokrine hills where they would camp for the day.

Shyla focused especially hard on her invisibility because she'd be moving quickly and pulled away from the wall where she was closely hugging. They both ran silently through the snow twisting around trees and lunging over rocks and holes, careful not to draw attention, and staying out of the sky, sure that Major Bradshaw ran sky patrols, scouting for intruders.

There was a cave deep in the woods that stretched back a good fifty meters where they had met up originally. Once they finally me up again at the cave, Shyla collected some partially dried out wood around the entrance, and Will started a fire at the very rear of the cave so that no light would drift off into the morning sky, keeping them very hidden from any possible sky patrols. As they felt the delicate warmth of the fire fold around their entrancing figures, exhaustion swept over them both like a thick wool blanket.

"So do you think the kids are down there?" Shyla asked.

"No doubt, especially with Major Bradshaw showing up, he must be getting ready for something big. Anyhow, get some sleep we can talk some more after we've got some rest."

Morning broke, and both Shyla and Will dozed off into a deep sleep hardly woken by a single noise, until once again dusk began to fall, and the embers of the fire cooled completely, turning a dark ashy coal color, and leaving them both chilled, before they woke.

Willem woke first, disturbed by something he'd seen in a thought, and quickly woke Shyla thereafter.

"What, what is it?" Shyla questioned, startled by the hasty awakening.

"That boy," he said.

"What boy?" She asked still confused.

"That one that knew Taylor, he's left, and I think to go after her and worse yet, he's been shrouded. I can't tell what he's doing. But pretty much the last thought I could read was him bringing her here, but I'm not sure how he plans to do that. We have little time to get those kids before everything goes wrong." Will frantically chocked out, catching his breath from the startled thought that woke him.

"Why are you like that?" Shyla pointed at Will.

"Like what," he replied.

"That," she pointed with one long golden and red furred finger again.

Will collected his thoughts and cleared his head glancing down at the ground where his bare feet were standing and then it hit him.

"Brrr, I'm f-freezing," he stuttered the words through clattering teeth. He was fully human. At some point during the day of sleep he must have shifted out of his gargoyle form and into his human form, strangely enough he still could read thoughts. He, like all the others could only use their special abilities when in gargoyle form, but it was one of the thoughts he'd read while monitoring the facility that awoke him from his cold sleep.

"Why'd you shift? You could catch your death in this cold. What were you thinking?" She began scorning him.

"I didn't do it on purpose, Jeez, lay off." He quickly responded in his defense. Clasping his arms tightly together holding in all the warmth that he could, he began to focus and return to his gargoyle form. The change only took a few moments, from the crowned ridges on his forehead to the silvery dragon like tail that jutted out behind him, he finished shifting back into his more comfortable and less weather affected body, just to notice a strange pulsing coming from the money pouch attached to his belt.

"That's strange," he mumbled, glancing into the pouch, only to see the small fragment of rock slowly release a faint glow of light in short dim waves. "Last time this happened Taylor was nearby or at least the other stone fragment was close, that's probably not good." He mumbled.

"Alright, well now that I'm ready, can you still shroud others with your invisibility?" Will asked.

"Course I can silly, what use would I be otherwise?" She jeered.

"Good, we'll enter using your invisibility. We'll wait until one of those scientists enters the eastern door on the far building, where you've been monitoring. That seems to be where most of the commotion is. Once we're in, we'll try to find the holding cells. If we can locate the kids then I'll slip away, cut the power, and cause a diversion, so that you can quietly release the holding cells and sneak the kids out of the base. Whatever happens to me, don't panic, get any of the children you find out of the facility and return here to the caves. Your main focus will be to make sure that no one breaks your invisibility. With any luck no one will even notice the children missing until you guys are safely gone with my diversion and your extremely exceptional cloaking ability." He finished tracing the plan out.

"Okay, so rendezvous here. We'll wait a day, but if you don't show I'm coming back in for you." Shyla responded.

"NO," he cut her off. "Those kids are the most important thing, keep them cloaked and if I'm not here in a day start traveling back toward the Chateau. No matter what, don't wait up for me any longer than that. If they get you or the children then it will all have been for nothing, understand?" Will clasped Shyla's hand, staring her down. "Stay hidden," he ushered one last time with urgency.

"Yes, Will." She looked away, "I will." She looked back up at his eyes, "promise me you'll be careful though."

He shrugged away and muttered a simple, "yeah."

"Promise, damn it," she shouted at him.

"Fine, fine, I promise," he planted the words firmly. "Now let's get going." And with that, Shyla pulled Will into her shroud of invisibility, and they sped off together flying through the air, carefree of being caught in flight. Flight would be the fastest way to get there and the most direct path to the eastern entrance of the northern building.

As they neared the facility, they noticed the usual guard standing at the southern entrance of the building and two patrol guards walking the grounds. The patrol guards were closer to the western front of the south gate and might be back towards the northern building within a half hour. It usually took them about two hours to walk the entire grounds before they started their rounds again. They should probably have waited for the two guards to finish the patrol before gaining entrance to the building, but to their luck a scientist was just on his way into the eastern entrance.

Most of the scientists appeared to take the side entrance to the building rather then the main entrance at the front, where the security guards were posted, but being that there was no guard at the side entrance, that was their first choice for breaching the facility.

"Okay, lets get right on his heal, and don't say anything to me I'll, read your mind. I don't want us to be heard, got that?" Will directed his thoughts to Shyla waiting for her thought response, until they both dropped down silently into the snow and followed delicately behind the man trying ever so quietly not to make any crunching noises in the snow that might give them away. Fortunately for the both of them it was very dark outside and there were few streetlamps scantly spattered along the road, and there was just enough roar from the wind, whipping around, that the snow was tossed about, lightly covering any appearing tracks.

"When he types in the code there is a momentary pause in the door before it closes. We'll slip in together and then wait against the wall, stay close to me." He spoke into Shyla's mind once again waiting for her little thought response to follow.

"Roger that," she responded comically.

The scientist typed in a six-digit code on the keypad inserted on the wall alongside the large steel door and waited for a confirmation buzz. With the buzz, the door slid open, and the scientist promptly walked inside, behind him silently and invisibly, followed Shyla and Will. Once inside, the door inevitably slid shut and the buzz sound became a few clicks acknowledging the door was locked shut.

They stood against the wall near the door and watched as the scientist walked up to a man at a desk, handed him a badge, and then walked off behind a door to the left of the desk. There were two doors aside from the obvious lobby door far ahead in the front part of the building. The two doors stood behind the guard desk, one to the left and one to the right. The guard stood up, looked around the room briefly and then began shifting his look from one side of his desk, pausing to focus at what must have been camera monitors, until he got to the end of the desk and then sat back into his seat.

"Follow me behind the guard, I'll bet there is something useful on those monitors he's looking at." Will instructed, as he tiptoed his way forward and around the desk, until they were both carefully standing behind the guard sitting at the desk staring at a basketball game on one of the monitors.

"He's distracted, that's good." Will commented in Shyla's mind.

They both looked from screen to screen browsing for any sign of the children. With any luck they would find a clue as to what direction they needed to head.

"Here, over here . . . check this one out." Shyla pointed to the left top two monitors. There was an empty hall with four doors two on one side and two on the other. There were security locks on each door and nameplates on the doors reading: Specimen F 203-207, Specimen F 208-210, Specimen M 134-137, and Specimen M 138-141. The monitor screen itself was labeled Barracks level 1 and the other monitor mimicked the first, only the numbers were different and the screen was labeled Barracks level 2. It was silent in the halls, on all the monitor screens, of course it was nightfall so hopefully nothing would change, at least until morning, which gave them plenty of time to rescue the children.

"Hey, look one of the scientists is coming off shift, down that door to the right." He pointed to the monitor. A tall man in a long white lab coat scuttled up to the door on the monitor screen which read 'Security Monitoring Hall Exit Door Right' and began punching in a code.

"Now's our chance to sneak in before the door reseals," Will whispered to Shyla's mind. Fortunately for Will, anyone inside of Shyla's invisibility cloak could see one another. No one else can see inside the hidden field of invisibility but they can see each other, allowing for them to easily stay close enough so that she could hold the field strongly together, hiding them in perfect sight.

Quickly they tiptoed over to the door just as the scientist exited, stepping inside before the door slid tightly shut.

"Hey there," the security guard shouted.

Both their hearts skipped a beat as they froze, just inside the door.

"Don't forget your cell phone, you left it here before going in. You know work policy; next time don't bring it to work, or I'll have to confiscate it." The security officer handed a small rectangular phone back to the scientist.

"Sorry, didn't realize it was in my pocket, won't happen again." The scientist responded, and then both Shyla and Will let out a long silent sigh as they realized the security guard wasn't talking to them, and then continued on down the hallway.

"Look elevators at the end of the hall, that's our best bet. Better hope the guard isn't paying attention to the screens." Will said.

They moved like serpents, silently crossing the hall without making a single noise, until they reached the elevator and pressed the down arrow button.

"Everything is underground," Shyla whispered. The idea made her nervous. If they got caught it would be much harder to escape from underground then it would be, from out in the open.

The elevator dinged open, and they slipped into the small boxed in room. The doors shut and Will looked up and down the small symbol panel.

*1 Main Lobby

-2 Lunch Hall & Cots

-L1 Barracks

-L2 Barracks

-1L Green Labs

-2L Blue Labs

-GND Basement

"This is where we part," Will pushed the –L2 button and then the GND button. "I'll drop you off at the lower Barracks level. Don't do anything until I've sent you a message. In case the guard notices the elevator, I don't want him to become alert until I make myself clear. I'm going to the bottom floor to see if there are some power generators there. Once I've cut the power and drawn all the attention to myself, you make your move, and start releasing those children. Take the stairs up and get them the hell out of here." Will spoke directly and sternly to Shyla, "Don't wait for me no matter what."

The words echoed through her head, "no matter what." Something felt wrong to her, but she had no time to think. The elevator stopped moving and the doors slid open and dinged as she stepped out.

"The invisibility will only hold until the elevator drops down another floor than I can't hold it over you anymore. Good luck," She loudly whispered.

"Same to you," Will responded, and with that, the doors slid closed leaving Shyla alone in the lower Barracks level. She raced over to the doors and peered inside, surprised to see several children silently asleep on small cots lined beside each other in each of the rooms. The F on the doors stood for the females and the M for the males because each room labeled was full of them according to the mark on the door. She waited by the door and focused entirely on keeping herself invisible meanwhile she felt the small tug as her hold on Will failed, as he dropped down to the floors below them.

"What the. . ." the security guard tapped on the elevator monitor screen, then reached over to the phone, picked it up, and dialed the security headquarters office at the front post.

"What's up?" The man at the security headquarters office answered the phone.

"Just got a malfunction with the laboratory elevator again, it's opened at the barracks level; no one is on it though. Pain in the ass I know, but you know protocol." The security guard spoke diligently into the phone.

"Okay we'll log it, probably just the wiring but keep an eye on it anyway. The boss arrived yesterday and said that with the girl here, we need to keep an extra sharp eye on things. Turns out she does not have her powers under control, and who knows what kind of mess that might mean. Thanks," the main office guard hung up the phone.

"Hmm," the guard set down the phone, and looked back to the game he'd been watching, catching the final score before glancing back into the elevator monitor.

"Shit," he reached over to the far side of the counter, spilling a mug of coffee, and flicked up a large red switch that was turned down, immediately sounding a loud steady stream of bursting blares, announcing an intruder all over the base, after noticing a large gargoyle like figure standing in the elevator where nothing stood moments before.

He picked up the phone to call the main guard post but before he had a chance to dial out, a voice came through from the other side.

"What the hell is going on over there?" A guard from the main post yelled through the phone.

"The elevator, it's not empty anymore, one of those escapes from the 80's is on it and getting off in the basement."

"Roger that, don't let anyone out of the building." The man hung up the phone.

The security guard ran over to the main door typing in a long security code that appeared to put the building on lock down, from here on, only specific codes would allow anyone inside the building or out. He pulled his pistol from his side and took his place, standing by the main door ready and waiting for further back up.

The alarm blared through the base, awakening anyone and anything remotely close to sleeping, along with the pulsing alarm came an announcement that repeated several times before it went silent. "Viper Task Force, report to the Northern Laboratory, there is a P-S-I Subject intrusion . . . Viper Task Force report to the Northern Laboratory," The announcement went silent after the third repetition, and the base intruder alarm fell silent another five minutes after that.

Will heard the alarm fall silent and continued down the darkened hallway after he exited the elevator. He made his way around several large steam pipes and past two rooms full of air conditioning units and high-pressure air systems. At last, he'd found a large room with two small generators running one on each side of the room and decided that destroying these would be the most efficient way to cut the power.

He glanced around the room, hoping to locate something to destroy the two generators with and without any luck he prowled around the generators themselves. He eventually found a speed trip, releasing both of them, on either side of the room, stopping the two generators and then he cut a hole in the oil lines and set fire to the room. If he couldn't destroy the generators, he could at least make it near impossible to restart them any times soon. Once the fire was set, he raced out of the room, hurrying toward the staircase located near the elevator, but before he could make it that far, two very large gargoyles launched out of the elevator, and another large reddish brown one, smashed his clawed fist right into his chest, from the stairwell.

Will wrestled around with the reddish brown one knocking him back toward the elevator. He smashed into the elevator and ripped a chunk of the steel door off, swishing it back in the air at Will. He ducked a few times, but one of the bone-etched gargoyles tumbled into his feet, knocking off his balance and then as he tried to knock away the darkish green one, the large reddish brown one laid a strong powerful smash to his skull with the steel chunk from the elevator door, and sent him reeling to the floor, where the other two braced his arms and carried him off up the stairs.

While Will was trying to set off a distraction, Shyla was browsing through each of the rooms silently trying to wake the children and ready them for an escape. She successfully reached her invisibility cloak inside of all the rooms, allowing the children to see her, and still keeping hidden from the cameras, until she saw him.

An almost flawless child, she once thought to be a dream. He'd short wispy golden blond hair that unlike his cheekbones didn't resemble anything of his Native American ancestors, and he had her little button nose and her beautiful cream-colored skin. His chin was small and narrow, and his brows thick and shadowy, but the most amazing recognizable feature that the little child carried was his eyes. They were like little globes of swirling fire, the same flaring color of her fur; blazing red mixed with the creamy undertones of yellow, but they were missing something. . . Life.

"Deon," she yelled his name, with no response.

"Deon," she yelled louder, waiting for a response until finally the lights went out.

She thought to herself, "Power is gone this must be my chance." She flexed her razor like claws and tore open the door-lock, carefully shoving the door open, and racing in alongside the little boy.

"What's happened to you?" She whispered tears streaming down from her face. "You're just a child?" She chided leaning down against him and swooping his little body up into her arms. She nestled his head in her hand and pulled it into her face looking at his eyes again. "What have they done to you?" She whispered, still totally focused on the child staring into his lifeless unyielding eyes. He had no responses to anything, even the little motions she made to move him affected nothing in his posture or responsiveness.

She pulled a blanket off of the bed he had be sitting stiffly besides, and wrapped him like a swaddled baby, and then tied it like a sling, around her small body, keeping one arm around him, supporting him closely to her body while she stepped up and over to the next room.

She frantically ripped open the door-lock with her razor claws gathering up the children in each room.

"Grab a blanket from your beds its cold outside," she repeated to each roomful of children and then motioned for them to follow as she found the stairwell near the elevator. "Stay close so that they might not see you, children," she said to them, and then they began to flood into the stairwell. After she had collected all the children from both of the barracks' levels, they slowly and silently escaped through the stairwell.

"We're scared lady," several of the children whispered to Shyla as they were climbing the stairs.

"I know children, but we must stay silent in order to get away safely." She replied.

"I want my mommy," another child cried and then Shyla could hear a couple of other kids sniffle in agreement but then they quieted down, for they could hear some shouting and banging coming from outside of the stairs.

As they got to the top of the stairwell, Shyla reminded the children to stay very close and not to make a sound. "Okay, we have to be very silent and very close together. We must sneak past anyone out there without them noticing, in order to get out of this place. Just be strong one last time children, please."

She gathered them all around closely, took one deep breath and pushed open the door hoping that with all the commotion outside they wouldn't notice the door open. The children slowly one by one filed into the main hallway, blankets wrapped tightly around each of them, and then they slowly moved down the hallway, keeping close to the wall, in case anyone needed to move through it. The security door at the end of the hall was fortunately open, and they filed through carefully, pausing and stepping aside, to allow a single man to run down to the end of the hall toward the elevator.

All the doors had been opened at the top of the building, with guards posted on each side and a truck was parked outside the main entrance with several men stationed beside it, like they were waiting on something.

Shyla quietly ushered the children out of the main entrance making sure to avoid any contact with any of the guards, and hurriedly rushed them into the snow. Once all of the children were together, she rushed them back behind the building into the darkest area, making sure that footprints wouldn't be noticed in the snow.

"The children are gone, search the grounds," someone near the entrance barked an order. "This was all a diversion, get them back and I mean now, and bring the kid up here to me." The man shouted, roaring with anger.

"Oh no," Shyla whispered. "Wait here children, and don't move." She abandoned the children for just a moment not actually moving far enough from them to break the invisibility and peeked around the end of the building.

And there, inside the building stood the very man who destroyed her life, finding every means possible to torture and dissect her, a man she once called father, Major Bradshaw. Beside him, was a team of four of the deadliest looking gargoyles she'd ever seen before. One covered in slithery scales like a snake, and another raptor like, all etched with bone brows and bone spikes coming from their joints. They didn't look anything like the gargoyles that she and her friends became, warm and graceful, but rather dark and horrifying.

She became distracted from the rage building up inside her as she saw, from out of the hall, two entirely bone etched gargoyles, dragging an unconscious human body, bloodied, and bruised.

"Will," she thought loudly, hoping that he'd wake up, but before she had a chance to remember what he'd made her promise. Promise to leave, and not come back for him no matter what, she was pinned.

"What the . . ." she shouted. "Get off me."

A large shimmering white daemon much like the one that Will becomes, slammed her against the wall.

"Here's one, I got her." He shouted to Major Bradshaw, grasping both of her hands and pulling them tightly behind her, leaving the sling with the small boy dangling from her shoulder.

"You don't know what you're doing, get off of me." She shouted some more, no longer holding her invisibility cloak.

Two more of the monsters joined the white one to brace Shyla in place and drag her alongside the unconscious Will and toss her on the ground. Rifles pointed at both Shyla and the child in her sling, one of them kicked her sharply in the ribs. "Move, and not only will I shoot you, but the kid will get it too." One of the random men spitefully shouted at her.

"I see you found the child you supposedly never had, Shyla," Major Bradshaw said, surreptitiously pulling aside the blanket and peering at the child's face. "A very gift from the God's, that one is." He commented tossing back the blanket, "but then coming from you what else could we expect." He finished and then stepped back. "Take him back to his room, and get rid of her," he nonchalantly ordered several of the team to dispose of Shyla.

"NO, Deon . . . no," she screamed as they pried him away from her, bracing her tightly as the large reddish-brown gargoyle stepped in and injected her with something that almost instantly made her body fall limp, allowing them to drag her off in the opposite direction that they carried the boy in.

Chapter XX: Vampire Repayment

"Wake up, Derek Willem," Major Bradshaw chided.

Will began to feel the painful throbbing of his head, and the sharp stabbing pressure of a bullet wound in his arm, as he slowly regained consciousness. He could feel his ribs bursting with pain and a cold trickle of blood dribbled down the side of his head, as his vision blurred in and out, slightly clearing up with each phase.

"Bring back the boy, Deon. I have a perfect task for him." Major Bradshaw ordered again.

"That's it boy, wake up," Major Bradshaw placed a foot on the fleshy bullet wound on Will's arm and twisted hard, causing sharp pain to shoot all up and down Will's arm and neck.

"Hey, the rest of the children are out here," someone shouted from outside.

"Good, get them back inside and lock 'em up. I've had enough crap for today. Go help the boys, Jake. Those kids are important." He turned to the white gargoyle and sent him away.

"So, there are children here? The same kids that were kidnapped from different schools," Jake asked?

"Don't be stupid boy, the government doesn't kidnap anyone. Now off with you," he ordered at once with no apparent desire to answer anymore of Jake's prying questions.

He realized that Taylor might not have been lying. He needed to be sure, before making a rash decision. There weren't that many children; maybe they weren't the kidnapped kids. The Major hadn't lied to him before, so why would he doubt him now?

"Don't be stupid kid, I know you're new to all this but you're on the wrong team." A strange voice echoed into his mind. "If you're not going to help, then stay out of the way, we're coming and we're coming fast." The voice commanded with more force than any voice he'd ever heard before.

"Am I hearing things?" Jake glanced around, before lunging off toward the back of the building, searching for the children that were now scattering about.

"Derek Ralph Willem, subject 2 5 7, you've got something I want." The Major's words gushed with lust.

"I don't know what you're talking about," Will managed to spit the words out gritting his teeth through the pain.

"That's okay, I'll just get Deon, to make you give it to me," after grinding Will's arm into the floor once more he looked over to child, Deon, who was absentmindedly staring off into space standing beside the Major.

In a tranquilizing harmonious voice Major Bradshaw stooped down onto his knees, looked Deon straight in the eye, pulled out a jewel, and spoke to him. "Deon," he said, waving the stone fragment back and forth at Deon, in a slow hypnotic motion. "I want you to reach into Will's mind and seize control. Once you've done that, I want you to return with him to their hideout and conceal yourself as a rescued child. I want you to wait there, living with them, controlling Will and keeping tabs on the activities that Dr. Ambler is involved with." Major Bradshaw waved the fragment back and forth like a metronome and then began to count backwards from five. "Five, four, three, two," and instead of saying one, he released the stone and let it fall until it stopped at the end of a tether.

As soon as the stone dropped, Deon shifted his gaze from Major Bradshaw to Will, and looked him directly in the eyes. He stood there for a moment with his little chest rising and falling with every shallow breath of air, which he sucked in, and continued to glare into Will's eyes.

"Ah, get out. . . out . . ." Will choked, as a new burning sensation seared inside his head. His fists were clenched tightly together, and it appeared as though he were fighting off some invisible entity, wrapping itself around his body until he finally stopped seizing. After a few moments, Deon stepped back, away from Will's motionless body on the floor, and once again unresponsively looked at Major Bradshaw.

Will's eyes went blank, and the little struggle he had left inside him disappeared. Suddenly he turned his head, looked up at Major Bradshaw, and without even recognition of pain stood up and addressed the Major. "I am in control now," the words came out of Will's mouth, but they really came from the little boy.

"I'll take that now," Major Bradshaw reached down and yanked the money pouch from Will's belt. He opened up the pouch and dropped the stone piece onto his open palm, examining the specimen victoriously, and then addressed the boy again. "Thank you, now to get you back without suspicion?" Major Bradshaw rubbed his chin.

"Excuse me Sir, I don't mean to interrupt," a light went on in the little boy's face as he began to speak. "There's a very large assault of extremely powerful Vampires on their way here. It seems that the Ancient One, Kamau Vanderhyte, is leading the assault, and with him, some other very powerful ancients. I fear you have less than ten minutes before they lay siege to the base." The little boy finished speaking, and then the light that illuminated his face went out, and he fell back into an expressionless stare, off into space.

"Sir, could that be right?" The large reddish-brown gargoyle spoke. "There hasn't been a Vampire recorded other than Kamau, in hundreds of years. There couldn't possibly be a large group of them." He nervously questioned the child's vision.

"Yes, we've never recorded anymore, but that was only because we could never get Kamau to surrender his race's whereabouts, and no matter what we did to him, he never betrayed them. That doesn't mean that there aren't more. Deon has never been wrong about anything, ever. So, notify the scientists and let's get the hell out of here. If this is anything like the towns that were mysteriously slaughtered in the 1400's, then we can't be anywhere near here when they attack." He shouted, staging Deon pathetically in the snow. "Remember, blend in with them." He whispered to Deon.

"Get the chopper ready," one of the guards shouted to a man in the truck outside. "We leave in five."

"Get as many of the kids as you can, leave the rest, anything the Vampires leave, we'll come back for later. Find Jake and Taylor, and bring them, against their will if you must." Major Bradshaw ordered to the Viper Task Force team members still remaining.

The Major shoved the stone back into the money pouch and placed it into his right Jacket pocket, running back into the truck where the driver was waiting, before driving down the road, until they reached a small landing pad where the helicopter was waiting. Several of the gargoyles caught up with the Major, gliding through the air, with Jake alongside, drifting over the cool breeze.

He swooped up under the helicopter, catching the ledge while it was taking off. He pulled his body up, into the open door, and stood beside the Major, gracefully and nonthreatening.

"You need me?" Jake reported.

"Yes, but where is your friend?" The Major coolly asked glancing down on the ground. "Just in time," he mumbled under his breath, noticing a large white cloud of snow, billowing up from the gate of the facility. A red trail of blood, soaking into the snow, remained as the deadly assault flew past the first two guards.

"I told her to wait. Why, are we leaving so suddenly?" Jake asked, facing towards the facility, looking out over the edge of the helicopter for any sign of Taylor. "Oh, there she is," he pointed to a girl, running just past some buildings only stories away. She stopped, shielding her eyes while looking up, with her silky hair whisking around in the icy breeze, Jake could see her mouth something, but couldn't make it out over the helicopter roar. The helicopter hovered over the ground momentarily as the pilot turned his head back, awaiting orders from Major Bradshaw.

"Jake," Taylor yelled louder, her voice barely breaking over the loud roaring wind and the helicopter blades. He turned facing Taylor, trying to shout in return.

As he was facing her, listening to her shouts, Major Bradshaw pulled out a long hunting knife with a serrated edge, and carefully placed himself in a position, to effortlessly run it into Jake's heart.

"No. . . Jake. . . watch out," she screamed so forcibly, with her arms outstretched, as if to send a bolt of lightning through the Major, but before the Major could stab Jake, Taylor was planted into the ground.

In a matter of seconds, the earth had reached up from the ground, wrapped its warm gloves of soil and roots tightly around Taylor's legs and braced her firmly, like an ageless ancient tree. The snow in front of her swirled into a ball of powerful electricity, spinning swiftly around like a small hurricane, each flake bumping into the other's creating a yellow and white vortex of snow, sparking erratically. And then finally, from what looked like the ground, a beam of energy shot up through her rooted legs, and out from her outstretched arms, pulling with it the electrifying ball of snow, launching directly at Major Bradshaw.

"No," Jake screamed, and without hesitation pushed the Major over bracing himself, as a shield, unknowing that the Major was about to kill him. There was a sudden flash, as the deadly burst of energy enveloped Jake's white gargoyle body, and then it began to fade away, as did the very breath of life that wisped out of his motionless body.

● ● ●

Jake wobbled from the ledge of the helicopter, without any visible sign of damage to his body, turned his empty eyes towards Taylor's, and then fell stiffly, like a statue, down to the ground, where the only sound made, was the echoed thud of his body hitting the snow.

"Jake. . ." Taylor screamed, racing over to his body, lying dead in the snow.

The white leather of his gargoyle body began to change back into the light tan skin and curly golden-brown hair of her oldest best friend. She crouched down beside him, wrapping her arms around his chest and pulling him in close to her. "What did I do," the words drowned her head, as fear and sorrow and overwhelming tears of sadness began pouring down her face. The brilliant blue of his eyes faded away to an absent grey as life vanished from his face.

"No . . . Jake . . . not you too," she sobbed and sobbed, weakly slumped in the freezing snow, completely unaware of anything around her, tightly holding onto her best friend's dead body. "Not you too."

The helicopter noise dwindled away as the helicopter disappeared into the distance. Screams and shouting followed by random rifle shots which began to fill the air, as Kam and his followers sped through the camp finding each and every guard, scientist, and worker left on the base.

A man ran past the helicopter pad where Taylor sat, holding Jake's body, quickly followed by an ivory ghost-like figure, gliding across the snow swiftly, after him. Just on the other side of the pad, did the Vampire catch up with the security guard, and with one long practiced movement; he split the air in half with his Katana and left two symmetrical slices of man, falling in opposite directions, onto the snow. He looked up from his dark embroidered cloak, after cleansing his sword in the snow and gave a small nod of respect to Taylor holding the body, and then glided off to rejoin the others in their deathly slaughter.

Taylor wasn't sure how much time had passed since she'd been holding Jake's body in the snow when Kamau gracefully slid across the snow, never leaving a single footprint, up to her and asked that she join them.

"I know this must pain you deeply my young darling, but I must ask that you come with us and return these children to the professor. They are freezing and my people will only give us protection until morning and then they must leave." Kam spoke to Taylor gently. His strong, hardened voice left her with little comfort, knowing that she would have to leave Jake's body behind.

"I'm afraid." Taylor chocked, looking up at Kam, her face swollen and red from all the crying. "I did this." She chocked back another wave of sobs, and then closed her eyes, knowing she couldn't live without Jake, and disappeared.

Kam watched as a black wispy cloud dissipated in the place where Taylor had been crouching and looked down at the body remaining.

"I know it's not much, but we will give him a burial for kings." He told the absence of Taylor, as a form of respect.

Once the slaughter had finished, Kam and the other Vampires began tearing apart some of the wooden materials they could find around the base and stacked them in a large pile.

One by one they created a pile long and flat, like a bed, not one of them speaking a word to another. They wrapped his body tightly in a sheet, and then placed him on the center of the wooden pile, raised just above their heads. One of the Vampires, a taller slightly darker in complexion female, tore open a large vat of oil, and poured it all over the body and the wood.

Everyone stood around the mound of wood, draped with the human body, the children huddled in one large mass alongside Shyla, who was battered and tightly coddling a little boy, beside Kam. Kam nodded to several of the statuesque figures, and they began to set fire, with some torches they had put together, lighting each end, and then tossing the torches on top, stepping back to pay their respects to the dead boy.

"Wherever Taylor is, I hope she is set free by this tragic event." Kam preached over the roar of the flames.

They watched silently, as the fire roared up over the mound of wood, consuming all the pieces, and melting away the sheet that exposed the burning flesh underneath. They watched until the fire had consumed most of the body, and the fire dwindled down to a large mound of scolding hot coals.

"We must be going now." Kam explained, placing an embroidered robe over Shyla's shoulders.

As dawn began to break the surface of the sky, several of the Vampires began dwindling away in singles and pairs, as they marched the children off through the woods. Shyla walked with the children huddled around her sides. She was carrying, in her arms, a little boy, with the same golden blond hair as the color of her fur, and Will walked beside them.

Deon watched as many of the Vampires that accompanied them, dwindled down to just one, gliding alongside Kam. She looked familiar, much like one of the images he'd found in Will's memory bank.

"We're surprised you showed up. How did you ever recruit all this help?" Deon used Will, searching for some clue as to where all the Vampires came from. He was diligently recovering information for Major Bradshaw, completely careless that he was back in his mother's arms.

"I know you don't know much about me." He explained, "but I can sometimes see into the future, not something I've ever made clear. Not always perfectly, but for the most part, fairly accurately. And as you saw with me earlier, I knew the rescue was going to fail. Your only hope was for me to leave. I've been owed a great favor from many of my kind ever since my capture by the government, and now was as good a time as any to collect on their debt.

"I thought Vampires were a myth." Deon commented again, using Will as his voice.

"Many things are not as they seem," Kam responded. "Obviously," he added.

"So then why do you stay with us and not return to your people?"

"We do not stay together as a people, most of us live alone. We have not got along for centuries, and we do not like to take orders from anyone, yet alone our own kind." He replied.

"So why do you work with us then? Instead of being alone," he asked again, wondering why Kam had stayed with Dr. Ambler instead of leaving with the Goddess-like vampire beside him.

"I have my reasons," he responded politely and then quickly changed the subject. "So, who is the child that Shyla is clinging so tightly to?" He nodded over to her tiger striped body, crunching in the snow.

"Just one of the rescued children, I suppose. I'm sure Shyla just feels close to him or wants to comfort him." He responded, as Deon said nothing further through Will, about himself.

"So how are we going to get all of these kids back to our hideout? Is Dr. Ambler picking us up?" Deon commented, not sure where the hideout was.

"You made the arrangements. I think Shyla called for the professor to pick them up, remember?" Kam raised an eyebrow at Will suspiciously. He wasn't sure if he was testing him or truly didn't remember, but either way, referring to the professor as Dr. Ambler was kind of strange.

"Okay, I'm going to go talk to Shyla now," he commented, retreating back to where she was walking with the children, comforting them.

Kam and the fellow female Vampire both bowed to each other, arms cuffed behind their backs, and then the woman glided off, over the powdered snow, south to an unknown destination. Kam turned northeast pausing briefly before making an announcement. "We'll be there momentarily, just kept up for another few minutes, and then you can relax, and vans will carry us off to safety."

"I've never seen him so calm and collected and assertive," Shyla whispered to Will.

"Yes, it is very strange." He mechanically responded.

"So, do you think Taylor is the one, the one in the prophecy?" Shyla asked.

"The prophecy," Will commented, and then Deon searched through his mind to see what he was talking about. "Honestly. . . No, I don't think it's her. I think someone more powerful and more experienced would be the one." He responded, as Deon discovered the prophecy. He would have to make sure Major Bradshaw found out. Major Bradshaw would love to know that he could control the world with the entire stone. All that would be needed now would be Taylor.

"Just around the corner children, the vans are waiting just around the corner." Shyla explained, hanging up the cell phone that she was talking on.

They walked another few minutes, turning around a large bend of trees, and to their surprise, on the other side, waiting, was the professor.

"Welcome children, you've been so brave, please come have some food and pick out some blankets. I'm sure you're all freezing and hungry and tired." He said, opening his arms wide. He pulled out a couple of boxes from the back of the van and started handing white paper sacks full of food to the kids in one hand and large, soft, fluffy blankets to the children in the other hand.

"Thank you." Some kids answered.

"Oh, wow, thanks," others answered. All readily snatching the sacks of food and the blankets and jumping into separate vans until they were all filled up.

"Where's Taylor, I thought she'd be with you guys?" The professor inquired, looking through the trees.

"Sorry, but I think she's left our world, for now. She has something she needs to deal with." Kam explained.

"It's true," Deon had Will add. "I can't find her mind anywhere."

"That's really strange, but I guess there's nothing we can do about it now." He stated, turning to Shyla. "Who's this?" The professor asked Shyla, as she picked up some food and a blanket from him with a little boy wrapped in her arms.

"My son," she replied, eyes wide and tired, but saying in one single look that you could never take him away from her again, ever.

Will seemed kind of distant for a little while until Kam finally got his attention, slapping a sack of food and a blanket against his chest. "Take that last van," Kam ordered, and with that they loaded the last of the children into the vans. Kam, Shyla, and Will loaded into separate vans allowing the children to be accompanied by at least one other adult, and they drove off, headed for the Chateau Le Cache where everyone would find a peaceful end to a long day.

Chapter XXI: Fragment Combined

It's been several days since the attack on the Cyndac Oil Refinery. According to authorities, one of the generators exploded setting off a series of explosions throughout the facility and ended in the tragic deaths of several of the workers and security guards.

"Land over there, by that burned pile of wood." Major Bradshaw commanded to one of his helicopter pilots. The man set the bird down beside the dark black pile, snow and black ash flying around everywhere as the rotors spun slowly keeping the helicopter ready for takeoff.

Major Bradshaw leapt out of the loading bay and stomped through the snow until he was standing on top of the pile of burned ash and wood. He browsed around, knocking bone away with his boot, until he saw it, the little fragmented piece of diamond looking stone. He pulled out of his jacket pocket, the other piece he had retrieved off of Willem, and then waved it nearby the piece sitting on the ground. Both pieces began to glow in bright pulsing waves.

A large smile pulled across the face of Major Bradshaw as he reached his free hand down and snatched up the fragmented piece of stone. He wiped the ashes off of the stone onto his shirt and then let out a deep low sinister chuckle. With one piece in each hand, he held them apart, correcting the position in his hand in which they fit together like puzzle pieces, and then pushed the two ends together.

Brilliant light flooded the area, jetting out past the helicopter, like a mini supernova and the two pieces reformed through the brilliant light. Once the two pieces were completely attached the light died down and the stone returned to its brilliant diamond looking crescent shape.

Major Bradshaw wrapped the stone in some cloth and placed it in his pocket, glancing down at the burned pile of ash.

"Poor kid; never had a chance," he mumbled, and then hopped back into the helicopter, and signaled for the pilot to head back to his new base.

~~~

Taylor was tired of the dark blank nothingness that consumed her thoughts. It seemed like she'd been hiding in it for an eternity. After what felt like a lifetime of deliberation, she decided she must return to reality and wake out of her hopeless dream, finally opening her eyes.

Bright streams of sunlight blinded her focus, causing her to shield her eyes with her ridged black claw. As a small island in the distance began to appear, the warm aroma of smoked salmon rushed into her nostrils and the cool crashing of waves broke against her feet. She was standing on one of the beaches back home at Salt Creek, or so it seemed, but it was different than she remembered. It was fresher, quieter, the traffic from the highway nearby was absent, and the road looked worn, almost abandoned. Something seemed off, but she couldn't put her finger on it, until she was startled by the same old man she had seen once before, leaning over a small fire on the beach, with a salmon spread open, smoking.

He looked up from the fire.

"Can't stay away from this time, can you?" He straightened out his back, before hobbling over with the same walking stick as the other dream.

She thought for a while before responding to his question. "What time is it?"

Jabbing his walking stick into the sand, causing it to burst out into a brilliant blue flame, he replied.

"The time you died to create!"

To be continued . . .

Coming Book 2
The Fallen Child

Made in United States
Troutdale, OR
10/04/2023

13417692R00145